BLOOD

ALWAYS TELLS

BLOOD
ALWAYS TELLS

HILARY DAVIDSON

A TOM DOHERTY ASSOCIATES BOOK

NEW YORK

BLOOD ALWAYS TELLS

A Forge Book
Published by Tom Doherty Associates, LLC
175 Fifth Avenue
New York, NY 10010

www.tor-forge.com

Forge® is a registered trademark of Tom Doherty Associates, LLC.

The Library of Congress Cataloging-in-Publication Data

Davidson, Hilary.
  Blood always tells / Hilary Davidson.—First Edition.
    p. cm.
  "A Tom Doherty Associates Book"
  ISBN 978-0-7653-3354-4 (hardcover)
  ISBN 978-1-4668-0230-8 (e-book)
  1. Travel writers—Fiction. 2. Murder—Investigation—Fiction.
I. Title.
  PS3604.A9466B56 2014
  813'.6—dc23
                                                        2013025068

Forge books may be purchased for educational, business, or promotional use. For information on bulk purchases, please contact Macmillan Corporate and Premium Sales Department at 1-800-221-7945, extension 5442, or write special markets@macmillan.com.

First Edition: April 2014

Printed in the United States of America

0 9 8 7 6 5 4 3 2 1

In loving memory of my grandmother,

MAUDE ELIZABETH DALLAS,

for teaching me that if you're going to sin,

sin big

ACKNOWLEDGMENTS

Every time I finish writing a book and start on the acknowledgments, I'm reminded of how many amazing people I know. First, I owe a giant thank-you to my editor, Paul Stevens, for trusting me to write a stand-alone novel, especially since my pitch for the book consisted entirely of the words, "I want to write a stand-alone novel." Paul's talent, wisdom, and dedication are exceptional. The entire Tor/Forge team is incredible, and I want to thank Aisha Cloud, Patty Garcia, Edward Allen, Seth Lerner, and Miriam Weinberg for always going above and beyond. Many thanks to my Canadian distributor, Raincoast Books (especially Dan Wagstaff and Jamie Broadhurst) and its partner Ampersand, Inc. (especially Vanessa Di Gregorio) for their work on my behalf. I'm also grateful to Judith Weber and the entire staff of the Sobel Weber agency.

There are many booksellers and librarians who've supported my work, and I'm grateful to all of them. Some who deserve special recognition: Scott Montgomery (BookPeople); Lisa Casper (The Tattered Cover); Ben McNally (Ben McNally Books); Jean Utley (Book 'Em); Barbara Peters (The Poisoned Pen); Maryelizabeth Hart (Mysterious Galaxy); Gary Shulze and Pat Frovarp (Once Upon a Crime); Lesa Holstine; Richard Katz and David Biemann (Mystery One); McKenna Jordan, John Kwiatkowski, and Sally Woods (Murder by the Book); Otto Penzler (Mysterious Bookshop); Guy Dubois (Maison Anglaise); Suzy Takacs (The Book Cellar); Nancy Frater (BookLore); Marian Misters and J. D. Singh (Sleuth of Baker Street); Walter Sinclair and Jill Sanagan (Dead Write Books); Dan Ellis (Armchair Books); Gary Baumbach (Woodstock Public Library); Dennis and Joan Jackal (Jessica's Book Nook); Don Ross (Manticore Books); Roy Skuce (Green Heron Books); Janine Werby (Merrifield Book Shop); John Cheyne (Book Express); Catalina Novoa (The Bookshelf); and Shonna Froebel (Barrie Public Library).

I'm especially grateful to the wonderful people I know in the crime-fiction community. It's too massive a list to include here, but it includes Megan Abbott, Jedidiah Ayres, Carole Barrowman, Judy Bobalik, Ken Bruen, Margaret Cannon, Kristin Centorcelli, Joe Clifford, Reed Farrel Coleman, David Cranmer, Laura K. Curtis, Barbara DeMarco-Barrett, Barna Donovan, Neliza Drew, Linda Fairstein, Kim Fay, Jacques Filippi, Margery Flax, Jen Forbus, Cullen Gallagher, Meg Gardiner, Allison Glasgow, Ian Hamilton, Chris F. Holm, Katrina Niidas Holm, Janet Hutchings, Jon and Ruth Jordan, Patricia King, Swapna Krishna, Ed Kurtz, Jenn Lawrence, Benoît Lelièvre, Laura Lippman, Jeremy Lynch, Susan Elia MacNeal, Catherine Maiorisi, Margaret McLean, Bobby McCue, Terrie Moran, Dan O'Shea, Sabrina Ogden, Chantelle Aimee Osman, Brad Parks, Keith Rawson, Todd Robinson, Janet Rudolph, Kathleen Ryan, Jackie Sherbow, Robin Spano, Josh Stallings, Steve Steinbock, Dennis Tafoya, Clare Toohey, Lisa Unger, Steve Weddle, Sarah Weinman, Chuck Wendig, Holly West, and Elizabeth A. White.

Heartfelt thanks, for a variety of reasons, to Christopher Jackson, Bethanne Patrick, Joan Chin, Pia Lindstrom, Katia Hetter, Mark Medley, Sarah Murdoch, Susan Shapiro, Jacqueline Kirk, and the very much missed Greg Quill.

Friends who deserve a special thank-you: Trish Snyder, Stephanie Craig, Ilana Rubel, David Hayes, Kathleen Dore, Shelley Ambrose, Darya Arden, Ghen Laraya Long, Helen Lovekin, Leslie Elman, Jessica DuLong, Ellen Neuborne, Jenna Schnuer, and Beth Russell Connelly.

Since taking up crime (writing), I've joined Sisters in Crime, Mystery Writers of America, Crime Writers of Canada, and International Thriller Writers. Also, my longtime friends at the American Society of Journalists and Authors and the Society of American Travel Writers have been incredibly supportive of my criminal ways. My thanks to all.

I'm grateful, as always, to my amazing parents, John and Sheila Davidson, for being so supportive from day one. (That goes double for my mom, my first reader on this book and all others.) I'm grateful to my aunts Irene McIntosh and Amy D. Cane for their tireless support. Huge thanks to my wonderful husband, Dan, for always being there for me — no matter how many pages I ask him to read.

Finally, I'd like to thank readers everywhere. What I do wouldn't be possible without you. Who'd think that someone with an imagination as dark as mine would be surrounded by amazing people?

PART ONE

DOMINIQUE

1

It didn't take Dominique Monaghan long to realize she wasn't cut out for the life of a criminal. She'd knocked back her conscience in the small hours of Friday morning with a couple of pink pills, and the results were worse than a hangover. *This is never going to work,* she told herself, mentally running down a checklist of all the reasons her plans would fail. At the top was the essential unreliability of Gary Cowan. He'd been as hard to grasp as quicksand back when they were together, and she had no reason to believe that anything had altered his character in the three months since she'd left him. It wouldn't be out of character for Gary to bail on their plans at the last minute. He wouldn't even think twice. In spite of the countless blows to the head the man had suffered in his line of work, he was an unparalleled genius when it came to excuses. Lies rolled off his tongue with the soft sweetness of a lullaby.

He won't show, Dominique told herself. *Something will come up and he'll bolt. He'll figure out I haven't forgiven him. He'll smell a rat.* Those thoughts soothed her. For all her maneuvering and plotting over the past month, since Gary had stepped up his attempts to win her back, she wasn't sure she could go through with her scheme. Better if he didn't show up and it all fell through, she reasoned. No harm, no foul, and Gary would never be the wiser. It didn't matter if he never found out just how much she loathed him.

She had a mild panic attack when Gary buzzed up from the lobby. "Hey, babe, I'm downstairs." His raspy voice was almost sweet. "I can't wait to see you."

"Sure," she said, feeling as awkward as she sounded, cutting the connection before Gary could say another word. She hovered in her foyer, tugging tendrils of hair this way and that, and double-checking that there was no lipstick on her teeth. Her face was a perfect oval, with wide-set brown eyes, smooth skin the color of powdered cocoa, high cheekbones, and a full mouth. She was broad-shouldered and statuesque, the kind of girl who'd been told by strangers as a teenager that she should be a model. That dream had brought her from Chicago to New York at eighteen, only to be dismissed by bookers for the big agencies, who told her she was too athletic and too old, and mid-level agencies, who informed her apologetically that they already had a black girl. She'd found a small agency to take her on and she'd worked steadily for a few years, but that career was over by the time she was twenty-seven. In the three years since, she'd worked—with far greater success—as a stylist on photo shoots. She didn't need to look perfect anymore, but the internal pressure never lifted.

Vanity of vanities; all is vanity. For a moment, Dominique could have sworn her Nana was in her apartment with her. She shook off that sensation, pulled on her coat, and picked up her weekend bag. It was time.

When Dominique's wobbly legs finally got her downstairs, some of Gary's sweetness had already worn thin. He'd parked himself in the lone, threadbare chair in what passed for a lobby in her new building. His head was tipped back and his eyes were closed. His long legs were extended as if he were deliberately trying to trip anyone who happened by.

"You took so long I needed a nap," he murmured, not opening his eyes. His complexion had faded over the past few weeks, leaving him a shade of yellow that suggested jaundice over St. Tropez tan. His sandy hair was shaggy, as if he couldn't be bothered to get it cut. There were purple bags protruding under his eyes. Gary had sported plenty of shiners in his time, but this looked brutal to her. Even though she didn't want to, Dominique felt the spindliest thread of sympathy tugging at her heart. Then she mentally kicked herself. *Remember how he treated you. Remember what he did.*

"If I wanted to string you along, I would've told you to drive up to your country house alone and wait for me," she said.

He laughed, his face cracking in a broad smile. "I know you want to rake me over hot coals." Gary opened his eyes. They were a startling shade of bottle green that made her shiver when they slid her way. Today was no exception. "I missed you, babe," he said, scrutinizing her face. "You have no idea how much."

He stood and reached for her hand, pressing his lips to it. When Dominique didn't shy away, he leaned in for a kiss, but she snapped her head to the side so that his mouth slid off, like a foolish baseball player who couldn't even make first base.

"You should try that line on your wife sometime," Dominique said. "See if flattery really does get you everywhere."

"She's got a heart of stone. Nothing ever worked with her, and I stopped trying a long time ago. But with you . . ." Gary tucked one lock of her hair behind her ear. "Maybe I just need to up my game."

Even the gentlest touch of his fingers antagonized her. The last thing she wanted was her carefully straightened hair messed up by a man she hoped to kick in the head before the day was done. She gave him a smile and turned her face to look out the window, hoping to bury just how fleeting and insincere that expression was.

"Aren't you going to kiss me?" he asked.

"Why would I want to?"

"You're still mad at me." Gary's voice was light, teasing. He knew he was stating the obvious, and it was clear he thought the whole situation was just hilarious. "I can tell."

She glanced at him, wondering how a man who bore more than a passing resemblance to Bradley Cooper could be so pathetic. He was thirty-seven, but he still looked like the golden boy he used to be, back when he was on the U.S. Olympic boxing team, going for gold. Not that Gary ever did anything for his country, or for anyone else. He was a striver; she'd always known that. It was his strength and his weakness, and it was what she was going to use to break him.

"You're not still mad about moving out of the condo, are you?" Gary asked.

"'Moving out.' There's a euphemism for you."

"What would you call it?" Gary's dark eyes were all innocence.

"Is there a synonym for being tossed into the street?"

Gary sighed. "That wasn't my fault. Trin forced that to happen. I had no choice." His smile faded and he rearranged his face to look serious. "I know that sounds pathetic. I know you hate me, and you have every reason to. But, I promise, I'm going to make everything up to you. All of it, babe. You'll see."

Trin was Gary's wife, an anorexic heiress whose sole occupation was, as far as Dominique could tell, showing up at New York Fashion Week every February and September to be photographed in outfits showcasing her flat ass and chicken legs. The rest of the time, the wife was alternately counting her family's massive pile of money and cutting endless lines of cocaine.

"I like this place, actually. It's a nicer building than the condo was."

"Really?" Gary pretended to look around. "No doorman. No concierge desk. I'm going to hazard a guess there's no pool or sauna or fitness club, either. What's to like?"

"The company's better." Dominique let her words sink in for a moment while Gary's brow furrowed. "Come on, let's get into your car before I change my mind."

Gary had parked farther east on Twenty-ninth Street, since the building's amenities didn't include a driveway, either. His car was a five-year-old Mercedes-Benz in a shade of muted green that Gary referred to as "the color of money." It had been a wedding gift from his father-in-law, and it was starting to show its age. That was Gary to a T, Dominique thought. Wealth and precious things surrounded him, yet there was something shabby about Gary, as if he were the poor relation who gathered the hand-me-downs. It didn't make him any less attractive to her. The well-worn jeans, dark blue shirt, and battered brown leather jacket all suited him just fine. It was the fake Rolex watch on his left wrist that bothered her. When she'd met him, he'd had the real thing. It had disappeared around the time he'd sold his condo. The sad truth about Gary, Dominique realized, was that it would never occur to him to buy a nice watch without a designer name attached. He had to have the best of everything, but if he couldn't secure that, he'd settle for a hopeless fraud. At his core, that was what was wrong with the man.

Gary took Dominique's bag and stashed it in the trunk, then opened the passenger door for her. When he got into the car, he said, "Trin thinks she's running the show right now, but that's going to change." Gary touched Dominique's face. "I know you don't believe me, but it's true."

"Mmm-hmm."

"Just watch and wait. I know you think I've been hit in the head too many times to think straight. But things are going to be different." He turned his head so that he was staring at Park Avenue South, and his husky voice dipped lower. There was an unfamiliar intensity in it. "I'm going to *make* them different."

"Sure you will." Dominique didn't mean to sound flippant. It wasn't so much that she'd heard the words before. She just didn't care anymore.

Gary inclined his head so that his eyes settled on Dominique again. There was a furtiveness in them, as if he'd forgotten she was in the car for a nanosecond, until her voice reminded him. "You still haven't kissed me, you know."

She gave him a look that was all cool innocence. "I don't suppose you've filed for divorce yet?"

Gary winced. "You need to trust me, babe. Give me time."

Time, sure. That was all he needed. She'd heard that song on repeat the two years they were together. It was one thing when the only obstacle was Trin. Dominique could deal with that. But she'd been genuinely stunned and dismayed when Gary suddenly decided to sell his condo, coldly informing her she'd have to find her own place for a while. That had stung, but mostly because the blow had landed without warning. Still, she could've handled that, if Gary had been honest with her. At the time, he told her he was desperate for cash and had no choice but to sell the place. He'd also mumbled something about lying low and not seeing each other for a few weeks. It was only later that she'd found out the real reason for Gary's change of heart: he was two-timing her with a featherweight blonde who looked like she'd been molded for a high school cheering squad. That was the last straw. It still made Dominique burn when images of Gary and his Lolita floated through her mind. She wasn't sure how long she could hide that fact from him, so she said, "I'm going to nap on the drive up."

"Would it bother you if I put music on?" Gary asked.

"No, that's fine." She closed her eyes and curled her body away from him. But when the first song came on, she flinched. It was Rihanna singing, "We found love in a hopeless place." That was what had been playing when Dominique first met Gary. Of course, it had been the song of that summer, and there were probably tens of thousands of couples who first caught sight of each other while that melody swirled in the background. Still, it scorched her memory and fanned her fury.

They didn't talk on the drive, even though Dominique was only pretending to sleep. Gary followed the narrow thread of the highway up to Ulster County in the Hudson Valley. The playlist was cleverly designed to toy with her emotions. Or was he trying to show how well he knew her? That was what she suspected when Laura Izibor's "Don't Stay" came on. "We break up and make up, and everything would be brand new. . . ."

Dominique paused it. "Do you mind?"

"I thought you liked that song." Gary shot her a sly glance.

"I'm sick of it." *And of you,* she thought, but that was more honesty than she intended.

They drove the rest of the way in silence. Gary never visited the country house in the summer, when his wife refused to let him use it. Trin rarely went up herself, but the property belonged to her, didn't it? Gary's visits were limited to the less appealing times, before new greenery bloomed or after the leaves turned and fell from the trees, and when the ground was marshy and squished underfoot, or once it was frozen solid.

When they pulled up in front of the house, it looked distinctly desolate to Dominique. It had been months since she'd visited, thanks to her breakup with Gary, but the hazy November sky lent the property an arid chill. It was a boxy structure that was supposed to imitate a Georgian house in the English countryside, but it looked like nothing so much as a gargantuan shoebox with rectangles cut out for windows. Back in the spring, when Dominique had last seen it, the place had been badly in need of a coat of paint, and it didn't seem that anyone had thought to take care of that. If she'd been feeling generous, she would have described it as a stately house, two stories of tasteful, expensive decoration, but there was nothing about it that ever made it feel welcoming to her.

Stepping over the threshold of the front door, Dominique noticed that the place looked different, but she couldn't put her finger on what had changed.

"I think we should start celebrating right now," Gary said. "I'm going to open the champagne."

"It's two in the afternoon!" Dominique protested. The last thing she needed was to get tipsy and ruin her plans. "You better have the fridge stocked with Diet Coke."

Gary looked rattled. Had he already forgotten what she liked? "The fridge. Right. It's not well-stocked right now, but that should be in there. . . ."

"Don't worry about it." It's not like she was planning to be there for long. "If you're good, I'll pour you a Scotch. Why don't you get a fire going?"

"Sounds good, babe."

Dominique made for the antique liquor cabinet, crouching to open it. "Hmm. These are all dusty. I'll be right back." She picked up a pair of cut-crystal Old Fashioned glasses and a bottle of single-malt Scotch and headed to the back of the house. The place was like one big icebox, but that wasn't the only reason she was shivering. She almost dropped the bottle in the hallway. When she found the kitchen, she set everything down on the counter and retreated to the powder room on the other side of the hallway.

She shut the door and put her back against it. Her heart was skipping beats like a scratched record. *You're nothing but a useless bundle of nerves,* she scolded herself, sounding like Nana. That only made the tightness in her chest worse. She heard Nana's voice in her head every day, and it was normally a comfort. Now, it needled her, reminding her she was doing wrong. Still, Nana was a ghost now, and Dominique could shut her out if she had to. Her brother was another story. The thought of Desmond's disappointment was painful. He was the most upstanding man she knew. Even so, if Desmond discovered how cavalierly and cruelly Gary had treated her, he would've beaten the man into a pulp. No matter how serene and wise he tried to sound, Desmond was like her under the skin. But he wasn't the family screwup; she was. One day, long after this

BLOOD ALWAYS TELLS   19

was behind her, she'd tell him what she did. She was certain he'd understand, even if he didn't approve.

On steadier legs, she hurried back to the kitchen and opened the fridge. It was notably empty, which made her wonder if Gary had believed she'd ditch him at the last minute. He'd been hopeful enough to buy a couple of bottles of champagne, which were chilling in the privacy of the top shelf. Gary liked his creature comforts, but so did his wife. Champagne was a food group to that woman, and the bubbly could have been lolling around since *her* last visit. Dominique wanted no part of that. Instead, she found a can of Diet Coke and downed it in a few swallows. Her mouth was still cottony, so dry it might crack. She put her fingertips to her temple, certain she had a fever. *It's just nerves,* she reminded herself. She poured a glass of Scotch for Gary, then immediately dumped it down the sink. In spite of everything, she had reservations about mixing alcohol and the tablet she'd carefully crushed into powder in advance. It would make everything easier, but at a greater risk. Instead, she opened a carton of orange juice and filled the glass.

If any man ever deserved this, it's Gary, she thought. But that didn't stop her stomach from flopping over in queasiness, or her hand from shaking as she added the powder to the glass.

2

When Dominique returned to the living room, glass in hand, she found Gary had lit a crackling fire. She had a tendency to overheat, and the room was almost too warm for her now. Gary was hunched over on the couch, elbows resting on his knees and his forehead resting on one hand, whispering into his phone. When he noticed Dominique, he hung up abruptly and tucked the device inside his leather jacket. Was he actually calling one of his other girls? That was a lot of gall, even for a dog like Gary.

"Business call," Gary said. "The last one this weekend, I promise. Thanks for the Scotch, babe." He did a double take. "Wait, this isn't Scotch."

"I decided orange juice would be better for you." Dominique handed him the glass. Gary frowned and set it on the coffee table. "Tell me about your business call."

"It's just something in progress. Nothing solid yet."

Dominique fought the urge to laugh. What business had Gary ever been in that hadn't been a spectacular failure? There was the chain of high-end boxing gyms that was TKO'd within a year. After that, he'd invested in an energy drink that turned out to contain a fat-burning chemical that was banned in thirty-eight countries. There was a deal with a video game company that would've been excellent, but it fell through when the company lined up a better-known fighter. Along the way, there was also the shoe manufacturer who'd offered Gary a whopping amount of money to hawk their cross-trainers—so much that Gary had turned down an endorsement deal from Nike—but had ended up on the ropes, in a desperate bankruptcy filing. Those weren't even the worst examples. Dominique had tried to forget about the hugest embarrassments, like the oversized blender with Gary's face on the front of it. *It could've been the next George Foreman Grill!* Gary claimed. It wasn't.

"Let me guess. Your buddy Tom Klepper is getting you into another bad deal that will tarnish your rep?" Dominique asked.

"Hey, lay off Tom. There aren't many people you can trust in this business."

"You can trust Tom to screw up."

"What do you have against him?"

"Well, he's kind of a parasite," Dominique said. "I met a lot of people like him in the modeling business. Hangers-on who offer you drugs. They want you weak and pliable."

"You think that's what Tom is doing to me?"

"No, of course not. It's just . . . everything he gets you involved with is messed up. He completely lacks judgment or business sense."

"Come on, babe." Gary smiled. "This is our reunion weekend. I've been looking forward to this since . . . well, since you left. I knew we'd get back together. We belong together."

"I'm sure you had plenty of things to keep you busy," she said.

"Too much. I need to relax. It's been a hard month. Hell, it's been a hard five years. I'm like an inmate at a North Korean work camp."

"Poor little rich boy."

He raised his eyebrows. "Go ahead and mock me. Maybe one day you'll marry some psychotic rich freak who will make your life into a living hell." Gary lifted the glass and took a drink. If he noticed anything amiss, he was hiding it well. But he set down the glass and pulled out his phone again, staring at his screen and jamming his thick thumb on a button. He'd taken only a single sip from the glass she'd given him. Could he smell what was in it? That was supposed to be impossible. Still, what did she know, except what she'd picked up from her friend Sabrina, who'd given her the pills, and Google.

"Do you want to talk about what's really going on with you?" Dominique asked.

"Not really."

Dominique drew her thumbnail across her fingertips, a nervous gesture that clacked against the empty air. She was starting to panic. Step One was getting Gary to the country house so they'd be alone and no one could interrupt them. Step Two was getting him to drink the unusually relaxing cocktail she'd prepared for him. There would be no Step Three without that.

"You're acting like . . ." Dominique struggled to hold her anxiety in check. She thought about Gary kicking her out of the condo, and that shot some venom back into her veins.

"What?"

"Like something's wrong." She knew she sounded lame. "You're making me nervous. Maybe after you finish the juice I'll get you some Scotch."

"Never thought I'd live to see you turning into a bad influence," Gary said, taking a long drink. He sighed. "I'm sorry, babe. I know I'm being an ass." His expression was contrite. "It's just . . . there's a lot going on right now. With Trin, I mean."

That was the worst thing about being involved with a married man, Dominique decided. His wife was always in the room, too, like some invisible, mocking ghost whose presence drew all the oxygen out of the air when you least expected it.

"I know this might sound crazy, but . . ." Gary took a breath and another drink. "I've found some things out, and I think she's plotting something."

"Plotting . . . ?" Dominique's throat was tight. If that ghost had hands, they were wrapped around her windpipe. Dominique was sure that, should she get another word out of her mouth, a squeak would escape with it.

"You think I'm paranoid, don't you?" Gary asked. "But part of me is starting to wonder if she had anything to do with that time I was kidnapped."

"What?" Now she was confused. For a moment, she thought Gary actually knew something, but he wasn't making much sense.

"You know, in Mexico?" Gary continued. "I told you that story. I know I did."

"Sure. I remember."

"I've had a lot of time to think about it," Gary said. "All the signs point back to her."

"The signs?" Was he toying with her? Dominique was on edge as it was. She could feel her face flushing. The last thing she needed was this complication. But Gary didn't seem to register her reaction. He was too busy staring at the screen of his phone.

"I mean, look at the situation," Gary said. "I go down to Acapulco to be a special guest at a boxing tournament. It gets canceled at the last minute. Then these three guys grab me at my hotel and hold me for ransom."

"Three guys? I thought you said there were four?"

"There *were* four. Three guys grabbed me in my room. A fourth guy was driving the van." His mouth twisted to one side, tasting bitterness. Dominique couldn't read how much of that came from his memory of what had happened. "It wasn't some kind of random kidnapping. They knew who I was. Doesn't that reek of a setup to you?"

"I guess, when you put it like that." Her words were halting, but Gary didn't seem to notice that, either.

"Trin set me up. She wanted me to die down in Mexico."

"But . . . didn't she end up paying the ransom, Gary? I mean, why would she do that if she wanted you dead?"

"Are you kidding? She never paid one red cent." Gary was usually sarcastic and cool, but his temper, which rarely flared in front of Dominique, was rising to a boil. "Her father finally coughed up the cash, after four days. To be fair to him, that was probably when he first heard I'd been abducted. If it had been up to Trin, I'd have been left for dead." He lifted his eyes from the screen and turned his gaze on Dominique. "You know she wants me dead, don't you?"

"That sounds extreme. She could get rid of you in other ways."

Gary scowled at her. "What does that mean?" His tone was annoyed, but he yawned, stretching the last word out of his mouth.

"Well, that agreement you signed with her family . . . you can't leave, but she could kick you out, right?"

"She can pull all kinds of crap to make my life a total hell, but she can't do that."

Dominique just stared at him. She knew he was lying. Maybe Gary realized that, because he kept talking.

"Her father wanted to make sure"—Gary yawned again—"that she couldn't ditch her husband. She has to be married, or else she's completely disinherited. He was a really sexist old coot. It's complicated. I think Trin believed getting a divorce would be possible after he died, but it's just as hard." He took another drink. "I went over everything with Tom, and—"

"Your buddy Tom isn't much of a lawyer."

"Hey, he's my friend as well as my lawyer. And it's not like I can show anyone else the agreement."

"You showed it to me," Dominique said.

"Yeah, I did," he admitted. "It was"—he yawned again—"important you understand the real situation."

He sounded drowsy yet lucid. That put him in the sweet spot

she'd been hoping for. "Hold on. I'll be right back," she said, grabbing her weekend bag and starting out of the living room. She needed a minute to get her things in order so she could do what she needed to, before Gary conked out.

"You know I love you, right?"

Gary's words stopped her dead.

"What?" she demanded. She turned her head so she could see him over her shoulder.

Gary was watching her. "You heard me."

The drug had done something stranger than Dominique expected. Her friend Sabrina, whom the muscle relaxant had been prescribed for, said it was like truth serum. Gary had never voiced an "I love you" before. He was too cool, too much of a player.

Dominique bolted upstairs, putting distance between them before her brain exploded from stress. *Restless legs,* her Nana used to say. *Runs in the family. Just like your mama.* She shoved that thought away. Her mama was the last person in the world she wanted to think about, especially right then. She raced to the bedroom at the back of the house, intending to drop her bag on the bed and extract the video recorder. But there was no bed in the room. There was nothing at all. The beautiful antique French furniture was gone.

She stared around the empty chamber. The walls were still covered in a rich blue silk. There were a couple of dark spots high up, near the ceiling, where a mirror and a painting by William Holman Hunt had once had pride of place. They had vanished, along with everything else. All that remained were the photographs of Trin.

That was what had been different downstairs, Dominique realized. Most of the furniture was gone. The house had always been choked with precious things, so many glittering, gilded objects crammed into each room that they seemed as unspectacular as weeds. There had been a speedy redecoration after Trin's father died, but those alterations were mostly about what hung on the walls: the mounted stag heads had come down, and so had the photographs of Trin's father and her three brothers. Up went *The Many Moods of Trin*, as Gary called it, a series of photos displaying his bone-thin wife awkwardly posing in couture. Losing the taxidermied animals seemed right to Dominique, but the family pictures were another matter. Whether the images of a quartet of dead men bothered Trin, she couldn't say. Maybe the woman cherished their memories in private. Somehow, Dominique doubted that. No one who unceremoniously dumped photographs of their relatives to make space for countless projections of their own image was anything other than a cold-hearted narcissist in her estimation.

Vanity of vanities; all is vanity. Dominique wondered what effect Nana might have had on Trin if she'd gone to live with her at the age of four, as Dominique had. Funny that the woman was clearing out the house, yet keeping her shrine intact. Maybe Trin was selling the property. Naturally, Gary would be the last to know.

Dominique continued down the hall to the master bedroom. It was missing some of its clutter, which was for the best, but it had lost a mesmerizing portrait by George Romney. That left Dominique momentarily forlorn, because the eighteenth-century lady in it had been the most cheerful thing in the house. At least the great-canopied bed still occupied the middle of the room. She set her bag on the tufted lavender silk bedspread and shrugged off her jacket.

She'd decided, well in advance, no matter what Gary said or did—and regardless what promises he made this time—there was no going back. Even so, his words about Mexico unnerved her. *This whole plan might be dead,* she realized. Gary had revealed that story about being held for ransom not long after they'd met, but he'd always treated it as a subject for mockery. Gary ridiculed everything around him, so that wasn't out of character. It was a trait that sometimes made Dominique wonder about his head. Who joked about being kidnapped? The man was a little too cool for his own well-being. Maybe that was why he had no trouble being a cheat and a liar, she thought. The irony wasn't lost on her: there she was, mistress of a married man, lit up with fury because that man was stepping out on her. What a fool she'd been. The shame and humiliation still burned inside her like a flame.

Vengeance is mine, sayeth the Lord. There was Nana's voice again, pressing on her like a weight from above. Today, Nana's ghost was on her case just like Nana herself had been when Dominique was a teenager. She pushed her away, but that cracked a door for the memory of her father to slip in. Dominique didn't remember him that well. Mostly, she had sensory images of warmth and rough skin that smelled of soap and lullabies sung in his deep baritone. She could recall standing on his polished shoes as he danced her around their living room. But those flashbacks only made her heart flutter in her throat. She missed him so. She had to push his memory away, too.

I'm really doing this. It's not just talk anymore. This isn't a fantasy. She fumbled with the recorder with shaking hands, then dropped it. It bounced on the floor and she grabbed it, furious with herself for turning into a schoolgirl with a crush. *What, one sweet word from Gary and you're ready to swoon?* she chided herself. She heard the front door open and shut and looked out the window. Had Gary wandered outside? The muscle relaxant was supposed to be a bit of a trip, enough to oil up his brain and tongue to pliable looseness, but not so much as to knock him out or actually incapacitate him. She didn't see him, and her mind was suddenly flooded with worry.

She rushed along the hallway and down the stairs, clutching the recorder and concerned Gary might hurt himself. In the living room, she stopped dead. Gary was perched on the sofa, staring at the fire with the curious intensity of a child. Behind him stood a tall man with a balaclava pulled over his face. He was holding a gun, and it was pointed at Dominique.

3

The man stared at her, unblinking. He was six three, her brother's height, with broad shoulders and a thick neck that had a gold bird with two heads hanging on a chain around it. The only skin she saw was a pasty white ring around the mask's small eyeholes. His pale blue irises were cold enough to be chipped from ice. He looked like a modern Viking in black leather and denim, a distressed duffle bag at his feet. "Get on the floor," he hissed.

"Who the hell are you?" Dominique demanded. Then she noticed a second figure cloaked in black, behind the tall man. This one was only five nine or so, wrapped in a leather trench coat that looked like a costume from *The Matrix*. The head was disturbingly insectlike, covered in a black balaclava with no eyeholes at all; instead, there were big, bulging patches of black mesh where the eyes should have been. The hands were encased in black gloves and one was holding a gun. For a split second, Dominique wondered if it was a person or a giant bug.

"What do you want?" Dominique asked. "My bag is upstairs. My money is—"

"Shut up." There was no life swimming behind the Viking's eyes. "Lie on the rug. Facedown."

Gary chose that moment to look over his shoulder, and his expression was a vague mix of surprise and delight. "Hello, Max." His voice was cheerful and hearty, as if greeting an old friend.

Max? Dominique thought. *How much muscle relaxant did I give him? How far gone is he?* There had been a doorman at Gary's condo named Max. He was a head shorter than the Viking with the gun and his skin was just a couple of shades lighter than the balaclava the man was wearing. If Gary was mistaking this white freak for Max, she'd screwed up badly with the drug. Even the second assailant, the Bug, seemed baffled. Its insectile head swiveled from Gary to the Viking and back, as if a Ping-Pong ball were bouncing between them.

The Viking glared at Gary, frigid eyes narrowed to slits. "Your phone?" he snapped.

"Yes." Gary said, holding up the half-hidden phone in his palm, as if hoping to show it off.

"Get it," the Viking ordered.

The Bug stepped forward and yanked it out of Gary's hand in one long, swooping motion. Gary's expression was openly baffled. He held his hands up, clearly believing the phone would be returned to him momentarily.

The Viking's eyes cut back to Dominique. "Lie down before I punch your face."

Dominique shot a look at Gary, who was watching the scene unfold as if it were a particularly fascinating play. His mouth was half-open. "You . . . you can't hurt her, you know." Gary sounded more confused than convincing.

"Shut up." The Viking didn't even bother to glance at Gary.

"Okay," Dominique said, lowering herself on the rug. "My wallet's upstairs. I have a little jewelry with me. It's in my bag."

The gunman's voice was contemptuous as he moved toward her. "If I wanted something, I'd take it."

"But obviously you're here because you want—"

"Enough." The man punctuated his words with the clink of metal as he secured her wrists. "Sorry, Dominique."

Her head snapped up. "How do you know my name?"

He didn't answer. Instead, he raised one gloved hand, and the Bug came closer, gun trained on Dominique's head. The Viking stood, extracting a second pair of cuffs from the back pocket of his jeans, and went to Gary. The ex-boxer just sat there like a muscle-bound dummy, staring at Dominique with a confounded expression while the man secured his wrists.

"It's going to be okay, babe. Don't you worry."

"Stand," the Viking ordered.

Gary got to his feet. The Viking looked over at his accomplice, jutting his chin in Dominique's direction, as if to say *bring her*.

Dominique glanced around the room, but she didn't see a way out. She was cuffed, Gary was bound and drugged, and both of their assailants were armed. All she could do was play along until one of them let their guard down. Her money was on the Bug. That one seemed like a little automaton who needed explicit instructions. Dominique was sure she could win in a fight. She'd always been extremely athletic—too muscular to be a truly successful model, in an era where emaciated, rail-thin girls who made Victorian maidens look tough as truck drivers were all the rage. She was a runner and a swimmer and she had a brown belt in tae kwon do. She didn't lack for confidence, either. All the Bug had to do was trip up in some small way, and she'd squash it.

"Okay." Dominique got up, pretending to find it difficult and stumbling a bit. "It's hard to stand with your hands cuffed behind your back, you know."

No one answered her. "Door," the Viking said. It was obviously an order, backed up with a gesture he made with his gun.

"Aren't you worried one of the neighbors will see you?" Dominique asked him.

"No."

Cocky bastard, she thought. "In *summer*, no one would be able to see a thing," she corrected him. "But it's the end of November, and the leaves are off the trees. There are a couple of houses across the creek that can see everything."

"Summer cottagers," he answered. "Move."

She walked toward the door, keeping her head turned to the side so she could watch the Bug with Gary. In spite of the gun, the Bug was timid. That certainty made Dominique's pulse race.

"Move," the Viking repeated, his voice almost a growl.

"Where are we going?" Dominique asked. "What's the plan?"

"Don't argue, babe," Gary said softly. He had all the spine of a jellyfish. Maybe he was legitimately woozy thanks to what she'd put in his drink, but that didn't mean he had to roll over for a pair of thugs, did it?

Seeing no other option, Dominique opened the front door. She scanned the horizon, weighing the risks of running and shouting against the hopelessness of doing nothing.

"The Holms have closed up their house for the winter, and the Jordans are in Montauk this weekend," Gary said. "There's no one out there, babe."

"Walk," the Viking said.

He nudged Dominique with his gun, forcing her to lead them around the side of the house. It was only then that she spotted the white van. It must have been parked there all along, waiting for her and Gary to arrive, she decided. There was no lettering on the side, but she noted the New York State license plate: FAF-72 . . .

The Viking yanked her hair so hard that her head jolted back. "Don't get—"

He was interrupted by Gary, who was suddenly wide awake and furious. "Don't you dare touch her!" Gary yelled.

The Viking spun around, and Dominique fully expected him to strike Gary. Instead, his frosty eyes were blinking furiously. "Okay," he muttered.

The Bug pulled open the door at the back of the van. There was a long metal bench on either side, with metal chains attached. It looked like a prison-transport vehicle. That made Dominique think of her mother and she took an involuntary step back.

"Wrong way," the Viking said. "Inside."

"Look, there must be some way we can work this out. You know he's married to a very rich woman, obviously. You can—"

"Inside *now*, and I'll recuff you with your arms in front," the Viking said.

She stepped into the van, followed by Gary, who was being nudged along by the Bug. Gary's arms were already cuffed in front of him, so all the Viking did was attach a chain to the cuffs, forcing Gary to hunch forward slightly. He didn't seem to mind.

"Your turn," the Viking said to Dominique.

"Why are you doing this?" she asked as he put the muzzle of the gun to the back of her head, unlocking one cuff. He turned her and pushed her down on the bench, restraining her and attaching a chain.

"Business."

His voice was so matter-of-fact it took Dominique's breath away. She flinched, even though his hands weren't on her.

"What's wrong with him?" the Viking asked after he attached her second cuff.

"Muscle relaxant."

The icy blue eyes narrowed again. "He take it himself?"

"No," she admitted, feeling heat in her face again. "I gave it to him."

The Viking smiled under his mask. "Thanks for making this easy," he said.

4

The Viking—Dominique couldn't help it, that was how she thought of the crazy big gunman—slammed the door shut and turned a key, locking them in. Dominique waited for the van's engine to roar to life, but it didn't. There were no windows in the back of the van, so she hadn't a clue what the thugs were doing. She strained her ears, listening for voices or movement, but she heard nothing.

"You all right, babe?" Gary asked.

"I'm fine. What about you?"

"I'm okay, just kind of . . . stunned, you know?"

"Do you have any idea who those guys are?"

"Sure," Gary said. "They work for Trin."

That startled her. Mob-related debt collectors was what she'd feared. "You recognize them?"

"No, but she must've sent them," Gary murmured. "She's pure evil."

Dominique closed her eyes and sighed. There it was, straight from the horse's mouth. It wasn't exactly a secret that Gary hated his wife. All you had to do was get a few drinks in him—or some muscle relaxant—and he bubbled over with dark accusations and recriminations about the woman. Dominique had been planning to get some of that on tape, along with certain key confessions. Instead, she was locked in the back of a van, chained in handcuffs, and forced to listen to Gary's ramblings.

"Please stop," Dominique said. "We need to figure a way out of this."

His eyelids were lowered to half-mast and made him appear punch-drunk. "There's no way out," he mumbled. "So sleepy." He lay on his side on the bench, as if he couldn't care less that his wrists were chained. He was still wearing his leather jacket, Dominique realized. He hadn't shed it inside the house. She thought of her coat upstairs with remorse. All she wore now was a delicate lace camisole under a whisper-thin merino wool cardigan. Whatever heat there was in her veins was battling with the crisp, late-fall air, and it was clearly losing. She wrapped her arms around herself as best she could, triggering a rueful memory of the time she'd posed in Jeremy Scott's straightjacket wedding dress. *This is insane,* she thought. She twisted her torso from side to side. She was going to freeze before the van even started up, at this rate.

Every so often, she checked her watch, grateful for the somber strip of yellowish LED lights above her head. Fifteen minutes in, the van's passenger door opened and slammed, but Dominique didn't catch any voices. Gary's gentle snoring filled the van. Five minutes later, the passenger door opened and closed again. A minute after that, she heard the door on the driver's side, and the engine revved up. Dominique's anxiety level rose—where the hell were they going?—but that was tempered with mild relief. Puffs of warm air were starting to venture through the vents. Maybe she wouldn't die of exposure after all.

The van backed up before turning and following the road out. There was only one, and it hadn't been repaired since Trin's father died. They hurtled over a particularly sizable lump, making it feel, for a heartbeat, as if the van's wheels had abandoned the ground. The landing knocked Gary's head against the bench.

"What the hell?" He lifted his hands, suddenly surprised to see them bound. The man looked painfully disoriented. "Babe? What's going on?"

"Two freaks with guns walked into your house, tied us up, and stuffed us in this van."

Gary looked around, still confused. "This is really happening, isn't it? I'm not imagining this."

"I wish."

"I think I was dreaming. I could've sworn Atlas was here." Gary put his head down on the bench again, stunned but resigned.

"Atlas?" The name tugged at her memory, but she couldn't place it.

"My mom's dog. I gave him to her. You've only seen pictures."

She studied him, wondering whether he was so befuddled by the muscle relaxant, a brain injury, or plain old stupidity. They were trapped by thugs, and Gary was talking about a dead dog. In the silence, Gary yawned. They were driving on a better road now, one that was well paved and smooth. He closed his eyes and drifted off to sleep again.

An hour passed. Then two. Dominique kept an eye on her watch. She didn't get the sense they were driving particularly fast—no doubt, the last thing the freaks wanted was to get pulled over for speeding—but she could tell they were on a highway from the noise. The van was warm enough that she almost could have taken a nap, if she weren't worried to death about where they were headed.

She'd stared at the van's interior for so long she'd memorized every crack and chip. She was wearing boots with slender stiletto heels, and she'd decided, early in the drive, that whenever they stopped, she'd kick the side of the van and scream to get attention. The heels would likely break, but she'd make some noise. But the van never paused, not for more than a few seconds.

"You look so afraid, babe," Gary said, startling her.

"You're awake. How do you feel?"

"Okay, I guess. Or I would be if that clown hadn't chained me up."

"Has someone been threatening you, Gary?" She had to ask. Gary was perennially short of cash and heavy on IOUs. "Did you borrow from a loan shark?"

"Of course not." He had the nerve to glare at her. "I told you, this is Trin's doing."

"Why on earth would Trin kidnap you? She doesn't want to see you."

"You don't understand," Gary said. "Whenever I talk to her—which is rare, I admit—Trin tells me she's already planned what to wear at my funeral."

"That's grotesque, but not what I had in mind. Has anyone threatened you?"

"No." He didn't sound very certain.

"Gary, think hard. Somebody with a gun just kidnapped you. He was out to get you. He said it was business. Who could that be?"

"Business," Gary repeated. "Huh."

"What?"

"I was never cut out for business." He turned his head to regard the van's ceiling. "That was my big mistake. I had money after the Olympics, endorsement deals and all that. But I thought I'd be a big shot who went into business. Instead I lost everything. I ruined my life. Why do you think I had to marry Trin?"

Dominique blinked at him. What had happened to the wry, sarcastic Gary she knew? This slow-talking version fascinated and repulsed her at the same time. Gary was never self-pitying. He mocked himself with the same relentless spirit he used against everyone else. He didn't wallow.

"Come on now, Gary. Think."

"You're not listening to me. It's Trin," Gary insisted.

"That's your delusional side at work again."

"You're not paranoid if someone really is out to get you. You can laugh all you want, babe."

"I'm not laughing." She held up her chained hands. "Anything funny about this to you?"

"No, of course not." He paused. "Dominique, I'm sorry about this. I dragged you out to the country and into this mess. I'm sorry about a lot of things."

"Let's worry about how we're going to get out of here. You can apologize to me later."

"Babe, I don't know how much later there's going to be. Listen to me, will you? Just for once, believe me. There's exactly one thing I know for sure."

"Which is?"

"Trin wants me dead," Gary said. "And she'll do anything to get her way."

5

Two hours and forty-seven minutes after the van had left the house in the Hudson Valley, it skidded to a halt and the engine went dead. It was almost six o'clock Friday evening. Dominique knew they'd spent most of the time on highways, but the past hour had seen them traveling along a series of roads with potholes like moon craters, before they hit pavement-free dirt paths. It had been a rough ride in the back of the van.

The driver's door opened and closed. "They're coming," Dominique said. "What do you want to do?"

"Not a damn thing," Gary warned her. "They've got guns. They're going to do whatever Trin paid them to do. Which means they'll hurt me but they'll probably leave you alone."

They waited for the door of the van to swing open, but it didn't. Five minutes crawled by, then ten. The only noise was the low growl of a plane overhead.

"You hear that?" Dominique asked.

"The plane?"

"A single-engine Cessna coming in for a landing."

Gary frowned. "When did you become an expert on aircraft?"

"My brother's a pilot. Don't you remember?"

"Sure, but Desmond flies choppers. That's not the same thing."

"He's trained to fly other planes. He used to co-own a Cessna with some other pilots. A couple of times, he flew to New York to visit me. He's taken me up with him." The memory almost made her smile. Desmond had a saying about flying, and she wracked her brain for it. It was something about running with the stars, only that wasn't it. *Running with the stars* sounded like a bad reality show about jogging in Los Angeles. Desmond's words were more like poetry.

"I don't remember any of that." Gary's voice was sour.

"He had to sell his share when he got divorced. It was before I met you," Dominique explained. "The point is, a small plane like that, flying so low, means there's some kind of airport or landing strip near here."

"You have no idea where we are! We could be anywhere!"

"We're less than a three-hour drive from your house," Dominique pointed out. "We've stopped somewhere near a runway. That's something to go on."

"That's not going to help us." Gary looked down, shaking his head. "Look, this isn't a movie, babe. You need to just go along with what these people want. They're not going to do anything to you. I'm the one they want."

Before Dominique could answer, there was the sound of a lock turning, and the door opened. Frigid air rushed into the van.

"We're here," said the Viking. He must have taken off his balaclava for the drive, Dominique reasoned, but it was back on his head now.

He stepped back and swung the beam of a flashlight around. Dominique saw trees all around them. They were in a clearing and the ground was muddy. The sun had already kissed the sky goodnight, but the stars were hidden behind a thick blanket of gray clouds. If it rained, the dirt roads out might well be impassable, she knew. Then she noticed the house.

When Dominique was a little girl, she'd nursed an obsession with haunted houses. She couldn't tell Nana the real reason—she thought they might help her talk to ghosts, and she had to hide that along with her curiosity about Ouija boards and other occult objects—so she pretended that she thought they were romantic. The more ruined they were, the more she loved them. The house in front of her could have been plucked out of her dreams. It looked as if it had been dipped in acid that was eating away at its façade. Most of the paint had been picked clean off, leaving the structure a weathered gray that was slightly lighter than the slate of its Mansard roof. There was a big verandah at the front, marked with a row of lean, elegant columns. The first-floor windows were boarded up. The place was so dilapidated it looked as if it were swaying slightly to one side. Or maybe it was bowing with a shaky grace, praying that someone would lift it from its torpor before it was too late.

"Please tell me this is a joke," Dominique said.

He leaned in slightly. "What?"

"That house will blow down with the first gust of wind. It looks like it's been standing since Noah's Flood."

He turned his head and shrugged then stepped into the van. "You first," he said to Gary.

"Leave Dominique alone," Gary snapped. "You can do what you want with me, but leave her out of it."

Dominique knew Gary was trying to do the right thing, but his words had the hollowness of secondhand speech picked up at the movies.

"Come on, tough guy," the Viking said, unlocking one cuff and hauling Gary to his feet. Gary swayed slightly, as if an opponent had just delivered a haymaker. She'd watched old videos of him in the ring, looking like that, big and yet childish, glassy-eyed but calm. The Viking turned Gary's body 180 degrees and shoved him, face-first, into the wall of the van.

"Don't hurt him," Dominique called out.

The Viking didn't answer, and she started to wonder where the Bug was. He finished recuffing Gary's back, then nudged him out of the van. He checked Dominique's chain, saw it was secure, and followed Gary out, jumping to the ground. He turned to look at her, then banged it shut. He didn't forget the lock, much to her dismay.

She struggled with the handcuffs and the chain, determined to be gone before he came back, but it was hopeless. In the glow of the LED lights, Dominique noticed for the first time that there was cushioning on the inside of the restraints. She pressed her thumb against one and it gave way slowly, like a rubber mat. Padded handcuffs? These weren't standard issue. When she started to really look at them, they made her think of fancy B&D gear they put in the window of Agent Provocateur. She could almost hear the Viking's voice, rasping on her name. She shivered, and not from the cold. For the first time, she wondered who the real target of the kidnapping was.

6

Twenty minutes after Gary was taken out of the van, the lock clicked again. The door opened a crack and a man poked his head inside. "Hi," he said casually.

"Hi," Dominique answered, stupefied that he wasn't wearing a mask. The man was in his late twenties, with bad skin and a scar on the left side of his face, bisecting his cheek. If anything, it made him more interesting than nature had. His black leather jacket was zipped open. Underneath was a T-shirt with PAGAN REIGN embossed at the top and an image of a clawed, golden bird underneath, with foreign writing Dominique didn't recognize. It looked a little like the bird on the necklace the Viking sported, but it only had one head.

"Bumpy ride?" he asked.

She nodded. He got into the van. He was the same height and had the same thick build as the Viking, but his manner was tentative.

"I'm supposed to unlock you, okay? Just promise you won't do anything stupid."

"Okay." She braced herself to run. Why the hell had she worn boots with four-inch heels? Still, she could sprint in them if she had to.

"Because here's the thing," the man said. "If you run away, your boyfriend Gary is going to get a bullet."

That brought her thoughts to a screeching halt.

"My brother is in the house with him right now," he said. "I'm not going to hurt you. No one's going to do that. But if you do something wrong, Gary will get hurt."

She stared at the man. His blond hair was just a little too long to be presentable, but it suited him. His nose had clearly been broken and not perfectly reset. That and the scar on his cheek made him look ready to take on the world. His cold blue eyes were just like the Viking's, which wasn't surprising since they were brothers. His were wide-set and angled upward at the outer corners, giving him the sly, suspicious gaze of a jungle cat. He was actually close to handsome, Dominique thought. The architecture of his face was impressively Slavic. If his nose had been straight and his skin weren't pockmarked and his eyes weren't so feral, he would have the makings of a model. So close and yet so far.

"Do we understand each other?" he asked.

She nodded. What else could she do?

He released her from the chains in the van and recuffed her hands. He stepped out of the van and politely helped her down. They crossed the clearing together, boots squishing in the muck. Inside the house, he shut the door behind them and locked it. He called out something in a language she recognized as Russian. She didn't know any words beyond *da* and *nyet,* but there were so many models from that part of the world, she caught the cadence of his speech without comprehending the content. No one answered him.

The hallway was only dimly lit, but Dominique could make out a broad staircase swooping up and angling to the left. The floor, the steps, even the paneling on the walls seemed to be fashioned from the same dusky wood. Gray slats of light filtered in from the rooms on either side of the hallway. A solitary lightbulb illuminated a living room with antique furniture covered in clear plastic. As her eyes adjusted, she could make out dust particles hanging in the air. She sneezed.

"Where are we, exactly?" she asked.

"At an old house in the middle of nowhere."

"Come on. Are you so worried I'll escape that you can't tell me where we are?"

"I'm not supposed to. That's not part of the plan."

The air inside the house was damp and sour. There was the distinct aroma of mildew mixing with mustiness and decay. More than that, Dominique couldn't identify, except to say it was all bad.

"So where's your brother and his other partner in crime?"

Something glinted in the man's eyes, and the corners of his mouth turned up. "You think I can't handle you without their help?" He nudged her down the hallway, toward the back of the house.

"Where's Gary?"

"Come into the kitchen," the man said. "I need to explain some things to you."

There was the smell of fish in the air, as if they were by salt water and not in the middle of a copse. Underneath it was an overwhelming scent of decay. Dominique's stomach was empty, but it heaved a little anyway, twisting to the side just like the house.

The hallway opened to a kitchen that looked startlingly modern compared to the decrepit, starchy formality of the entryway. Unlike those in the musty rooms at the front of the house, its window wasn't boarded over. Dominique stared through it, absently noticing how different the view was from the house in the Hudson Valley, even in the dark. There, it was all manicured yards and flowerbeds and a big, white gazebo that could've come out of a storybook. Here, the woods were thick and dense, with old trees growing so close to one another that they blotted out the moonlight. They were losing leaves, but there was enough of a canopy overhead to make the stormy sky even darker and more forbidding. She'd always been a city girl, first Chicago and then New York. Being around people energized her. To her, empty countryside was only so much dead space, waiting for people to come liven it up.

"What's that smell?" she asked.

The kitchen would almost have been cozy but for the rank odor that hung in the air like a shroud. Something had died there recently, and the body hadn't been cleared out.

"What happened in here?" she breathed.

"It's a good thing I don't have a strong sense of smell," the man said. "At first, I thought your pal Gary was faking it—he said he was going to throw up—but it's pretty bad, isn't it?"

"Where's Gary?"

"He's fine. Don't worry about him right now." The man cleared his throat. "You want something to drink?"

It was as if he were playacting as host, Dominique thought. In spite of what Gary insisted about his wife being behind their kidnapping, that theory didn't sit right with her. What Dominique had planned for that day would ultimately benefit Trin, and even though she'd never had a conversation with the woman, she suspected Trin knew something about what was going on.

But it was more than that. What if she hadn't doped Gary with that muscle relaxant? Would Gary have been a match for the Viking? The Bug had seemed ready to scuttle off at the flick of a finger. Would she or Gary have been able to call for help, or run away to a neighbor's house? She'd never know, but the possibilities filled her with regret. She was largely to blame for the situation they were in.

"Diet Coke—any pop—would be good. Thanks." She hated saying *thanks* to the man, even if he wasn't as awful as the Viking. It didn't roll off her tongue because of Gary's warning. It was her Nana's training, bred into her since she was a small child.

"Just so you know, there's no food," he said, walking to the fridge. "Take a look inside."

He opened the fridge, and Dominique reared back. The stench increased tenfold, fanning out like a swarm of insects. Dominique couldn't even look at first. When she did, she saw that the fridge was fully stocked, and not with human heads, as she'd imagined. The door was lined with cans of Diet Coke and light beer. There were bottles of wine resting on their sides across the bottom shelf. But the light inside the fridge was off and everything that wasn't in a bottle or can—meat, vegetables, milk, cheese—must have spoiled.

"What happened?"

"We filled it on Sunday," the man explained. "There was supposed to be enough food in here for a week, just in case things went wrong. And then the power must have gone off, and it never came back on in the fridge. Maybe it blew a fuse."

"Is there any other food?"

"A box of crackers. That's about it." He cocked his head. "Good thing you're a supermodel. You're used to starving."

"Wow. You're not exactly the world's most competent kidnappers, are you?" Dominique said. "You don't even have food for yourself, let alone us."

The man's icy eyes turned baleful. He was obviously offended by her criticism.

"You know what I think?" Dominique went on. "You should quit while you're ahead. No harm, no foul. You pack us back into that van and take us to the first stop on the highway. We won't tell a soul. You and your crew get away scot-free and nobody will be the wiser."

"You're not in any position to negotiate, you know," the man said. "You're going to help me clean out the fridge."

"Excuse me?"

"You heard me. Then I'll let you have something to drink. Don't do it, and you and Gary will both die in this house of thirst. It's up to you."

"Why do you care about cleaning out the fridge if you can't smell anything?"

He made a dismissive snort. "Gary, Mr. Macho Ex-Boxer, almost barfed in here. I don't want any messes to clean up, especially anything involving DNA."

"I think you mean your brother wants you to clean this mess up, since he's boss of this operation and you're not." She wanted to view his reaction, see if there was any daylight between him and the Viking. He looked resentful, but he shrugged. She tried a different tack. "What can I do with my hands cuffed?" Dominique asked. He had let her keep her hands secured in front. Small blessings, as Nana would say.

"You get to hold the garbage bag."

Dominique had cleaned plenty of refrigerators in her life—she was obsessed with details like that, which was another trait she'd picked up in Nana's neat-as-a-pin house on Chicago's South Euclid Avenue—but this mess was impossible. Whoever filled it with food hadn't cleaned it out first, so there was grime in there that she was sure was breeding new life forms. There was enough fish and meat and chicken to feed a small army, plus wilting heads of lettuce and brown broccoli florets. Bringing up the rear was the smelliest part, a cheese selection dominated by Roquefort, Stilton, and something called Pont-l'Évêque. That last one made her gag.

She listened for footsteps while the man filled a couple of trash bags, but there were no sounds from the hallway or upstairs. It didn't sound like anyone else was in the house, but obviously Gary was, and someone was minding him. The man never took off his gloves, she noted. He had a gun tucked into the back of his jeans that she only caught a glimpse of when he bent toward the fridge.

"Let's take a break." He closed the fridge door. "I can't believe how disgusting this is."

He glanced at his phone, then set it on the kitchen table, faceup as if he were expecting a call. It wouldn't take her but a second to swipe it, she knew, but what did she do afterward? Would she have time to dial 911? It was almost a bad joke: in the middle of a forest, would anyone even notice?

The man went to the back window and stared out into the darkness. The glass was made up of tiny panes, and whatever was happening on the other side of it was holding his attention. Was there an accomplice watching the grounds? A lot hinged on that. If a second gunman were inside the house, all bets were off if she or Gary could make it outside. But if the kidnappers had even more help, who knew what might happen?

"Is somebody out there?" she asked him.

"Just one of our guys."

So there was at least one person outside, watching the grounds. Good to know. "What if someone wanders off the road?" she asked.

"We're more than three miles from the nearest road." His voice was reproving, as if she should have known better, even if she had been smuggled there in the back of a van. "No one's coming here."

"Do you have any tick spray?"

"What?"

"We're in a wooded area. Even though it's November, you must've thought about Lyme disease, right?"

His mouth fell open, as if the idea hadn't crossed his mind. Before he could string together an answer, his phone rang. The noise made their eyes arc in the same direction. The screen of the phone had come to life, filled with an image of a white woman with highlighter-yellow hair with a bright pink streak shot through it. The woman was wearing enormous sunglasses in the picture, but that didn't hide her identity. Dominique would've recognized her anywhere. That was Gary's wife.

7

Hold on," the man said to Dominique as he picked up the phone. "Hello?" He headed out of the kitchen, as if moving a few feet away conferred some shield of privacy. He halted just beyond the entryway, his eyes flicking furtively at Dominique.

Her mouth was dry again. She hadn't believed Gary when he'd claimed his wife was behind this, but she'd been dead wrong.

What did she even know about Trin, after all? Dominique had spotted her countless times over the years at fashion shows. It was impossible not to notice Trin, even in a crowd, since the woman was always dressed outrageously, had her hair dyed hues that didn't occur in nature, and carried odd props in one hand—one year a monocle, another a vintage Japanese fan—and a cigarette in the other. Trin sometimes showed up in designers' showrooms for private viewings of a collection; her access was guaranteed by the fact that she spent a mint on couture. She never entered into conversations with models, preferring to treat them like thoroughbreds who'd respond to hand signals and sharp commands. "STOP. Turn around!" Trin would bark, in a clipped voice that aspired to be a British accent but couldn't quite make the leap across the Pond. The ladies who collected couture were an odd flock of fine-feathered birds, usually billionaires' wives insulated from reality in gilded cages built with money from oil and gas and coal. Even in that rarified air, Trin stood out. She was a caricature of an heiress, so oblivious to others that it seemed as if she floated along in a bubble.

When Dominique first met Gary—at a photo shoot to promote that stupid, toxic energy drink he'd bought into—she'd been curious about him, because she knew he was married to the notorious Trin Lytton-Jones. He'd shown up not only without a wedding ring, but also without a tan line where the ring should have been. He'd been so laid-back and self-deprecating and charming that Dominique was intrigued. How could a handsome former athlete, a man who liked baseball and bowling, cold beer and hot jazz, be married to such an alien creature?

The truth is, we're not really married, Gary told her later, when she asked.

That's a great line. What would your wife think if she heard it? Dominique had fired back.

She wouldn't care. Our marriage is a publicity stunt, nothing more. We don't have any relationship at all.

Gary had pursued her, and Dominique had laughed him off. Any married man who wanted to sleep with a girl would say he was estranged from his wife, and Dominique wasn't that kind of girl, anyway. But she was fascinated, and more than a little attracted to Gary, and so she dug deeper. There were people in the New York fashion world who knew about Trin and Gary's strange arrangement, and everyone agreed it wasn't a real relationship. Trin's far-out, avant-garde style had always made Dominique think of a bejeweled stick insect, one that injected its mate with poison after sex. Gary eventually explained that he wouldn't know anything about that, since he'd never slept with his wife.

Then why are you with her? Dominique asked.

It's a business arrangement.

You made a business arrangement with Trin to marry her as a publicity stunt?

No. The arrangement is with her father.

Trin's father had forced her to get married, Gary explained. After auditioning a series of candidates—all athletes, because Mr. Lytton-Jones wanted his grandsons to be tall and strong—Gary had been selected. He wasn't exactly thrilled at the prospect, but he'd explained to Dominique that he'd desperately needed the cash. He'd lost everything he'd made through endorsements, and he'd borrowed against future earnings. The companies he'd tried to start up had gone belly-up and left him deeply in debt. Worst of all, his mother had been on the verge of losing her house because she couldn't afford her medical bills; getting cancer had pretty much bankrupted her.

That unexpected bit of sweetness in Gary pushed Dominique over the edge. The man was willing to pimp himself out to pay for his mother's cancer treatments and mortgage. She hadn't expected that from such a glib, sly player, and it impressed her. She'd never imagined she'd get involved with a married man, but Gary wasn't *really* married, after all. At Christmas, Trin jetted off to be with her father while Gary spent the holidays with Dominique. After a while, he'd shown her the massive document—really, it was almost a textbook—that revealed the deal he'd made with the devil. It had made Dominique's jaw drop. Gary hadn't fabricated any part of that story.

I'm only showing this to you because I need you to know what I'm up against, Gary said. *I want to leave her, but I can't right now, because if I do, I have to pay back every dime I got, plus a penalty fee.*

No court would enforce that.

I walked into this with my eyes open. My lawyer went over it. Tom says it's an ironclad agreement.

"This isn't a good time," the man said into the phone, dragging Dominique back into the present. The musty house, the nauseating mess. That was where her affair with Gary had led her. The shame that she'd avoided in two years of dating him pressed down on her chest at that moment.

The man turned his face away. "Can't right now," he murmured, moving farther down the hall from the kitchen.

Dominique's eyes panned around the room. No knives. No obvious way to escape. What she noticed instead was the old cellar door with a big, shiny steel bolt on it.

The kidnappers had probably stashed Gary in the basement, she realized. That's why she hadn't heard so much as a creak from the floor above. It would be easier to stuff him down there, no matter how much of a cobwebby mess it was, than to take him upstairs and risk him jumping out a window. She shot a glance down the hallway. The man had turned his back to her, and he was moving away, whispering so she couldn't make out a word. She took a couple of breaths, eased back the bolt on the cellar door, and inched the door open.

She wanted to call out Gary's name, but she didn't dare. It was pitch-black down there. She pulled open the door a little wider and reached one hand in, forgetting for a second that she was still handcuffed, so one hand trailed after the other. Her fingers fluttered over the wall. She found the light switch, but when she flicked it on, nothing happened. She tried again a couple of times. Was electricity out completely? That was impossible, because there was a light on in the kitchen and there'd been one on in the front parlor. Either this was a bad connection, or there was no lightbulb.

Her ears strained for some sign of life, but she heard nothing.

"Okay. Goodbye," the man said.

Recoiling from the darkness, she shut the door and slid the bolt back in place.

8

Was that one of your accomplices?" Dominique asked the man.

He shrugged. "Let's go upstairs."

"We haven't finished cleaning the fridge out."

"Leave it. Someone else will take the trash out. We're going upstairs."

"What's upstairs?"

"Your guest room, Calendar Girl."

"What did you just call me?"

He gave her the hint of a smile. "I used to have your swimsuit calendar."

She felt a hot flush over her face. To think of this man with a gun tucked into his jeans playing visions of Dominique in a bikini in his head . . . that made her feel ill. Nana had been firmly opposed to Dominique's desire to model. *Think of the strangers pawing over you in their heads,* she'd warned. *They'll believe you belong to them.* If Nana hadn't suffered a stroke and died when she did, she probably would have barricaded the door to keep Dominique from going to New York. Now, Dominique suspected Nana was right all along.

"You don't want to call me that again," Dominique said, "because, gun or no gun, I'll crack your head open."

He frowned, but he didn't answer. Dominique stormed out of the kitchen, back through the hallway and up the rickety old staircase, which creaked loudly in complaint. The house must have been grand a lifetime ago, before it was abandoned and started crumbling. Dominique noticed the remnants of crumbled molding on the walls just under the ceiling.

"How did you find this place?" she asked.

"I have a friend who works in real estate. I came out here and had the agent show me a bunch of places in the area. I knew this one would be perfect."

"You rented it? That's a pretty great way to let the police know you were involved. Maybe your partners want to leave you holding the bag."

He made a dismissive noise.

"Seriously, if they connect Gary with this place, that will come right back to your doorstep," Dominique went on. "You got a good defense lawyer lined up? 'Cause you're going to need one."

"Thanks for your concern," the man said. "I didn't rent it. It can't be connected with me."

"That's what you think."

"It's what I know."

"You research the neighbors around here?"

The man sighed. "I didn't need to. There aren't any neighbors."

"Neighbors. Campers. Hunters. There's always somebody around."

"This house is on sixty acres. Totally private. There's a fence around it."

"A fence? Big deal."

"Electrified fence," the man said, through gritted teeth.

"Oh, an *electrified* fence." Dominique didn't even try to keep the mockery out of her voice. "I wonder if the power to it went out, just like the fridge."

"Shut up!" the man barked. "I don't want to hear another word out of you."

Now it was Dominique who made a dismissive noise in the back of her throat. His frustrated outburst made him sound just like the

Viking, and she knew she was getting under his skin. She was quiet for a minute, until the man led her inside a bedroom that was lit by a bulb hanging crookedly from a wire on the high ceiling. The room was small and square and had no furniture at all. There were nails embedded in the walls, as if the room had once held dozens of picture frames. But they were empty now, and the paint on the plaster had faded to a watery, pale blue. In some places, the color had been replaced by long streaks of rusty water damage, as if the paint had been bled away.

What caught Dominique's attention was that the room had a window. Not a boarded-over window, like the ones at the front of the house. This one was smaller than the kitchen's, made of many small panes of glass with thick black iron lines holding the rectangles together. It wouldn't be an easy window to open or to break, but Dominique was determined to try.

"Where's Gary?"

"He's got his own private quarters."

"In the cellar?"

"You never give up," he said. So, Gary really *was* in the cellar. That was a good thing to know. "You get the room with a view," he added, leading her over to the window. "Kind of nice, actually."

"The trees creep me out. Imagine being surrounded by that all day long."

"Some people would like that."

"It's like they have eyes," Dominique said. "They're watching, all the time."

The man gave her a strange look, then turned his head away with a shake of his shaggy blond mane. "It's way better than being in the city. I hate it there. I can't wait to get away from it."

"It's freezing in here," Dominique said.

"We're going to get the furnace working. In the meantime, use the blanket."

"What blanket?"

The man pointed to a corner of the room. The nubby fabric was the same drab brown as the floorboards.

"It looks grungy."

"It's new. I bought it at Target." He sounded exasperated. He really wasn't a very good kidnapper. Dominique didn't believe he had a clue what he was doing. Maybe it wasn't his plan, and his brother roped him in. How long did they think they'd be able to keep Gary and her at this house? The beginnings of a plan started to form at the back of Dominique's brain.

"I need to use the bathroom."

He sighed. "Fine. It's off the hallway. Come on."

He led her to a white-tiled cell with a cracked claw-foot tub. She was disappointed to see that its lone, tiny window was boarded up.

"The toilet and sink work," he said. "Leave the door open."

"I am not leaving it open, you pervert!"

"How about I lock you in your room and leave you there for a few days? How would you like that?"

She was silent. She'd been pushing him, needling him, to see how far she could go. It wasn't very far.

"You can close the door most of the way," he offered. "But you have to keep talking. It's not like you ever shut up anyway."

"Fine," Dominique muttered. She would've fought more, but she really did need to use the bathroom. "Can you unchain me?"

"No. It's not like I bound your wrists with duct tape. You've got a three-inch chain between the cuffs. I chose them for comfort, you know. They're padded so you don't hurt your wrists. Gary's are, too. I'm—we're—thoughtful like that."

She thought it was interesting, how he shifted from sounding as if he were in charge to making it appear as if decisions were made by committee. There was no way this creep was the alpha. She went into the bathroom and pushed the door closed, as far as he would let her.

"Keep talking," he warned.

She looked around the bathroom, but there was nothing but a bright pink cotton towel and a fresh bar of soap. The medicine cabinet had been torn off the wall. There was nothing to use as a weapon.

"My hands are tied. It's not like I can do much." *Otherwise I'd stuff the soap down your throat,* she thought. Taking a deep breath, she noticed that the bathroom, unlike the rest of the house, had a pleasing scent, almost as if it contained a bouquet of red roses in bloom.

"Complain all you like, just keep up the chatter."

"What do you want me to talk about?"

"You can recite the alphabet, for all I care."

"How come you're doing this?" she asked.

"Did I tell you that you could ask me questions?"

"You said I could complain or recite the alphabet," Dominique pointed out. "I figured questions were okay." She looked around, trying to figure out where the fragrance was coming from. Maybe the towel had been washed in some special detergent? It was odd.

"I don't mind questions. Just don't expect answers."

"So, why are you doing this?"

"Why don't you ask Gary?"

"I would if you'd let me see him," Dominique said. "Can that be arranged?"

"Not right now." There was an audible sigh.

"Is this just about money?"

"Obviously." His tone was derisive. "What about you? How come you're here?"

"Um, I'm here because you dragged me here." She stretched out each syllable, unsubtly pointing out how stupid the question was. "Did you forget that already?"

"No, I mean, how come you're with Gary?"

"What, you think you're Oprah now?"

She flushed the toilet and it made a giant whooshing noise.

A moment later, the man said, "Gary's a loser, you know."

"How do you figure that?"

"He was never much of a boxer. He failed in everything he tried afterward. Then he married a rich woman and had affairs. He's just a piece of garbage."

"You sound like you've got a personal dislike of him," Dominique observed. When she picked up the soap by the sink, a shock of electricity coursed through her. It was by Jo Malone, an expensive brand she loved, and even though the packaging had been discarded, it was clearly Red Roses, Dominique's favorite. That was the source of the fragrance in the room.

The discovery unnerved her. What a bizarre thing for the kidnappers to do. It was almost as if someone put it there to please her . . . but that couldn't be right. Could it? Her face was hot but her thoughts were sending chills down her spine.

"It's just business," the man said. "The person I feel sorry for is you."

"Why?"

"Because, if you get killed, it will be Gary's fault."

9

He took her back to the room with the ratty brown blanket. "You probably think you can escape out the window," he said. "You can't. It's been sealed so it can't be opened. You could try knocking out a pane of glass, but the metal is solid and you're not going to get through it. If you somehow *did* magically find a way to get through, you find that the roof isn't solid. You might go through it, or you might get stuck in it. Either way, it's pretty bad. There's no hospital around here."

"Thanks for the warning," Dominique said. "Having you around is like getting my own private hotel concierge. Any other advice about the neighborhood?"

"You're funny as hell." He gave her a tight smile that said she was less amusing than rotting cheese. "If you knock out a pane of glass, you'll end up freezing. That blanket can only do so much."

"You promised me a drink for helping with the fridge."

He gave her a long look. "So I did." He hovered in the doorway. She could sense that he wanted to talk to her, but his yearning was tinged with reluctance. Was it a mistake to encourage him? She wanted nothing more than to get out of that house, but maybe the best approach to that was to engage with her captor.

She gave him a long look. "What is it?"

"I'm curious. My brother said you had a flip camera with you back at the house. What were you planning to do with it?"

She didn't see any point in lying. "I brought it along to film Gary."

"In a compromising position?"

"You mean naked? No, that wasn't the plan."

"What then?" he persisted.

Dominique took a breath. It had all seemed so straightforward when she'd talked about it with her friend Sabrina, or with the lawyer. But looking at her scheme in hindsight made her feel incredibly stupid. "Gary had signed a document a few years ago, one he wasn't supposed to talk about."

"You mean his agreement with his wife."

"You're well-informed." Of course he knew, Dominique thought. The wife had hired him. "That's the one. It has a confidentiality clause. Basically, Gary could lose everything for talking about it."

"And you were going to get him to talk about it." He nodded to himself. "I get it. But did it never occur to you what Gary would do to you to keep you from releasing it?"

"He wouldn't do anything to me. He wouldn't dare."

"Don't be so sure. Gary's a thief, and a con man, and a liar. More than that. Gary is a murderer."

"No. I don't believe that," Dominique said. "Yes, he's a liar. Maybe a bit of a con man. But the rest . . . no."

"Speaking hypothetically, if you loved a man, and you found out he was all of those things, would you still love him?"

"You mean, would I stop loving someone because of things he'd done? No. Definitely not." Her words made her feel like a hypocrite. Did she love her mother? No. Was that because of what her mother had done? Damn straight. She looked out the window, blinking back a tear and forcing her thoughts in a different direction. *You're not being two-faced,* she told herself. Think about your brother. Desmond had been in all kinds of trouble when he was a teenager. She was a decade younger, and too much of a baby back when he ran with a rough crew to remember the details. As an adult, she'd never wanted to learn more about that time. What purpose would that serve? What she knew was enough. Desmond had always been patient and loving and gentle with her. After her father died and her mother went to prison, Desmond changed. He was serious and grave, suddenly bearing the weight of the world on his shoulders, but his innate sweetness was still there. "What about you?" she asked.

"As the old saying goes, 'Love is evil, you can even fall in love with a goat,'" the man recited.

"What on earth does that mean?"

"It's Russian. It's basically like the English saying love is blind," he explained. "By *goat,* it really means bastard."

"Okay. Your turn. You're working for Gary's wife, aren't you?"

"No."

"Don't stonewall me. I saw her photo on your phone," Dominique said.

"Sure. Because one of the kidnappers just happened to leave his phone on the table for you to see."

His low, insinuating voice set off alarm bells in her mind. It had seemed very convenient that his phone had been on the table for her to view, but the image of Trin's face had startled her and chased cautious thoughts away.

"You're saying I was meant to see that?"

"How hard do you think it is to set a phone so that photo comes up when a certain number calls?" the man asked.

That shook her hard. "Who the hell are you really working for?"

"I can't tell you that. Just be sure to ask Gary about that."

"Why? What does that mean?"

"It means he knows."

"He knows *what*?"

The man just shook his head and stepped back, shutting the door. Dominique heard the key turn. A moment later, she was across the room, rattling the door. It wouldn't budge.

She went to the corner and picked up the blanket. As the man had promised, it was new and notably free of mildew. Dominique wrapped it around her shoulders like a cape—an awkward process, since her hands were still cuffed—and went to the window. She hit the glass with the heel of her fist, but it didn't budge. She leaned closer, tracing the outline of each panel with a fingertip, searching for the flaw. There had to be one somewhere, she reasoned. This old house was ready to cave in. There was no way a window that big was free of cracks. But as she explored it, she noticed the window was double the expected thickness. There was Plexiglas reinforcing the window from the inside.

That only made her search harder for a weakness, because she was nowhere close to admitting defeat. But there was heavy weatherproofing material all around the frame, inside and out. There was no way to open the window. She couldn't escape that way.

A low rumble caught her by surprise, and she searched the dark sky for a plane. There wasn't any sign of one, and the more she listened, the less right it sounded. She moved over the metal vent in the floor and felt a surge of warm air passing through it. So, the kidnappers had finally turned on the furnace. That was something, at least.

She went over the room looking for anything she could use as a weapon. The nails in the wall were a possibility, if only she could get one out. She pulled and pried, damaging her perfectly manicured fingernails in the process, before finally extracting one. It was two inches long, with a flat head and a dusting of plaster dappled over its surface. Lying almost weightless in her palm, it didn't look like much of anything, let alone anything dangerous. *Some weapon*, she thought. She went back to the window, scratching at it with the nail. If Plexiglas could laugh, she thought, it would have quite the chuckle right then.

Maybe I could pick the cuffs with the nail. That wasn't exactly her skill set. Desmond could have done that with his eyes closed, at least as a teenager, but he'd never taught her how.

While she was contemplating the possibilities, she heard a key in the door. She put the nail in the pocket of her jeans and glanced at her watch. It was close to nine. The man eased the door open gingerly, as if expecting an attack.

"I've been thinking," he said, "and I have an offer to make you."

"Oh?"

"I'll let you out of here. Kidnapping you was never really part of the plan, so I'll let you go. But on one condition."

"What's that?"

"You help me kill Gary first." He smiled, revealing perfect, even teeth. His tone was nonchalant, almost playful. "How about it?"

10

Dominique stood stock-still, balanced between shock and horror. "Say that again," she told him. "I don't think I heard you right."

"You heard me just fine."

"Maybe I did, but I don't believe you," she answered. "What you're talking about isn't just crazy. It's evil."

"I'm not suggesting you kill an innocent person. This is about Gary."

"He's a good person, at heart."

"You know that's not true," the man said. "He's a sleazeball who married a woman he didn't even like for her money."

"His mother had breast cancer and was on the verge of losing her house," Dominique pointed out. "I think that had a lot to do with his choice. Gary took good care of his mother until she died."

"He took great care of himself, too. Only the best would do for him. He was a golden boy, raised to think he was better than everyone else. Handsome. Athletic. The type who always got the girl." The man lifted his big shoulders in an impassive shrug. "He got addicted to a lifestyle he couldn't afford. And that made him a monster."

"Did Gary hurt someone you cared about? Is that why you kidnapped us?"

"No." The man shook his head with obvious impatience. "I told you, this is just business."

"Then why are you obsessing about him?"

"He reminds me of a certain type of person I hate. So smug. So superior. The golden boy who wins at everything. The rich man who uses people and calls them his helper monkeys. Personally, I don't care about Gary one way or the other. But make no mistake: he's a killer."

"Who did he kill?"

The man cocked his head to one side. "That's a complicated question."

Anger flared under Dominique's skin. She hated people who played head games, especially when she couldn't walk away from them. "In other words, you're making this up."

"No. It's just . . . I'd love for Gary to explain it to you himself. It's quite a story."

Dominique racked her brain. There had been a story once, something about a boxer Gary had knocked out cold in the ring. The man had suffered a serious concussion, and he'd gone on to develop chronic traumatic encephalopathy. His life had been circumscribed by memory loss, aggression, and depression, and eventually he'd killed himself. "Carlos Murcia," she said.

"What?"

"The boxer. Gary always felt bad about what happened to him. Like he contributed to his condition."

"I don't know what you're talking about," the man said. "This doesn't have anything to do with boxing."

That only left her more confused. Who else had Gary harmed? "Why don't you explain?" she prodded.

"It would take too long. Anyway, I don't care. It doesn't matter to me if Gary lives or dies. It only matters to the person I work for. And make no mistake about it: Gary is going to die."

"No. You can't."

"The only question is whether you're going to die with him. Do you want to?"

"What kind of fool question is that?"

The man's mouth stretched back in a smile that lasted for a nano-second. "You're beautiful, and you're kind of amusing. So I'll make you a deal. If you'll kill Gary, I'll let you live."

"That's your idea of a deal?"

"What's wrong with it?"

"I would've expected you to say you'd let me live if I sleep with you."

"Obviously, that's also part of the deal." He was so cool as he said it. Dominique didn't feel the slightest spark of desire from him or any heat from his skin, but those feral eyes of his said *I have you in my power and I can make you do whatever I want.* "But that's just a given. And sleeping with me wouldn't keep you from going to the police and telling them what I did. But killing Gary—that makes this a completely different game. You do that, and you can never go to the police."

"Really? You think the police would blame me when you're threatening me?"

"I'm not threatening you. Gary dies in either case. That's not a threat. The only question is what *you're* going to choose. Because I believe you're quite capable of murder."

"You're wrong."

"I know all about you, Calendar Girl," he added.

"You obviously don't know the first thing about me."

"I've looked you up."

"Have you been Googling me out here?"

"We're so far from civilization, there's no Internet service. But I've already read about you. I know all about your mother."

Dominique clenched her hands into fists. The metal chain of the cuffs rattled. "You don't know a thing about her."

"I only know what the newspapers said. But I also know that blood always tells. Your mother was a murderer. You're capable of killing a man just like she did."

"You listen to me." She could feel her own heartbeat pulsing in her throat. "My mother didn't murder anyone."

"Your mother went to prison for putting a bullet in your father's head." The man spoke slowly, driving his words home with frightening precision. He wasn't just a control freak. He was a sadist. "Her lawyer tried to claim it was self-defense, but there was no evidence your father ever beat her. No bruises, no doctor's visits, no hospital visits. The jury didn't take much time to convict her, either. Everyone knew she was guilty."

"The gun went off by accident." Now that she was cornered, she found herself clinging to the same story Nana and Desmond had told her, the one she'd always refused to truly believe. She'd grown up hating her mother for taking her father away from her, but hearing the same charge from a stranger made her recoil. "It wasn't murder."

"A shot in the head at point-blank range. That was no accident."

Dominique backed away from him, bumping into a wall. She had been four years old when her father died, and her memory of that night was shadowy and vague. Her mother had given her a bath and put her to bed as usual. Then, later—she didn't know when, because there was no clock in her room—there was shouting and firecrackers. It was like the Fourth of July, she'd thought, and she'd gotten out of bed and pulled back the shade over her window. But there were no sparkly lights in the sky. It was raining. She remembered seeing Desmond streak across the lawn, and she watched, fascinated, when a police cruiser pulled up in front of the house. The police had been very nice to her, taking her to the station and giving her candy and pop. Early the next morning, Nana came to collect her. *There's been a terrible accident,* Nana said. *Your daddy has been hurt.* Nana wouldn't say *dead,* but that was what she meant, only Dominique wouldn't learn that until later. Nana never wanted to talk about what happened.

Later, when she was in elementary school, she asked Nana about that night.

Your mama said it was an accident, Nana replied.

Don't you believe her?

She swore to me she never meant to shoot him. That means it was an accident.

She'd never been able to get Nana to say more than that. As she'd gotten older, she'd lost the desire to know more. It was a tragedy she wanted to bury. Dominique took a deep breath. "Is that how you want me to kill Gary? Put a bullet in his head?"

"That would be appropriate, don't you think? History repeating itself, in a way." He was as relaxed as if he were offering to grab some takeout for her. "You'd never be able to tell anyone. Think of the stories. 'Like Mother, Like Daughter.' It would have to be our secret."

"You're serious?"

"I give you my word," he answered. "I'll let you live if you kill Gary. I can't be any clearer than that."

Dominique held out her hands. "You going to uncuff me?"

His expression made it clear that he didn't really trust her, but he fished a small key out of his pocket. "Don't make me regret this," he said as he released her.

He pocketed the handcuffs as she rubbed her wrists. "Where's the gun?"

He pulled it out of the back of his jeans. It was all black plastic, like a stunt gun. "Don't get all excited," he said. "It's not loaded yet."

She pointed it at the window and fired. Click, click, nothing. So much for her fantasy of nailing him in the chest. "You don't trust me?"

"I don't trust anyone."

"What about your brother?" she goaded.

"He's a psycho. You don't want to mess with him."

"And your other partner?" Dominique kept her inflection casual, determined to mine him for as many details as she could. So far, she counted three kidnappers, and she suspected there weren't any others. From the quiet in the house, she wondered if the other two were outside.

"More trustworthy than most, but requires heavy supervision." He grinned wolfishly. "Never questions orders, though."

"Nice. Where's Gary?"

"In the basement. Come on."

He led her out of the room and along the narrow hallway. On the stairs leading to the first floor, Dominique dropped the gun. It clattered down a few steps, and the man reached for it. "Nerves must be making you clumsy—," he was saying when Dominique palmed the nail, putting her thumb against its flat head and jabbing it into the left side of the man's neck.

He shouted at her as he started to tumble down the staircase. He flung one arm out, seizing the railing to steady himself, but the wormy wood crumbled in his hand and he thudded down, down, down, his big body slamming against one step after another in rapid succession. The wood cracked and groaned in response, one stair splitting open as the man bounced off it. He collapsed on the landing at the bottom, bleeding from his neck.

Dominique held her breath, ready to run and barricade herself in the broken bathroom.

The man crawled to his hands and knees. He retched, but nothing came out of his mouth but a dry gurgle followed by a gasp. He was down but he wasn't out. He unzipped his leather jacket, putting a hand inside to press against his ribs. Had one of them cracked? He turned his head toward Dominique, but his movements were achingly slow.

"You rotten bitch," he spat. He paused again, catching his breath before spewing a stream of invective at her. His eyes were wide with rage, but his words were weak to the point of inaudibility. She'd been waiting for him to regroup and charge up the stairs, but he didn't have enough left in him for that.

Finally, he stopped ranting and stared up at her. In the gray light of the hall, he looked distinctly pale. He put his hand to his neck and stared at the blood. He took a deep, shuddering breath, as if testing his ribs from within. "You've dug your own grave," he said in a stronger voice. "Enjoy it."

With that, he stunned her by stumbling to the front door. He pulled it shut behind him with a decisive slam.

She waited for him to return, wondering what he was going to come back with. Her guess was a powerful gun, but he could have been hunting for one of his partners. All she had was the nail, which she was still holding. She heard an engine fire up and she rushed down the steps, opening the front door in time to see the white van's taillights disappearing down the narrow path through the trees.

11

Even though the wind was freezing and she was in four-inch heels, Dominique ran out of the house and down the dirt road. She didn't believe anything the man had told her, not about the sixty acres or the electrified fence. Her instinct was to get out and get help. But as the van's taillights were swallowed by the darkness, she panicked. There was no sound except for the rustling of the skeletal trees. She turned in a circle, without seeing any lights or other signs of civilization. Something near her cracked a branch on the ground, and there was some rustling and another snap. Was it human, or an animal? In the Hudson Valley, there were sightings of black bears, but she didn't know where she was or what might be stalking her. She ran back in the direction she'd come from. Frightening as that decrepit old house was, it was better, in her mind, than the *Blair Witch Project* possibilities in the woods.

When she got back to the house, Dominique shut the door and locked it. Aside from the slip-covered furniture in the living room, she didn't see anything to barricade the entryway with. Her heart was pounding in triple time. She looked at her hand, realizing she was still gripping the nail. She'd actually forgotten she was holding it. The gun was on the floor, where the man had dropped it as he'd fallen. She pocketed the nail and knelt to pick up the gun. Had that man really believed she would kill Gary for him? Or was it just some prop in a bigger game?

For all she knew, Gary was already dead. That thought stopped her heart for a split second.

Dominique hated to admit it to herself but, in a confrontation between Gary and the gunman, her money would be on the latter. For a former boxer, Gary wasn't much of a tough guy. Mockery was the main weapon in his arsenal.

She started toward the kitchen, picturing the new lock on that crumbling cellar door, but she froze up. It was as if there were a pane of glass in the hallway, blocking her. She could see past it, but not move beyond it.

"Gary!" she shouted. There was no answer, no footsteps, no sign that anyone heard her. If Gary were in the basement, wouldn't he be yelling back or pounding on that door? Unless he was already dead. . . .

She shivered and wrapped her arms around herself, even though it wasn't cold inside. The movement brushed the metal of the gun against her skin, and she cringed. She couldn't face the thought of finding Gary dead, and so she rushed upstairs. She returned to the little room the gunman had stashed her in, setting the gun on top of the blanket she'd left lying on the floor. M&P22 was written in large letters on the side. Under that was SMITH & WESSON SPRING-FIELD, MA U.S.A. It was a mix of black plastic and metal, and even though it had been light in her hand, she felt a residue from it on her palm. There was no powder or oil on her hand that she could see. It had to be psychological. She hated guns. After what happened to her father, was that any surprise?

She backed out of the room, keeping her eyes on the weapon as if she expected it to jump up on its own and start firing. Shutting the door, she kept her hand on the knob, steadying herself. She didn't want to see that gun again. But without the light from the jaundiced bulb in that room, the hallway filled with shadows. There was a creak on the stairs and Dominique stared over the railing, but no one was there.

"Gary?" she called.

He didn't answer. She watched the landing at the base of the staircase, seeing the shadows on the wall quiver. That was just the hanging bulb, she told herself, picturing it on its crooked wire. The warm air in the vents could be making it dance. The house was heating up; maybe that was why the wood was calling out. It didn't have to mean someone was creeping around.

She crept forward, keeping her eyes on the first-floor landing and brushing her hand against the wall until she touched metal. What else did the kidnappers have stashed away? Given how fast the gunman had run, she was willing to bet he'd left things behind. All she needed was a phone.

She turned the knob and inched the door open. There was no light inside and she brushed her hand against the wall, finding a switch. The room was even more spartan than her small cell, lacking even the comfort of a blanket. Its window had been boarded up.

The next one was different. She knew that even before she found the light switch, because the combined stench of the damp and mold of the house was replaced by the sweetness of roses. This room was large, big enough to be called a master suite. It had a queen-size bed decked out with a raspberry satin duvet and plush white pillows. There was a walnut dresser with carved drawers and brass knobs, and a large wardrobe with delicate flowers painted on the front.

What the hell? Dominique thought, momentarily dazzled. It was nothing like a hotel suite or Gary's country house, but, compared to the rest of the ramshackle old building, it was a palace. Was this where her kidnapper was planning to seduce her? He'd worked everything out in advance, or at least, he thought he had.

Her next thought was that the wardrobe was big enough to stash a man's body.

She approached it, listening for any sound behind the pretty, painted doors. Holding her breath, she pulled them open. Swaying slightly in front of her eyes were two men's dress shirts, all freshly pressed and redolent of starch. They were broad enough in the shoulders to fit the gunman, but for all she knew, they'd been hanging there for some time.

Next, she turned to the dresser. In one of the top drawers, she found a folded bundle of white silk. Touching it gingerly with the tips of her fingers, she lifted it, unfurling a stunning full-length negligee with lace insets. It was made by La Perla, and it was Dominique's size.

She dropped it, deeply disturbed by thoughts of what the gunman had been planning for her. What he was *still* planning for her, for all she knew. She had to find a phone. Or a big sweater, or anything that would let her go outside without freezing. Naturally, there was nothing like that, but inside a large drawer at the bottom of the dresser was her purse. She unzipped the top, peering inside. There was her wallet, with cash and credit cards intact. Her makeup. Her jewelry case. The one thing that was missing was her phone. She went through every compartment, but it wasn't there. She zipped the bag closed and returned it to the drawer, dazed.

Catching her breath, she made her way to the en suite bathroom. There was a bottle of Jo Malone Red Roses Bath Oil—her favorite scent in the world—waiting next to a cracked white claw-foot bathtub. There were fancy bath salts, too, and plush white cotton towels. On the vanity counter was an unfamiliar black toiletry kit. When Dominique unzipped it, she found a new toothbrush and an unused tube of toothpaste, along with hand-sanitizing gel, aspirin, Band-Aids, and condoms.

There was no window in that bathroom, but Dominique felt eyes on her. She looked around, but no one had crept in. The only ghostly presence was a haunted image of herself in the rust-edged mirror over the sink. Returning to the bedroom, she stared outside at the clearing. It felt to her as if the trees were crowding in on the house, moving closer to it in the darkness.

The forbidding forest terrified her, but so did the house itself. There was no safe place around her, and in desperation, she sought the faint pinpricks of light in the sky that were fighting their way through the cloud cover. She wished she could remember Desmond's saying. It wasn't running with the stars, but that was close. She re-created the faint echo of his voice in her mind, but she couldn't recall the precise words. Still, thinking of him was a comfort.

The last thing she wanted was to go to the basement, but she knew she had to. She couldn't hide out in the bedroom, inhaling the sweet scent of roses, while Gary was trapped. Nana's voice crept into her head. *Every man shall bear his own burden.* There was no way around it. She had to find him.

Dominique crept down the stairs to the first floor, then made her way to the back of the house, where the kitchen light still burned. The stench still hung in the air, but it was weaker, and the garbage bags were gone. Standing in front of the cellar door, she reached for the bolt. The house had had a little time to heat up, but that deadbolt was cold as death. She held her breath, pulled it back, and opened the cellar door.

"Gary?" she called into the darkness.

There was no answer.

She stood still, listening. Even if Gary was gagged and couldn't answer, she expected moaning or crying, or maybe even retching. Instead, there was nothing. Dead air.

"Gary?" Her cry bolder and more desperate this time.

Nothing.

She tried the switch on the wall again, but no light came on. There had to be a flashlight in the kitchen, she reasoned. The gunman was carrying one when he appeared, and no one was fool enough to wander into that darkness. She hunted until she finally found a tiny penlight that went on when she twisted the top. It would have to do.

She pushed a wooden chair in front of the cellar door so it couldn't close suddenly, trapping her in the basement. Then, shining the thin beam on the rickety wooden steps, she moved down. There was no railing to hold on to, and the steps were in such poor condition, she expected one to give out under her. When she reached the bottom, she shone the penlight across the floor. There were spiders and other multilegged creatures making their way across it. The sight of them made her skin itch. She shone the light in front of her but saw only yawning darkness. What was this place? Was there some kind of pit Gary had been tossed into? She could see rough walls next to the staircase and a little to either side of her, but then everything vanished into a void.

"Gary?" she called again. Her voice was high and thin, as if her heart might pop out of her throat at any second.

Still no answer. No sound at all.

She inched forward, her light on the floor. A centipede wound its way toward her, retreating when she pointed the dim light on it. She watched it on the ground, moving along until it reached the dark edge. Then it disappeared into it. Dominique didn't understand how that was possible. There was nothing but an abyss that light and bugs disappeared into, a black hole in the center of the basement.

Nana's voice pushed her on. *The Lord is my light and my salvation; whom shall I fear?*

She took a step closer, then another. There was nothing but darkness in front of her. She reached out with the penlight, poking it into the unrelenting black void.

The void rippled.

She jabbed it again. Her hand brushed against fabric. Drapes, she realized. There was a set of blackout drapes bisecting the basement, rendering part of the space invisible. She trained the light on the ceiling. It wasn't easy to see the track, but once she knew what she was looking for, it was evident.

Running her hand across the drapes, she found an opening. Pulling it aside, she had the shock of her life. There was Gary, lounging on an overstuffed sofa. He had a blanket pulled over his feet. On a table in front of him was a glass of orange juice, an open beer, and the remnants of a bag of tortilla chips. Gary had white headphones plugged into his ears, which were in turn plugged into an iPad. His hands weren't in cuffs. He wasn't in any kind of restraints at all.

When he noticed Dominique, he smiled.

"Finally." He tugged out the earphones. "What took you so long, babe?"

12

W hat the hell is going on here?" Dominique demanded.

"Not much. I'm watching *Die Hard* again." Gary looked like the proverbial cat who'd just swallowed a canary. "How's tricks with you, babe?"

"What . . . ?" Dominique felt her world crumbling under her feet.

"Were you coming down to check on me? That's sweet. It's nice to know that even though you wanted to drug me into oblivion, you're still kind of fond of me. What was that you gave me earlier?"

"It was a muscle relaxant." She answered automatically, not believing what was in front of her eyes.

"Really? What were you trying to do to me?"

"I was going to tape you saying all the horrible things you normally say about your wife."

"You were going to blackmail me?" Gary's squared-off jaw dropped a little. "Don't you think that's hitting below the belt?"

Dominique didn't answer. It was good that Gary had instantly leapt to a conclusion, especially a wrong one. It meant she wouldn't have to explain, and that was a relief.

Gary sighed. "Never mind. Like Mike Tyson says, everybody has a plan until they get punched in the face." He waved his hand at a small aluminum fridge against one wall. "You want something to drink? I've got plenty of beer, but there's champagne in the kitchen fridge if you want it."

"Champagne . . ."

"You look like you could use a drink, babe. Come sit down." He lifted the blanket and swung his legs off the sofa. "It's cozy over here."

She didn't want to, but she moved toward him. Her body was on autopilot, and her mind was spinning. "I don't understand any of this," she said, reaching the sofa just before her legs gave out under her. "You know a couple of guys kidnapped us, right?"

"Right. We've been kidnapped this weekend. Isn't that perfect? We could use some alone time. Plus, we're in the middle of nowhere, so you can't leave."

"Gary, what's going on?"

"You look like you just saw a ghost," Gary said. "What do you want to know? We can play twenty questions."

"I'm not playing a game. Just tell me what's going on."

Gary shrugged. "That's not a question, you know. But it will be interesting to see your reaction, so okay. Welcome to the wonderful world of kidnapping. It can be done for fun or for profit. For all kinds of reasons, actually."

She stared at him, her face blank.

"Don't be so glum. Look around." Gary gestured expansively with one hand, palm up. "What a nice place for a romantic retreat."

"Where are we? New York? New Jersey? Connecticut?"

"Nope. We're not far from the Delaware State Forest."

"We're in *Delaware*?"

"No, the Delaware State Forest is in Pennsylvania. You ever hear of the Pocono Mountains? We're near them." He shrugged. "It doesn't really matter. Point is, it's Nowheresville. We're so far from civilization, we don't even have Internet out here. No phone. So private. So quiet. We're just in our own little world here. Pretty perfect alibi, don't you think?"

"Alibi for what?"

"Come on, babe, you're not even trying."

"None of this makes any sense. I thought you might be—" *Dead*, she was going to say, but her eyes filled up with tears and she gasped.

"That's sweet. You still care. I was kind of wondering." Gary picked up her hand and kissed it. "I suppose, since this is your first kidnapping, it must be very confusing for you. You had no idea your mission for this weekend was to be a good girlfriend and back me up."

"You set this up?" She pulled her hand away from him.

"Of course I did." Gary looked pleased with himself. "Just like I set up everything for my last kidnapping."

"Your *last* kidnapping?" Her mind reeled, snapping back into the present with a force that made her body jolt forward. "That time you were kidnapped in Mexico . . . you arranged that?"

Gary nodded. "I knew you'd figure it out eventually."

"Why? Why on earth would you do something like that?"

"That time, it was for money." Gary shrugged. "Cheesy, but true."

"You kidnapped yourself . . . to make money?"

"It was the only way to get anything out of that psycho I'm married to," Gary explained. "I've been too embarrassed to explain all of it to you, especially the allowance. It's like I'm a pet on a leash."

"An allowance?"

"I used to get a thousand dollars a week for being married to Trin. It was more when I first married her, a lot more, but her father got annoyed and cut it back."

"This is about money?"

"No, the *Mexico* kidnapping was all about money. Trin's father blamed me for not giving him a grandson. He told me at one point that if I were a real man, I wouldn't give Trin any choice on the subject. Can you believe that? He basically wanted me to rape his own daughter. What kind of sick bastard thinks like that?" Gary's green eyes looked genuinely distressed. "I'm not saying I'm a good guy, but I've never laid a hand on a woman who didn't want me to. And, believe me, Trin *never* wanted me to." He drank some beer. "Bad as Trin's father was, she's a thousand times worse. After daddy dearest died a year ago, Trin cut me."

"She did what?"

"I mean she stopped my allowance." He made a face. "I know I sound like a spoiled brat. What thirty-seven-year-old man gets an allowance? You've been dating a loser, babe."

"We've talked a thousand times about you getting a divorce," Dominique said. "You always said you couldn't because of money. But if she cut off your cash flow, why stay?"

"You forget the iron-clad prenup. I'd have to pay millions back to her family. You think I've got any cash? I've had to scrounge through sofa cushions for coffee money."

"You could have left!"

"Without getting paid for the misery I've been through?" Gary's eyes narrowed. "Don't give me that holier-than-thou attitude, babe. I know you. For someone who's up on her pedestal, looking down at me, you've got some rich tastes and no way to fund them. You think your job styling photo shoots would pay for nice trips and dinners and all your clothes?"

"I never asked you for any of that." She was still too much in shock to take in everything Gary was saying. He'd arranged for them to be kidnapped? Those men with guns were, what, actors playing a role?

He cocked his head and reached for her hand again. "Don't look so miserable, babe. I wasn't lying about desperately wanting a divorce. It just took me a long time to realize I was never going to get one. I've gone over it again and again with Tom—with my lawyer—and there's no way out."

Dominique sat straighter. She knew Gary wasn't telling her the truth, but she had to be careful. She could never let him know how she'd become so well-informed about his situation. Sure, he'd shown her the agreement, but it was hundreds of pages and she couldn't pretend she'd read and memorized it.

"Maybe you don't know this, but there's a rumor in certain fashion circles that Trin wants to divorce you. They say she could do it, now that her father's dead."

That got Gary's attention. "Who said that?"

"Might've been one of Tom Ford's people. Why? Does it matter?"

"Fashion people are crazy. They live on a different planet." Gary shook his head. "Of course, I have to keep quiet, while Trin or her houseboy could babble away to whoever they want. Figures." He took a long drink. "It's true that Trin could divorce me, especially now that her father's dead, but she won't."

"Because of the money?"

"She doesn't want to part with one precious penny, but that's only part of it. She could divorce me, but she'd have to get married again within thirty days. And whoever she marries requires family approval."

"But her whole family is dead."

"Which means that approval is left up to her father's best friend, who happens to administer the trust fund Trin so desperately needs to be the parasite she is."

The conversation was veering into dangerous territory, as far as Dominique was concerned. She'd never been a good liar, and she was pretty sure Gary would know something was off. "Who would she marry, anyway?"

"Well, she's been eyeing the poor houseboy for a while. He's perfect for her: gay, ridiculously handsome, loves fashion. I don't know if she's serious about it, but it made me start poking around the family finances. Now, I'm not great with numbers, but even I can tell that the balance sheet is off. Things aren't as stable as her father led the world to believe. I think there's some kind of Ponzi scheme going on. I showed some stuff I found to Tom, and he said it didn't add up."

"What do you even care? You don't need her money!"

"I'll go out of my mind if I have to keep this charade up much longer. I'm out of cash and out of options, so I had to do something drastic."

"You mean you kidnapped yourself—again—so your wife would pay your ransom and you'll have some spending money?"

"No, I'm planning to inherit it this time around." Gary's grip on her hand tightened. "We're here this weekend so I'll have a rock-solid alibi when Trin's body is found."

13

Dominique heard an echo of the gunman's voice in the back of her head. *Make no mistake: Gary is a murderer.* Was this what he'd meant? He wasn't talking about a murder Gary had already committed; he was aware of what Gary was planning.

"Back up," Dominique said. "Alibi?"

"That's what I said." Gary's eyes were flinty.

"How does being trapped in this house, where no one can see us, give you an alibi? That makes no sense."

"You're thinking of an alibi in the traditional sense. Like, we could go down to Palm Beach, stay at a fancy hotel, let people see us."

Dominique nodded.

"Here's the problem. I haven't got enough cash to buy a Happy Meal, but to the rest of the world, I'm a rich guy. That means, if I go to a fancy hotel with my girlfriend, and my so-called wife is murdered while I'm out of town, I'll still get blamed for everything. The police will say I hired someone to do her in."

"But you can't—"

"On the other hand, if we're kidnapped this weekend, and Trin is kidnapped, too, and she happens to die, that means we were all victims of a crime. Trin's had death threats for wearing the most obnoxious furs. You've seen them. They've still got the fox's head attached, bobbing over her shoulder. It's disgusting. Who's to say some radical group wouldn't hold us for ransom, and get Trin killed in the process?"

Dominique closed her eyes. Tears were trying to squeeze out behind her lids. "Please tell me you're saying this to punish me for what I did," she whispered. "You're not a killer, Gary. You wouldn't do that."

"I've got no choice, babe. I thought things would get better when her father died, but they're actually worse. See, the father cared about appearances, which meant he'd throw money my way so I'd show up at parties and events to be photographed with Trin. But Trin herself couldn't care less. She's got Zachary Amberson backing her up, too."

Even though Dominique was in shock, she had the presence of mind to say, "Who?" at the mention of Amberson's name, albeit a couple of beats late. She was afraid Gary would realize that she knew full well who Zachary Amberson was and, once he did, it wasn't but a hop and a skip to figuring out who she'd been making that tape for.

But Gary was too wrapped up in his own story to notice. "That's her father's best friend. Also his lawyer. He's been working for the family his whole life, but I think that's so he can collect their souls and bring them back to hell. I swear, there's this smell of brimstone whenever he's in the room."

That hadn't been Dominique's experience with Amberson. The attorney had called her about a week after she'd moved out of Gary's condo. *Miss Monaghan, I don't want to intrude, but I understand that Mr. Cowan has, ah, recently changed his living arrangements. We would like to keep that story out of the media's hands.* He'd offered Dominique money, but she had turned him down flat. But Amberson was quietly persistent, sending her a big bouquet of pink roses when she moved into her new apartment and touching base occasionally. When she'd discovered that Gary was cheating on her with a young girl who looked barely out of pigtails, it had been Amberson she'd turned to in her fury.

"Hold on. You're calling this lawyer the devil while *you're* plotting to kill your wife?" Dominique kept her voice steady.

"First, she's not really my wife. She's a crazy cokehead who thinks other human beings are toys. She deserves whatever she gets."

"Gary, you're not going to kill your wife. You're not going to do it for any reason, but especially not for money. That's insane. And evil." She was repeating herself, she realized. Those were the words she'd used when the gunman had asked her to kill Gary.

He leaned closer to her and raised his eyebrows. "You're going to give me a lecture on evil? You're the one who plotted to blackmail me, babe."

"That's not the same!" she insisted. "You can't compare those two things."

Gary laughed, but there was no joy or mirth in it, just brittle bitterness. "You were mad enough to want to hurt me, though."

"That's true." She stood up, moving slowly, circling the small oasis Gary had carved out for himself in the cellar. "When did you find out what I was up to?"

"I had no idea until today. I guess you've been plotting for a while, getting ready to drug me and get me talking about Trin and our sham of a marriage. Max filled me in on the details."

"Max?"

"You know, the guy who kidnapped us. The one who works for me."

Max. She remembered Gary saying that name when the kidnappers first appeared. The muscle relaxant had loosened his inhibitions and his tongue. She had no idea how well it had actually worked.

"Max works for you," Dominique repeated.

"Him and his crew."

"Either Max or one of his crew told me he was going to kill you."

Gary chuckled. "Of course he did. He probably told you all kinds of crazy things. You were supposed to be scared."

"Terrorizing me was part of your plan?"

"Of course not. Max was supposed to rough me up a little bit back at the house, but he knew he couldn't lay a hand on you except to put the cuffs on and off. We were supposed to be kidnapped and brought here. Then, I was going to surprise you with champagne and filet mignon and mind-blowing sex. Kind of like an awesome weekend away. Only, you decided to be evil to me. So that part went wrong, and the stupid fridge broke, so all the gourmet food went bad. One of Max's buddies is getting us food, but he can't go to any dinky little general store near these parts, and the nearest city is Scranton, so you're going to be hungry for a while, babe."

"A guy put a gun in my hand and told me he'd let me live if I killed you."

"A gun? With real bullets and everything?"

"No bullets," she admitted.

"You'd have trouble shooting me without ammo, you know."

She took a deep breath. "He talked about my mother."

That caught Gary's attention. "He did *what*?"

"He said she was a killer, and so am I." Her voice was soft and steady, but her mind was churning. Upstairs, she'd been startled and afraid as well as furious. Now that she knew it was all just a setup, she was angrier than she'd ever been in her life.

"Babe, I'm so sorry." His expression was contrite. "I *never* told anybody to do that. Max knows who you are and he must've looked you up. That won't happen again."

She gave him a terse nod of acknowledgment. "How did you find this guy? Is he an actor?"

"No."

When he didn't say more, her temper flared. "What rock did he crawl out from under?"

"Tom knows him."

Dominique's mind reeled at that. She'd always detested Tom

Klepper. He was nothing but a sycophant who clung to Gary's coattails. The awful part was, Gary lapped it up. Dominique had always suspected that Tom was some kind of father figure to him, since Gary had never known his own dad. That was the only reasonable explanation she had for why Gary would put up with the creep.

"I should've known Tom was mixed up in this," Dominique said. "What I can't believe is that you'd go along with any plan Tom came up with. Haven't you learned anything from the mess he's helped you make of your career?"

"I told you, *I* came up with the plan," Gary insisted. "Tom has just been helping me out."

"Is Tom supposed to kill Trin for you?"

"Of course not. One of Max's people is going to handle that."

"How is he going to do it?"

"Can't tell you that part. But, let's just say, confidentiality is guaranteed."

"What does that even mean?" Dominique put her hands up to her temples. She was dizzy and confused and she wanted to scream. How had she ever become involved with a man who was such a fool? Worse than that, he was prepared to get blood on his hands for money. He was willing to become a murderer.

She took a deep breath. "Gary, I want you to listen to me." She took her seat beside him again and clasped his hand. "You are going to call this off. There is no way you're going through with this psychotic plan. You have to call Max and tell him to stop."

Gary shrugged. "The plan is in motion, babe. I can't stop it now. It's too late."

"No, it isn't. As long as Trin is alive, it's not too late."

"Don't tell me you don't want her dead, babe. This is as much on you as it is on me. I'm doing this for us, and deep down, you know you want her dead."

"That's not true!"

Gary laughed. "You're the worst liar ever, Dominique. The only person you fool is yourself."

"You have to do something! You can't kill her."

He yawned and stretched, already bored with her reaction. "You know what's crazy? You haven't even thought about how you're in danger."

"What's that supposed to mean?"

"I set up this little scenario so I'd have an airtight alibi." He put one hand on her thigh. The gesture was suggestive, even if his tone was lackadaisical. "You should be thinking about how you're going to be so nice to me you'll make me forget how mad I am at you for wanting to blackmail me."

Dominique turned and punched Gary in the face. There was no doubt or regret in her mind. Blood poured out of his nose. He put his hands to his face and yelled. "Ow! What the . . ."

Dominique leapt up and ran, ripping the curtain down as she passed it and sprinting up the stairs. She slammed the cellar door shut and locked it. It took a minute for Gary to start pounding on the other side.

"What are you doing? Let me out of here!" he yelled.

She moved the wooden kitchen table against the door. She had no idea if that would hold, so she ran upstairs to the bedroom and grabbed the gun Max had handed her when he'd told her she had to kill Gary.

14

She paced across the pitted wooden floor, occasionally peering out the window, wondering how her life had come to this. She'd had a two-year affair with a married man who'd murder his wife for money? That realization was so painful and sickening she was ready to run headfirst into that terrifying forest just beyond the house and let it swallow her whole.

The most horrifying part was hearing Gary rationalize everything. You didn't plan to take a life and try to pretend it was no big deal. Killing another person was only justified if your own life was at stake.

She prowled around the room, trying—and failing—to block out Gary shouting and banging on the cellar door. She needed help. Pulling her handbag out of the dresser, she turned it upside down, dumping the contents on the bed. She must have missed her phone on the first search. If Gary had hired the kidnappers, there was no reason to take it, was there? But it was gone. Gary wanted her to have no way to contact the outside world. He wanted to make sure she couldn't stop him.

Deep down, you know you want her dead, Gary had told her. That was a lie. She'd gotten wrapped up in a horrible situation, with her ex spinning a web of an alibi around her. She didn't wish anyone dead, but she was involved in this mess up to her eyeballs.

For the first time in a long while, she thought of her mother and didn't push her memory away. Ever since Dominique understood that her father was gone and wouldn't be coming back to tuck her in at night, she'd blamed her mother for taking him away from her. But she couldn't imagine that her gentle, soft-spoken mother wanted him dead. Somehow, her mother had been holding a gun and it had gone off in her father's face. Her mother must have been horrified by what she'd done. Once it happened, it didn't matter that it was an accident; she was responsible. She had killed a man who didn't deserve to die. Dominique suddenly felt that she understood why her mother hadn't offered any defense at her own trial, why she wouldn't even testify on her own behalf. The guilt had eaten her up. And Dominique understood that even though she hadn't plotted Trin's death with Gary, she wouldn't be able to live with herself if his plan succeeded.

She was so overheated that her skin felt moist, but when she tried to open the window, she couldn't get it to budge. There was a pounding behind her temples that was only growing stronger. Part of her wanted to cry in frustration. But she'd been raised by Nana to have steel in her spine and she wasn't going to fold. Instead, she dropped to her knees beside the bed—just as she had when she was a little girl—and started to pray.

"Lord, I need your help," she whispered. "I'm not proud of what I've done, and I know I should be asking you for forgiveness right now, but that will have to wait. Please don't let that woman be harmed." Even in her prayers, Dominique realized she couldn't quite bring herself to say the woman's name. "Trin Cowan. No, not Cowan. She hates that name. You know who I mean, Lord. Protect her from Gary. Protect her from whoever he's hired to kill her. Any bad thoughts about her I've had, Lord, please know I didn't mean them."

She stood, calmer now in spite of Gary's racket from the basement. "You'll be sorry!" he shouted. Did he have another way out of the cellar? She had no idea. He did have an iPad, and that made her wonder what other electronic gadgets he had down there. A phone would be very, very helpful.

Picking up the gun, she held it for a moment, considering the past. She didn't know what had happened between her parents. Deep down, she wasn't sure she wanted to. Her father had a temper, and she remembered him shouting—never at her or her mother, but at Desmond. He didn't curse, but he'd say things like "I'll make you sorry!" That wasn't so different from Gary at that moment, howling in the cellar. The parallels struck her suddenly, and she set the gun down carefully, afraid it would go off, even though it was supposed to be empty.

Everything that had happened that day showed her she was trapped in the middle of other people's games. Gary had hired some very bad people to kidnap them and to kill his wife. But there was something off about the kidnapper who'd shown her his face. His hatred for Gary was real. *Golden boy,* he'd called him, and there was poison flowing under the words that could only come from envy. *A sound heart is the life of the flesh, but envy the rottenness of the bones.* Nana, again, always with a quote from the Bible at the ready.

Dominique shut the drawer. She was going to end this game.

As she went down the stairs to the first floor, she felt light-headed, almost tipsy. She aimed to be quiet, but every movement caused a creak or a groan.

"Don't think you can keep me locked up, because you can't!" Gary shouted.

The implicit threat meant nothing to Dominique, except that it reminded her of the time. It was almost ten o'clock at night. She didn't know when the kidnappers would be back, and she wasn't looking forward to that reunion. She needed to find a phone. With that in mind, she headed for the kitchen. Gary was banging on the door.

"Cut that out," Dominique ordered. "I'm going to open the door, and we're going to talk. But you need to stop shouting and carrying on like a fool."

The thudding stopped. Dominique pulled the table away from the door and reached for the lock. Deep breaths, she told herself. Three. Two. One. She slid the bolt back.

Gary pushed the door open. "I thought you were going to leave me trapped down there."

"I thought so, too. Lucky for you, I had a change of heart."

He stepped into the kitchen. There were streaks of blood on the front of his shirt from his nosebleed. "You've got a mean right hook," he said. "Anyone ever tell you that you should've been a boxer? You'd be an awesome lightweight."

"I should never have hit you. I'm sorry." She wasn't, not really, but she knew Nana would be ashamed on her behalf, and that was bad enough.

"I deserved it. Pulling a stunt like this, what did I expect?"

There was an awkward pause while he studied the floor. Dominique watched him, but he wouldn't meet her eyes.

"You know this is all wrong, don't you?" she asked.

"I'm not pretending it's right. But I don't have a choice." He finally met her gaze. "I'm trapped and I've got no way out. It's sink or swim for me. I don't expect you to go along with it. All I ask is that you try to understand how desperate I am."

"I know."

They weren't good at talking about serious things together. They never had been. That had always been their biggest obstacle, and Dominique couldn't see a way around it at that moment.

"There are clean shirts in the bedroom upstairs," she said. "There's also a bathtub that looks clean. Why don't you take a bath and rest?"

"Sure." He reached forward, as if he were about to touch her face, but he lost his nerve and tucked a stray bit of hair behind her ear. "What are you going to do?"

"I think I'll open that bottle of champagne you keep talking about."

"Pour me a glass. I'll be down soon."

Gary went upstairs, and she ventured into the basement. It was less scary this time, since the blackout curtains were open, but it was no less buggy. She found Gary's phone in the inside pocket of his jacket. The power bar was below fifty percent, but that was enough for what she had to do. She felt relieved for a moment, but the pounding in her head wouldn't let up. She hurried upstairs and to the front door. She could hear water filling the tub upstairs. The sound was booming through the house as she let herself out.

15

It was pitch-black outside, and so cold Dominique hunched her shoulders and pulled her neck down, turtlelike. She was wearing Gary's jacket, which was so large on her that cold air blew into the sleeves, preventing it from warming her up much at all. She forced her tired feet down the front steps and away from the house. It was raining lightly, and there wasn't a single star visible in the sky to give her the slightest ray of hope. The only lights were the ones on inside the house, and they were more forbidding than the darkness.

At night, the forest was more alive than ever. There was a light crackling noise of creatures moving about, but nothing that sounded big enough to be a bear. She pressed the phone's power button, and it came to life, its bright screen like a beacon in the darkness. She stared at it, grateful for the lone half-bar that indicated shaky service, and moved a little farther into the trees, putting as much distance as she dared between her and the house. The last thing she wanted was for Gary to overhear her. Something brushed against the back of her head, and she stifled her scream, realizing it was only a branch swaying in the wind. Dominique looked back at the house with longing. Awful as it was, it felt safe compared to the invisible horrors swirling around it.

She dialed 911. An operator answered, sounding briskly impersonal. "What's the nature of your emergency?"

"I want to report a . . . um . . . an attempted murder." Dominique gulped on the last word. That hadn't come out right. She didn't feel like herself at all. "I mean, a murder that's being planned."

"Are you in danger ma'am?" The coolly efficient voice of the operator did not sound convinced.

Dominique shook her head as if the operator could see her. "No, no. You don't understand. There's a woman in New York. Someone is going to kill her this weekend."

"Just to be clear, ma'am, no crime has taken place?"

"No. Not yet. But a woman is going to be killed. Her name is Trin . . ." Her voice trailed off. What the hell was Trin's last name?

"Is that a first or last name?"

"Um, I'm blanking on her last name. Hold on." Dominique's headache had subsided a little in the crisp air, but it was hard to focus. "Lytton-Jones, that's it. Trinity Lytton-Jones."

"Look, ma'am, if the crime hasn't happened, you need to call Crime Stoppers." The operator sounded exasperated.

"I need to talk to the NYPD. Can you transfer me?"

"Ma'am, I have to ask, have you been drinking at all tonight?"

"I'm not drunk! This is real. Listen! Her name is Trinity Lytton-Jones. Her husband's name is Gary Cowan. He wants her dead." The words tumbling out of Dominique's mouth reflected her train of thought, but not what she actually wanted to say. They were twisting around her and getting tangled up.

"Ma'am, I hope you know it's a crime to prank-call emergency services."

"I'm not! I just—"

The line went dead. The operator had actually hung up on her.

Dominique put her hand over her mouth, fighting down her panic. Why wouldn't the operator listen? Her head pounded again and she couldn't quite catch her breath. It was so cold her teeth were chattering. Her next thought was to call her friend Sabrina.

That was the only person she'd ever really talked to about Gary and his wife and all that drama. Sabrina was in New York and would be able to call the police for her. But the call just went to Sabrina's voice mail. Dominique glanced at her watch. It was well after ten, which meant Sabrina had gone to sleep. Her friend was ill with lupus, and even though she was an incredibly active person, she needed a lot of rest. She wasn't going to be able to help her now.

There was only one other person Dominique could think of to call, and that was her brother. Desmond knew Gary from his annual visit to New York City, and he was aware of the relationship's sketchy background. Still, it was hard to imagine spilling this mess in his lap. Desmond was steady and calm, and if he wasn't flying his plane he was probably parked with his nose in a philosophy book. She couldn't imagine what he'd think of her situation, or of her. The last thing on earth she wanted to do was explain all that to her brother, but she was going to have to tell him some of it.

She dialed Desmond's cell. "Pick up, pick up, pick up," she whispered as it rang.

He didn't. The call went to voice mail and Dominique almost threw the phone into the woods in frustration. This was too much. There she was, stuck in the middle of nowhere, with no way to get out, and the only people she trusted were out of reach.

"I can't believe you won't answer your phone! You never answer your damn phone. The one time I need you, when I really need you, you're nowhere to be found. Here I am in the middle of . . . of nowhere, Pennsylvania . . . no, the Delaware State Forest, or . . . whatever it is, I'm here, and I've tried to call the police, and they won't talk to me. I don't know what to do!"

She hit the button to end the call, wishing she could slam it and have that reverberate in his ear. She knew she was being ridiculous, and she was just as aware of what she had to do. Gary's phone was in her hand. She could call his wife directly. That was in her power.

Only, she was pretty sure she'd rather be struck by lightning than call. But what choice did she have?

"Fix me," she whispered, recalling a spiritual Nana had been so fond of. She couldn't sing it, but even whispered, it had power. "Fix me so that I can go on despite the pain, the fear, the doubt, and yes, the anger."

She called up Trin's number, and she held her breath while the phone rang.

"Who is this?" demanded the voice that answered. It was clipped and vaguely British and completely artificial. It was a sound that Dominique loathed long before Gary had entered her life. It echoed loudly through the designer showrooms. *STOP. Turn around.* Trin's perennially bored visage was seared into her memory.

"Hello, Trin. This is Dominique Monaghan. We've met before." Her voice was hesitant.

There was silence on the other side of the call.

"Um, this is Trinity Cowan, right?"

"Cowan?" The outrage carried over the line loud and clear. "I'd rather stick pins in my eyes than be called that. It's Lytton-Jones. Cowan is so very common."

"Right. Sorry about that. Look—"

"So it's true, then?" Trin asked.

"What's true?" Dominique was completely baffled.

"That Gary's dead."

Dominique shuddered. "Where did you hear that?"

"The police called tonight. Costa, what was the name?" A man's voice answered in the background, but Dominique couldn't hear him clearly. "A Detective Lee called. He said Gary had crashed his car at the country house. He's supposed to be dead. That's why you're calling me from his phone, isn't it?"

"That didn't happen. Gary is just fine."

"Are you sure?" Trin sounded chagrined. "I was *so* hoping it was true. I never go to the country house at this time of year, but I thought I'd see his body."

Dominique swallowed her disgust. "Whoever called you is lying. Where are you now?"

"I don't know. On a highway somewhere. Costa, where—"

"Listen to me. You're in danger."

"What do you mean?"

At that moment, Dominique realized she couldn't come out with the precise truth. Crazy as it sounded, she couldn't do that to Gary. For all she knew, anything she said could end up in court later. So she improvised. "There's something strange going on. Gary is just fine. I think someone's trying to lure you out to the country house. Turn around."

She half-expected the woman to laugh at her words, which sounded ridiculously vague to her own ears, but Trinity's voice got serious. "I've been expecting this."

"You have?"

"Everyone is jealous of me. Jealous of my family." She murmured something Dominique didn't catch, then raised her voice again. "You're one of Gary's little creatures, aren't you?"

Gary had mentioned Trin's cocaine habit on many occasions, and Dominique had encountered plenty of people in the fashion business who indulged that particular diet. She'd seen the drug encourage delusions of grandiosity and paranoia, but mostly it made people incredibly boring to listen to. Trin had the first two traits down pat, but this conversation was anything but dull.

"I'm his friend."

"You're a tramp. For all I know, *you're* conspiring against me."

"I'm trying to save your life, you idiot."

"I'm the last one, you know. The last of my family," Trin said. "My brothers were murdered. Oh, it was all handled quite cleverly, to make the series of tragic events look like accidents. Misfortunes. Misadventures. The world doesn't believe it, but I know the truth." She didn't sound sad; her voice was almost triumphant. "I suppose I should thank you," Trin added. "But since I detest Gary so much, that sentiment extends to his little creatures, too. I hope you rot in hell together."

16

The wind kicked up and Dominique sank to the ground, clutching the phone after Trin hung up on her. Leaves swirled in the air. At least, that's what she hoped they were; there could have been some bats mixed in, for all she knew. She was sure there was something terrible waiting in the darkness for her. *Let it come,* she thought. *I don't care anymore.*

The phone rang and she considered crunching it under her heel, just so she wouldn't have to hear Trin's voice again. But when she looked at the screen, her heart rose in her chest.

"Dominique?" said a voice in her ear.

"Desmond? Is that really you?"

"You just screamed so loud at my voice mailbox that I couldn't resist calling you back." Desmond's deep voice was warm, but a little on edge. Her uncharacteristic outburst had alarmed him. "You want to tell me what that was all about?"

"I'm in trouble, Des. I don't know what to do."

"Someone hurt you?" His tone was sharp. Desmond had always been an overprotective older brother. Dominique held a lot back from him, things that would've upset him, but she always knew she had him in her corner, no matter what.

"No, it's not that. It's just . . . I'm so lost right now."

"Take a deep breath, baby girl. Start from the top for me."

"Okay. You remember Gary? The guy I was dating?"

"Sure, I remember him." Desmond's voice oozed disapproval.

"What does that mean?"

"Sarcastic, smug, looks like a model for Wonder Bread. He's married but couldn't get out of it for whatever reason. I thought you broke up with him months ago."

"I did. Except that I decided to teach him a lesson by blackmailing him."

"You did *what*?"

"I made plans to spend this weekend away with Gary at his country house. I was going to tape him saying some things he shouldn't be talking about. But we got kidnapped instead. Only it's not *really* a kidnapping, because the guy who did it is actually working for Gary, and he's going to kill Gary's wife."

Telling Desmond what she'd done made her feel like a naughty child again, but she had to come clean. There was a deafening silence on the other end.

"You there, Des?"

"Is this some kind of early April Fool's? You know it's the end of November, right?"

"Please listen to me. This is real. I honestly thought we were being kidnapped. I even memorized the license plate of the van. FAF-7, uh, something. I forget the rest. I had no idea what was really going on."

"Baby girl, you've been involved in some crazy things, but I don't even know where to start with this."

Dominique could picture her brother's expression. It would be stern right now, his brow furrowed in worry. He had a strong moral code he lived by, and nothing she'd done in the past twenty-four hours would survive his scrutiny. Hell, not much from the past couple of years could.

"I can't explain it all right now, Des. The important thing is—"

"You've been seeing a married man. I thought you were done with that, but it's still going on." His voice was flat.

"I told you I broke up with him, and I did."

"If you weren't still involved, you wouldn't have come up with a harebrained scheme to blackmail him." Desmond was doing his level best to sound neutral, but he wasn't succeeding.

"He wants to murder his wife."

"Please don't tell me you're involved in that." His voice was sharper now.

"I'm not. I'd never."

"Okay. Where are you? You said something about Delaware in your message."

"Delaware State Forest, but it's in Pennsylvania. The Poconos, I think. There's an airstrip nearby. A few tiny planes were coming in earlier, but nothing since it got dark."

"Probably a grass landing strip. Okay, that's good. You near a road?"

"We were in the back of a van with no windows, so I didn't see the route. There's no road here, just a dirt path. The house is supposed to be on sixty acres with a fence around it. I don't know if that's true, but it's what the kidnapper said."

"You ever go out there before?"

"Never."

"Who's helping Gary with his crazy plan?"

"He hired a guy named Max. He left a little while ago." She didn't want to elaborate on that subject. She knew Desmond had only contempt for Gary, and this would make it worse. "Do you remember me telling you about Gary's creepy pal Tom Klepper? He helped set all this up. Someone is supposed to kill Gary's wife this weekend, while we're captives at this house. I just called Gary's wife to tell her. Someone was trying to lure her to her country house, but I warned her."

"Where's Gary?"

"In the house. I told him I was going to get some wine, and I got his phone instead."

"Is he trying to hurt you?"

"No, it's nothing like that. He's not violent, he's just . . . desperate." Dominique sighed and turned her head up to the sky. Her headache wasn't so bad now, and the wind must've been blowing the clouds past, because she saw the first flicker of light in the sky. "Gary's been trying to convince me he had no choice. It's . . . it's a long story, but he's got this whole saga where he's the victim of Trin and her family."

"Trin?"

"That's his wife's name." There was a loud beep and Dominique stared at the phone. The low battery icon was blinking furiously.

"Of course it is." Desmond's tone made it clear that he doubted all of this was happening. "I'm only worried about you. Where can you stay so you'll be safe until I get there?"

"You're going to come here?" Dominique whispered. Her heart was already a little lighter. Desmond would take care of her. He'd take care of everything.

"Of course I am. But you'll have to sit tight for ten or twelve hours."

"You're at home?" Even though she'd lived in New York for a decade, metro Chicago was always home to her.

"Yeah, I—" There was another beep, which cut out something he said. "In the meantime, sober up. You're slurring your words a bit."

Dominique was outraged. "You're the second person who said I sound drunk."

"Tell your nerves they'll answer to me if you drink another drop. Have some water."

"I'm not drinking!"

"I'm kind of hoping you are. Like, maybe this is all a bad dream. See you soon."

"Wait!" Dominique said. There was another beep. "What's that thing you say, about running with the stars? I've been thinking about it all day, and I can never get it right."

"'Dwell on the beauty of life. Watch the stars, and see yourself running with them.' That's Marcus Aurelius."

"That's it." She stared at the sky. It was only beginning to reveal itself.

"Don't do anything crazy. Or anything even more crazy than what you've already done, I mean."

"I love you," Dominique said. She wasn't sure if he heard it. She felt guilty about landing him in such a mess, yet relieved for herself. It didn't matter that she was thirty. Desmond was her big brother, and he always took care of things.

She got to her feet, suddenly much steadier. There was still no sign of any car on the dirt road. She didn't want to think about what would happen when Max got back. As much as she wanted out of the house, it was too damn cold to hide outside. She'd wait for him upstairs.

17

The first thing Dominique noticed when she walked into the house was the silence. She'd expected Gary to yell at her when he realized what she was doing. But, given how he seemed to suffer from attention deficit disorder, he'd probably gotten distracted by a spider or his iPad. She'd never feared Gary in her life. Why would she? He was snarky and laid-back and about as harmful as a puppy, excepting those recent murderous impulses toward his wife.

She tiptoed into the kitchen, planning to return Gary's jacket and phone to the basement. She thought she could do it quickly, but there was Gary, sitting at the kitchen table, drinking a glass of champagne. He was wearing one of the freshly pressed shirts from the wardrobe upstairs and he smelled, faintly, of roses.

"There you are," he said. "I was going to send a search party, but then I decided to give you some privacy for your phone call."

"Gary." Dominique didn't know what to say. She sat in the chair across from him. There was an empty glass on the table in front of her.

"Who did you talk to?" Gary lifted the champagne bottle and poured her a glass.

"My brother."

"Oh, sure, Saint Desmond." Gary set the bottle down. "Does he ever get tired of flying rescue missions for puppies in his spare time? Or flying little children for surgery around the country?"

"Don't mock him. He just tries to do the right thing."

"Unlike a loser like me, right? Only, I seem to remember you telling me that his wife left him because he was never home. He was always out, doing good deeds for other people."

"Gary, stop it."

"You're the worst girlfriend in the history of the world. You're taking Trin's side against mine. You have no idea what she is. She wants me dead. I have to kill her before she kills me. It's self-defense."

Dominique sighed. "You could leave her and declare bankruptcy. They couldn't come after you for the money."

"Nope. Believe me, I thought of that. But I checked everything with a lawyer, and I'd still be screwed."

"Let me guess. That's what Tom Klepper said."

"Of course."

"Tom is nothing but trouble. He's the creep who steered you into this lousy deal with Trin's family in the first place. Maybe there is some way out of the deal, but Tom's too stupid to find it."

Gary shook his head. "That's your problem. You don't trust people. Tom's a great guy. He's just not much of a lawyer compared to a sociopath like Zachary Amberson. That's why Trin has been able to stomp all over me. The devil's got her back." Gary lifted his glass in a toast. "To everybody getting what they deserve."

"You sure that's what you want to drink to, Gary?"

He clinked his glass against hers and took a long drink. "I knew I'd never be able to keep the truth about what I was doing from you, babe. That was the real reason I didn't want to see you. I thought I'd be able to get rid of Trin and the coast would be clear for us."

"Oh, really? What about you and your new girlfriend?"

Gary frowned at that. "What's that supposed to mean?"

Dominique leveled her eyes on him. "It means that I know all about your little blond pal. You know, the one who looks like a slutty cheerleader."

"What are you talking about?" Gary looked and sounded genuinely baffled for a moment, until that familiar sardonic smile crept across his face. "You've been screwing around with someone else, haven't you? So you're going to try projecting the blame on me. Nice try, babe." He took a drink. "Not going to work, but nice try."

"I haven't been seeing anyone else."

"Sure."

"Don't play innocent with me! You kicked me out of your condo."

"I had no choice about selling it. That was my only asset. How the hell do you think I financed this?" He waved one hand. "What do you think I used to hire those guys? They don't work for peanuts."

"This?" Dominique looked around the kitchen. "Seriously? If that's true, you're a bigger fool than I thought. How was the plan supposed to work? Why are we at this house? Why here?"

"This house is expendable. Max was going to shoot Trin in the head, and her houseboy if he was along for the ride. Then he was going to bring their bodies here, and we'd burn the house down. We couldn't do that in the Hudson Valley—that house would take forever to burn, and too many people would see it. The fire department would take care of it. But here, in the middle of nowhere? The house would burn down and all the forensic evidence would be gone with it. Bye-bye, CSI."

Dominique closed her eyes. She felt queasy, understanding the method behind Gary's madness. "So we were going to run from the house, like we'd escaped the kidnappers, and Trin and Costa hadn't?"

Gary nodded. "Don't you feel the least bit, just the *teeniest* bit flattered, that I want to kill my wife so I can marry you?"

"Nana used to have this saying, 'What a man will do with you, he'll do to you.'" Dominique set her glass down. "That's what comes to mind."

"Well, you're wrong. I'd never do this to you. I'd never do this to anybody but Trin."

"Yeah, I kind of get the sense it's mutual."

Gary leaned forward. "Don't tell me you called her."

Dominique grimaced. She expected him to explode in a rage, but he just put his head in his hands. "You're killing me here. I'm dating Pollyanna. If you didn't have such a bad temper, you'd be a saint."

"I'm saving your ass, too," Dominique shot back. "I didn't tell her what you did. You two can go back to your Cold War tomorrow."

"You never got to meet Atlas," Gary said. "You would've liked him. He definitely would've liked you." Gary rubbed his forehead. "He was my mom's dog, a Jack Russell terrier who couldn't help but get into trouble all day long. But he was also the sweetest thing." The edges of his mouth quivered, and he looked almost wistful. "After my mom died, Atlas moved in with me, which meant he also moved in with Trin, and that . . . that was a disaster. He liked to chew on things. Like shoes. And he got into one of Trin's closets and . . . well, let's just say the results weren't pretty."

"I see where this story's going."

"No, you don't. Maybe you're thinking she made me get rid of Atlas, but that's not what happened." He cleared his throat. "One day, I came home and Atlas was gone. Just . . . gone. Trin's apartment is huge, so I looked for him, then figured he was napping somewhere. I asked Trin, and she said she hadn't seen him. A while later, I got back to looking for him. Nothing. He's the world's friendliest dog, so I knew something was wrong. I keep looking, I ask the doorman if Atlas could've gotten out. No one's seen him. Then, he suddenly shows up in the middle of the living room."

"Where had he been?"

"The taxidermist's. Trin had him killed, then had him stuffed."

Dominique's breath escaped in a little whoosh. "No. No one would do that."

"She did. She called it a gift. She said he was old and decrepit and how wonderful it would be, now that I could enjoy him forever."

They were both silent for a minute.

"The worst part was I promised my mom I'd take care of him. Then he's dead in my care within a week. . . ." His voice trailed off.

"That's horrifying." She turned it over in her mind. "Was it some kind of revenge, because of you seeing other women?"

"Trin's never cared about me sleeping with other women. She doesn't want to be with me. She only married me because her father told her she had to be married by thirty. He arranged the whole thing." He rubbed his temples with his fingers. "She's an evil person. I know she had a screwed-up childhood. Her father was a crazy control freak, and she was never allowed to see her mother. That would mess anyone up. But at some point, you have to be more than a collection of all the rotten things that ever happened to you. I mean, I had a crappy childhood. My dad tried to make my mom get an abortion, and when she wouldn't, he walked out on her. And you . . . you had a truly awful childhood, babe. Look at you now."

His words made a part of her that was usually hidden twist inside. "It wasn't awful. Just sad. Daddy . . . it was a terrible accident. But I had Nana and Desmond to take care of me."

They were quiet again for a long time. Dominique wasn't sure how it happened, but they were holding hands. Gary yawned and stretched back in his chair.

"Do you want to go upstairs and lie down?" Dominique asked.

"This has been one hell of a day." He yawned again. "I feel like I just went nine rounds with Sugar Ray Leonard. My head is a mess. I'm so tired, I almost fell asleep in the bath. I don't have the energy to drag myself upstairs."

"I'm going to get you some aspirin. I'll be right back."

She went to the master bedroom and got a couple of aspirin out of the toiletry kit. She'd meant to ask Gary about why he'd chosen pretty things for such a macabre place, but she'd forgotten the question with everything else going on. By the time she returned to the kitchen, Gary was slumped over the table, snoring gently. She ran her fingers through his hair, set the pills in front of him on the table, and realized she should have taken one herself. Her headache was hammering under her temples. She picked up her wineglass and went back upstairs. She took some aspirin, then sat on the bed. After a moment, she got up and turned the lights off, then returned to her perch on the bed. She wanted to watch for Max. From the curtainless window, she had a bird's eye view of the dirt road through the trees. When he came back, she'd know.

She sat there for a long while, taking a sip of champagne every now and then. The events of the day had sapped every last bit of energy from her veins. She wondered what Desmond was doing, and where he was just then. She thought about Trin. Just considering the ugly possibilities made her whole body leaden. She curled up under the blanket and put her head on the pillow, but her eyes stayed open and on the points of light outside. Something jabbed at her hip, and it took her a minute to realize it was the nail she'd dug out of the wall. She pulled it out of her pocket and held it in her hand. The sky was perfectly clear now. The thundering hooves in her head wouldn't stop stampeding, but there was some comfort in gazing at the way the stars hung in the sky, like glittering jewels laid out on black velvet. They never changed. She knew that she might be looking at points of light that had fizzled out thousands of years ago, but it didn't matter. From where she lay, they burned bright.

Dwell on the beauty of life. Watch the stars, and see yourself running with them.

That was such a beautiful thought to her. That Desmond. Always so wise.

She drifted into sleep imagining herself soaring up to the sky.

She was a little girl again. Her restless legs were in motion and she was blissfully happy. She was suddenly aware of Nana beside her, reaching for her in the darkness. She clutched her hand and they both smiled, racing to the next star together.

Part Two

DESMOND

18

If Desmond Edgars had his way, he wouldn't be making the drive from the Chicago suburb of Hammond, Indiana, to Pennsylvania alone. Hell, he wouldn't be taking a trip at all. He had plans for the weekend, an arrangement he'd been looking forward to for some time. On the phone with his sister, he hadn't been entirely truthful. Not that he'd straight-out lied to her, but he had company over when she called, and he didn't want the interruption. When Gary Cowan's name first popped up on his phone, he was annoyed that his sister's lame-ass ex was calling him. Then, worry crowded in. Concerned that something might have happed to Dominique, he played the message. There was no turning back once he heard the panic in his sister's voice. When he called Dominique, he had a hundred different questions he wanted answers to. But she rattled off that crazy story of hers in her rapid-fire way— too much information flying at him all at once—while his lovely companion, the one with almond-shaped eyes and legs that went on for days, did her level best to distract him.

When he got off the phone, regret weighed heavily in his voice. "I hate to say this, but I've got to cut this visit short."

"But, baby, we barely got started." She put one manicured hand on his left shoulder, stroking the flame-breathing panther tattooed there. One languid finger looped around the words SPIT FIRE underneath it.

"I know." He slid off the bed, half-turning to put on his shirt.

Pointless modesty, he told himself, but it didn't make him turn around. "But I have to be somewhere else."

"You can't just go, baby. We have plans."

"Don't worry," Desmond said. "I booked you for the weekend, and I'll pay you for the weekend." He glanced at her. "I'm still holding out hope for Sunday."

"Okay, then." That mollified her, at least a bit. "You remember it's extra for house calls, right?"

He did.

Desmond could no more ask that sloe-eyed girl to make the drive with him than he could ask her to take the controls of a plane. Even if she were willing—and he had serious doubts on that front—you didn't draw strangers into family business, and anyone who wasn't family was a stranger. That was his grandmother's rule, first and foremost. He adored his baby sister, but Dominique was a magnet for trouble. She'd never been a bad girl, not by a long shot, but she had a penchant for bad boyfriends and that led her into some hard places. He never heard exactly where until things went sideways into a ditch, though; Dominique didn't ask for his help unless she was desperate. That was why he was willing to drop everything and go to her, but he'd never ask anyone else to do that.

So he made the drive alone, speeding along endless stretches of highway across Indiana and Ohio and into Pennsylvania. A series of composers kept him company on the ride. He started with Francis Johnson's "The Princeton Grand March" and went from there. The music kept him alert—especially Edmond Dédé's "El Pronunciatiamento," which he played several times. The nineteenth-century Creole composer's perfect balance of harmony and discord kept him on edge, yet distracted him from worry. Most of the time, at least. It troubled Desmond that his sister didn't answer when he phoned her from a gas station near Akron. He tried Gary's cell phone as well as her own, but the calls went straight to voice mail.

He wanted to think maybe she'd gotten a little tipsy and carried away. Maybe she was sleeping it off now. But those beeps toward the end of their call meant the battery was dying, so she could be waiting on tenterhooks for Desmond to arrive and spirit her out. He wondered about calling the cops, but swatted that thought away. What could he tell them? Besides, if Dominique wanted them involved, she wouldn't have called him.

He made excellent time, getting to the Delaware State Forest a little after eight in the morning after almost ten hours on the road. But it took him the better part of two hours to find the house. Dominique's directions were good, given she hadn't even seen the route to the house with her own eyes. She'd been sure an airport was nearby, and that narrowed down the possible area to the land between the Delaware State Forest and the grass landing strip at the Flying Dollar Airport in Canadensis, Pennsylvania. If he were unlucky, he might have to go southwest in the direction of the Ponoco Mountains Municipal Airport. But he was sure he needed to look west of the forest. There were no landing strips to the east, not until you passed other state parks.

It all seemed sage in theory, but once he'd spent an hour driving through trees, his confidence wore down. There were too many dirt-road turnoffs and too few signs. After conversations with a gas station owner, a couple of hikers, the owner of a 1950s-era cabin, and the staff of the diner where he grabbed breakfast to go, he finally found the dirt path that led him to his quarry. Desmond knew instantly he'd found the right house when he pulled up in front of it: locals talked about the old mansion that had empty windows that stared back like accusing eyes. The other houses in the area were mostly modest, clean-lined cabins, not overbuilt monstrosities like this.

Desmond knocked on the front door and waited. Nothing. He searched for a doorbell but couldn't find one. There was an old black Honda parked out front with mud smeared over its plate. Was that what Gary was driving these days? Quite a comedown from the Mercedes-Benz he was so proud of.

No one answered, and Desmond started to wonder if he'd just driven some seven hundred miles on a wild goose chase. Gary's heart and soul were in that car. If it wasn't there, then he and Dominique probably weren't, either. Curious and more than slightly annoyed, Desmond made a circuit around the house, peering into the windows that weren't boarded up. The place was only sparsely furnished, but what little there was in the rooms looked attractive in an old-fashioned way. His mother would've politely called it quaint, but his grandmother would have deemed it pleasing. Even so, the house was ragged enough that a strong wind might just sweep it off its feet.

When he got around to the back, he saw a man slumped over the kitchen table. The window was made from panels of thick Coke-bottle glass that made it impossible to see inside distinctly. Desmond had met Gary a couple of times. The sleeping man's coloring and build was a match, but his face was turned away and Desmond couldn't be positive it was him. There was an open bottle of champagne on the table and a glass lying on its side, as if it, too, had passed out drunk.

Desmond rapped on the window. "Gary?" He knocked harder on the glass. "Wake up, man. Open the door."

The man didn't stir.

Desmond didn't like the feeling that settled in his gut just then. He hurried back to the front door, ready to wrangle the lock, but it pushed open without offering resistance. It was the countryside, so why lock a door? Desmond hoped that was the idea. He didn't want to consider the alternative.

Inside, the house smelled as if someone had busted open a can of Lemon Pledge. He went straight back to the kitchen. "Gary?" He recognized the face and put his hand on the man's back, noticing a phone on the table. Gary wasn't breathing. There was no pulse when Desmond touched his neck, and the skin was cool. Gary's eyes were closed and his face was flushed, as if he'd run a marathon before drifting off to sleep and dying.

The rooms on the first floor were empty. Desmond took the freshly polished stairs to the second story two at a time. "Dominique!" he shouted. No answer.

Desmond saw an open door as he reached the upper landing. He ran to it and saw Dominique curled up in bed like a cat.

"I'm here, baby girl," he rasped, rushing to her. "Wake up."

Her chest wasn't rising and falling, but he refused to believe his eyes. The moment he touched her cheek, he knew she was dead, but he couldn't process the thought. Her soft brown skin was cool under his fingertips, yes, but her cheeks were flushed. If anything, she looked relaxed and healthy, dreaming of things that made her lips curl in a smile.

"Wake up," he ordered, his voice barely a whisper. He said it as if she were still the rebellious eight-year-old who told him he wasn't allowed to go into the military and leave her behind. Twenty-two years had gone by since then, but that didn't matter. She was still his baby girl, and she was lost to him.

19

He stood, rooted to the spot and gasping for breath. He couldn't lift his hand to wipe his eyes. There were no bruises on his sister, no serious cuts or wounds. He held her hands, and when he gently pried hers apart, he discovered she was holding a rusty nail. It was a couple of inches long, and he held it up to the light. That wasn't rust. It was blood. Was it Dominique's? He wrapped the nail in a tissue and put it in his coat pocket. Why would his sister be holding on to a thing like that? Her nails were painted hot pink with little gold stars, but the tips were ragged and broken. The damage wasn't dramatic enough to be a defensive wound, but it was completely out of character for a girl who never left the house with a hair out of place. Clearly something had happened. How could Dominique be dead? Had Gary killed her and committed suicide?

Desmond touched his sister's throat, seeing no sign she'd been strangled. Her eyes were closed, as if she had drifted off to sleep and never woken up. *Una nox dormienda,* the Romans called it. A long sleep, after the pain and suffering of life. But a healthy thirty-year-old woman wasn't supposed to sleep like that.

Death hangs over thee. While thou livest, while it is in thy power, be good.

The familiar words ran through his head. Desmond rocked back on his heels. Dominique was the only family he had left, and she was gone. His first impulse was to throw himself out the window. Instead, he straightened his back and looked around. There was a glass on the nightstand. He sniffed at the pale remnants. Chalky, like champagne. He thought of the open bottle downstairs, on the kitchen table. In his mind, the scenario started to unfold. Gary had poisoned Dominique and then killed himself. Maybe Gary had even swallowed the same toxin. That could explain why they both looked like they'd peacefully drifted off to sleep.

Part of him—a bigger part than he'd admit existed—wanted to go downstairs, find an axe, and chop off Gary's head. But that was foolishness now, even he could see that. He had to attend to things properly. Responsibly. That was his job now, and he took it seriously.

He choked back his tears and dialed the police. Words tumbled out of him, first the bare bones of who he was, where he was, and what he'd found. Then, without thinking, he added, "I think it's a murder-suicide."

"Please don't touch anything, sir. It might be important," the operator warned him. She kept him on the line, saying it would be helpful to them to track his signal to find the house. Helpful, sure. His sister was dead and they wanted him to be helpful. And don't touch anything. That wouldn't be helpful. For some reason that one word, *helpful*, grated on him. He'd driven through the night to help his sister, but there he was now, being helpful.

He paced the bedroom, staring at the walls as if they were part of a cage. It was like a hothouse in there, and the window wouldn't budge when he tried to open it. He wanted to take off his coat, but he had nowhere to put it. The only available surfaces were the night table, the dresser, and the bed. He kept his coat on.

"Are you all right, sir?" the operator asked him at one point.

"My sister's dead. How can anything be 'all right'?"

"You sound disoriented, sir. You keep repeating things."

Was he? He had a jackhammer pounding away behind his eyes,

and he felt exhausted. But he'd been driving all night, and all the coffee he'd swallowed was taking its revenge by making his limbs weak and jittery. You didn't have to be a medic to figure out the pain in his chest was caused by the sight of Dominique's lifeless body.

"I'm fine," he answered. "As much as I can be right now."

He was determined to make his way through the house before the police got there. In his initial shock, he'd forgotten something important. Who was the other man Dominique had mentioned on the phone? He couldn't remember. There was an echo of his sister's voice in his head, but it was hazy. Whatever name she'd said was wrapped in a cloak of fog. Desmond had an excellent recall for facts and dates and details, a holdover from his military training, so this lapse gnawed at him as he made his way through the rooms on the second story of the house. They were empty. There didn't seem to be anything to find outside of the bedroom. He went back in and touched her hand again, hoping he'd been wrong about everything. He wasn't.

There was a noise downstairs, like the hinge of a door moving, and the floor creaked. Desmond realized he'd been wrong about one thing. He wasn't in the house alone.

He took the stairs down to the main level, moving as stealthily as he could. On the foyer, he thought he saw something move out of the corner of his eye. He turned toward the parlor, ready to attack, but there was nothing there.

He made his way back to the kitchen again, bracing for a confrontation. But the only person there was Gary, still slumped over the table just as Desmond had left him.

"I think there's someone in the house," he murmured to the operator, before realizing he wasn't holding his phone anymore. He didn't remember putting it down. What the hell had he done with it? He stared around the kitchen, and his eyes fell on the cellar door. It was open, just a little. Had it been that way when he'd first come in? He didn't remember that.

He moved closer to it. There was a sound coming from the basement.

He opened the door wider and saw a light burning downstairs. He started toward it, hearing the sound of a voice. He was halfway down the stairs before he realized the sound was coming from a television. *It's a trap,* he realized. But as he turned to go back, the cellar door slammed and the lock slid shut. He raced up the stairs, throwing his body against the door. He did that again and again, and the splintery wood gave way. As he shouldered his way through the cellar door, he felt as if his legs might give out under him any second. Gary hadn't moved, but Gary's phone was gone.

An engine started up outside. By the time Desmond reached the front door, the Honda was disappearing into the trees. Desmond wanted to go after it, but he tripped down the wooden steps, falling into the dirt on his hands and knees. *Get up,* he commanded himself, but his body wouldn't obey. His limbs were shaking as if a puppeteer were pulling his strings. *Get up. Get up.* He couldn't even lift his head.

He heard the sound of a vehicle approaching the house. For all he could tell, someone was coming back to finish what they'd started in that house. He staggered to his feet, but he fell again, and this time, everything went dark.

20

"How does it feel to be a canary in a coal mine?" asked the woman hovering above him.

She was very pretty. Desmond, even in his quasi-awake state, noticed that. Her skin was a tawny gold, like honey. Her long dark hair was parted in the middle, framing her perfect oval of a face, and her amber eyes were flecked with pale green that looked like bits of old jade. As he came around, he noticed she was wearing a white coat and a stethoscope, even though she looked too young to be a doctor. He wasn't entirely willing to trust that she was real, even though the noise filtering into the room from the hallway—shoes clattering, voices speaking, chairs scraping—didn't belong in a dream.

"A canary?" Desmond's brain tried to process that. He had been drifting in and out of consciousness and having strange visions. He'd come to when people lifted him onto a stretcher, back at . . . back at that damned house. He started to remember it all. It had felt as if a gorilla were crushing his chest, and he'd tried to call out. The sensation eased when they put a mask around his nose and mouth. Next thing he knew, he was in a hospital, lying on a gurney in a busy hallway. He'd talked to another doctor and a couple of nurses. He didn't remember their names. They'd asked him questions. He knew they hadn't answered his: how did his sister die? Somehow, he'd fallen asleep again. When he woke up, he was in a semiprivate room, but the other bed was empty. There was a hospital bracelet on his wrist. He was still in a fog of exhaustion, but he focused on pushing through it.

"That entire house was filled with carbon monoxide." The doctor's voice was soft. "It looks like there was a problem with the furnace. The leak probably started as soon as they turned it on. By the time you arrived at the house, it was full of carbon monoxide from top to bottom."

Desmond swallowed hard. "I didn't smell any gas."

"You wouldn't. Carbon monoxide is colorless, odorless, and tasteless. It's not even irritating, at least not for a while. It's almost impossible for people to detect." She gave him a wan smile. "I'm Dr. Torres, by the way. We're going to do some tests now, if that's okay with you."

"What if it's not?"

She raised an eyebrow. "What do you think?"

"You'll do them anyway. That's what I thought." He lifted his left arm to look at his watch, but it wasn't on his wrist.

"It about four o'clock," Dr. Torres said, answering his unspoken question.

But Desmond was distracted by something he didn't expect to see. "What's that on my hand?"

"It's checking the amount of oxygen in your blood. We're going to do a complete blood count and a—"

"Blood count? I wasn't bleeding."

"We check to see if you have enough red blood cells to carry oxygen, white blood cells to fight infection, and platelets for clotting. We'll also do some metabolic tests. That's mostly to see if the pH level in your blood has changed. Then we'll put you into a hyperbaric chamber."

"Sounds like fun."

"Because you passed out, we're also going to assess your car-boxyhemoglobin and methemoglobin levels. That way, we'll make sure there's no carbon monoxide in your bloodstream."

"Is that what killed my sister?" Desmond asked.

"That's what it looks like. From what we could put together, your sister and her friend were in the house for hours before the CO killed them. They probably went in, turned on the furnace, and had no idea they were slowly being poisoned by it." She touched his arm. "I'm very sorry about your sister. I don't know if this is any consolation, but it's a painless death. Carbon monoxide makes people drift off to sleep, and they just don't wake up."

That wasn't any solace to Desmond, not just then. The shock of Dominique's death was too fresh and too raw. Returning to con-sciousness meant that the pain of discovering her cold body hit him all over again. He swallowed hard. "Her boyfriend, Gary, he died the same way?"

"Yes. There hasn't been an autopsy, but it's pretty clear without one."

He'd built up such a case against Gary in his mind. It was hard to let go of it. Gary was a victim, too.

"There are a couple of officers from the PMRPD who want to ask you a few questions," the doctor went on.

"PMRPD?"

"Pocono Mountain Regional Police Department," Dr. Torres ex-plained. "They seem to have a pretty good picture of what happened at the house, but they want you to clear up a few details."

His brain fog was thinning. He remembered what had happened in the house. "I want to talk to them, too."

"I told them they only get five minutes right now. We need to get you into the oxygen chamber."

The state troopers were waiting in the wings. One introduced himself as Tyson; his partner was Westergren. Tyson did most of the talking. "We wanted to check in with you. Did you know both of the deceased?"

"Dominique Monaghan is my sister. I met Gary Cowan a couple of times. I don't know him well—didn't know him well—but I recognize him."

"What, exactly, was the nature of their relationship?"

"My sister was seeing Gary for the past couple of years," Desmond answered. "But Gary was already married."

Westergren nodded. "We figured it was something like that."

"Champagne, condoms, fancy lingerie," Tyson added. "Kind of obvious what they were up to, you know?"

Desmond gave him a cool, appraising look, and Tyson recoiled slightly, but he didn't look apologetic.

"You've talked to Gary Cowan's wife?" Desmond asked. Dominique had cared more about saving that woman's life than she had her own. He had to know.

"We tried to," Tyson said. "She's not home."

"We tried calling her. Someone from the NYPD went to her apartment to notify her of her husband's death." Westergren was frowning. "She wasn't there. The doorman said she and her houseboy had left in a rush last night and never came back."

"Houseboy?" Desmond asked.

"Rich people can be weird. Kind of makes you wonder if she and this houseboy have something going on, huh?" Tyson wriggled his substantial eyebrows.

All eyes went to him, but no one said a word.

"Well, her hubby was cheating on her, so maybe she was screwing around, too. She's probably not going to be sad he's gone," Tyson added. "Anyway, she's a billionaire heiress, so it's not like she was counting on her hubby to support her."

Desmond remembered how upset Dominique had been when she'd called him. His sister had been agonizing about the wife. Gary had been plotting the woman's death. Only, the world had turned upside down and Dominique and Gary were dead instead.

"Trin," Desmond said slowly. "That's the wife's name."

"Trin Lytton-Jones," Tyson answered. "The names rich folks give their kids, huh?"

"She ran off?"

"Yeah. Why?" Tyson frowned at him.

"Dominique was worried about her last night."

"There's a record of a 911 call your sister made last night from her boyfriend's phone," Westergren said. "She was talking about a woman named Trinity who was in danger. The operator thought it was a crank call."

"Well, we know now what happened," Tyson said. "The doc explained how CO fogs up the brain until you're so confused you can't tell which way is up. So, Dominique Monaghan maybe thought to call 911 because she and Gary weren't feeling well, but then she got confused on the phone." Tyson nodded to himself, as if all the pieces were coming together tidily in his mind. "It's sad. All this could've been avoided if the house had a CO detector."

"It's a tragedy," Westergren said. "I'm sorry about your sister."

Desmond's experience with the police didn't allow him to trust them. He wasn't prepared for this sympathy and obvious credulity.

"Whoever rented them that house may be criminally liable," Tyson said.

"What?"

"Sorry, not them. Whoever rented Gary Cowan the house, I should've said," Tyson explained. "Fellow named Jake Weston. We've got him coming in."

"*Gary* rented the house?" Desmond asked, unsure whether he could believe his ears. Bits and pieces of Dominique's conversation with him were coming back. He remembered what she'd said about being kidnapped, only to find that Gary had really planned everything. Only, how stupid was Gary, if he staged a fake kidnapping at a house he could be easily traced to?

"Yes. Can't imagine why. It's a wreck."

"There was someone in the house when I went in," Desmond said. "What about him?"

Tyson and Westergren looked at each other. "Who?"

"There was a black car, an old Honda, parked in front of the house when I got there. When I was in the house, someone locked me in the basement. I had to break the door to get out."

Tyson shook his head. "There wasn't anybody else there. There was no car, except yours."

"I noticed that," Westergren piped up.

Desmond and his partner stared at him. The kid couldn't have been more than twenty-two.

"I noticed that your sister and her boyfriend didn't have a car there, even though there are tire tracks," Westergren explained. "You'd have to use a car to get to that house. It didn't make any sense."

"Huh." That was all Tyson had to offer.

"That was weird," Westergren said. "That and . . ."

"What?" Desmond asked, but the doctor was there, interrupting them.

"I'm sorry, but we really need to get Mr. Edgars into the hyperbaric chamber," Dr. Torres said, just as Desmond's body shot some adrenaline through it and his brain was heating up. "Any other questions will have to wait."

"Wait," Desmond panted. "You were saying—"

"Hyberbaric chamber, now." The doctor's voice didn't brook any argument. Westergren retreated. Tyson was already gone.

21

The oxygen treatment in the hyperbaric chamber took ninety minutes. That gave Desmond plenty of time to think, with no questions or accusations flying around him. It hadn't occurred to him how the scene at the house would look to the cops. He'd walked in, armed with the knowledge of Dominique's scheme to blackmail Gary, and Gary's horrible plan to rid the world of his wife. But, mentally backing away from that information, he saw how the police eyeballed the scene. A couple having an illicit affair went to a house in the country for some alone time. While they were there, they both fell ill. They never knew the cause and they died from invisible but insidious carbon monoxide pouring out of a faulty furnace. You put those puzzle pieces on the table, and however you arranged them, they added up to the same thing. It was a tragic accident. That was all.

Desmond remembered Dominique saying that the guy Gary had hired to play kidnapper had left. Max, that was his name. The situation started to look awfully convenient, all of a sudden. Maybe Max knew there was something wrong with that furnace. Dominique had told him Max worked for Gary, and he had a co-conspirator who was going to kill the wife. But maybe that series of links fit a different way, too. Maybe Max's unnamed helper worked for Gary's wife, and Max was supposed to get rid of Gary. Maybe it all came down to who was willing to pay more for murder.

What didn't track, in Desmond's mind, was method. Max could have killed them any number of ways at that isolated house. Instead, someone had rigged the furnace to fill the place with carbon monoxide, sending both Dominique and Gary to a quiet death. Was Max such a coward he couldn't face his victims to kill them? Or was he just a very organized killer, one who knew that the state police would have to investigate bullet wounds, while they could write off CO inhalation as an accident?

Desmond realized that his own arrival made the death scene look even less calculated. Dominique had called her brother, and he'd come running to the house, only to end up poisoned by carbon monoxide himself. That was a credible accident.

It all fit the murderer's design perfectly.

There were so many angles Desmond couldn't quite figure, but that one was obvious to him. Someone had planned for Dominique and Gary to die in that house. His sister had been so frantic about the danger Gary's wife was in, she never saw the danger to herself.

Lying in the metal-and-glass cylinder, unable to move, Desmond pushed his thoughts toward the best way to proceed. He could tell the cops everything he knew, but what would that accomplish, exactly? Desmond wasn't eager to reveal that Dominique hadn't been on a romantic getaway with her boyfriend, Gary, but a mission of blackmail. He pictured that detail making it to the tabloids—as it undoubtedly would—and he knew his sister's reputation would be dragged down into the mud.

No, it was better to focus on his own experience. Someone had been in the house when he barged in. He'd never caught a glimpse of the person. For all he knew, there'd been a whole team of assailants there, but he would've bet his life that it was just one coward, working solo. All he'd really seen was the car. Unlike his sister, who'd had the presence of mind to memorize the plate of the kidnapping van, he'd barely glanced at the black Honda. The plate hadn't been visible, and he hadn't investigated.

So, who was there, and what was he doing? That led Desmond's mind back to the elusive Mrs. Gary Cowan, otherwise known as Trin Lytton-Jones. There was an ugly thought coiling around the back of his brain like a snake: Dominique thought Max was working for Gary. But what if Max was actually working for someone else . . . like, say, Trin? The woman who just happened to run off with her houseboy. How convenient was that?

When Desmond was pulled out of the glass coffin of the hyperbaric chamber, Dr. Torres was waiting. "How are you feeling?" she asked.

"Fine. Unusually clear-headed, actually. When the troopers brought me in, did they give you my phone?"

"Yes. One of them said you dropped it before you passed out."

"I didn't pass out," he countered, gritting his teeth. "But I need to call some folks."

"Of course. You must have so many people to call, and arrangements to make. I hope you don't feel you have to do everything at once. I can't imagine how difficult that would be. Do you have other family that can help?"

"No."

"Oh. I'm sorry. This is so sad for your parents."

He didn't have the heart to tell her his parents had been dead for some time. He wasn't about to open the story of the death of Dominique's father, either. It had been many years since Desmond had willingly spoken the man's name, and he didn't think he could say it without injecting poison into it. Let that sleeping dog lie.

"I guess I'll rest for a bit," he announced when they got back to his room. After the doctor left, he got up and found his clothes. He had no intention of lingering in the hospital any longer than he had to. He needed to go back to the death house. He suspected the local cops would sign off on accidental death sooner rather than later, and he wanted proof that his sister had been deliberately killed.

When he was ready to leave, he opened the door and found Dr. Torres waiting for him.

"How was your nap?" she asked.

"Don't you have sick people to take care of?"

"That includes you."

"Don't make me sneak out of this hospital," Desmond said. "That would be undignified, but I will if I have to."

"You lost consciousness from carbon monoxide poisoning. You don't realize how serious that is."

"I feel fine." He shrugged. "Maybe a little tired, but otherwise I'm good."

"You can have symptoms come up afterward, things that might seem unrelated. CO messes with your body at the cellular level. You could end up with memory problems, or lack concentration or the ability to keep track of things."

"My teachers told my mother I was a hyper kid. They said I couldn't concentrate on anything but wreaking havoc."

"This isn't funny. You can have mood swings, or you could suddenly have food or chemical sensitivities."

Desmond didn't try to hide his incredulity. "What, I'm going to be allergic to peanuts all of a sudden?"

"For all we know, yes."

He waited for her to smile, but those amber eyes were intense. "You are kidding, right?"

"Not even slightly. Look, I'm not saying it's likely. You could be perfectly fine. But you're walking through a minefield with CO exposure. You could have tremors or headaches or fatigue. You have no idea how bad it could get."

"I'll turn into a hypochondriac if I listen to much more of this."

"Better that than an invalid. You're a pilot, right?"

"How did you know that?"

"It was easy to guess from your membership cards to the Professional Helicopter Pilots Association and the Black Pilots of America, plus the other ID in your wallet. I'm guessing you don't want to give that up. You know a doctor could get your license pulled, right?"

That rocked him to his core. Desmond loved flying. There was nothing in the world like the freedom he had in the air. Taking that away from him would be a kind of death.

"I want you to have another treatment in a hyperbaric chamber. Maybe more than one. Will you do that?"

"Sure."

"You won't. I know your type. You think you're so strong that nothing can touch you. What's so important that you have to leave the hospital right now?"

"Seriously?" Desmond gave her a look. "'A man is only worth as much as the things he concerns himself with.'"

Dr. Torres's eyebrows lifted. "Are you quoting philosophy at me?"

"Marcus Aurelius."

She paused for a moment, thinking. Her eyes were bright like a hawk's. "The Roman emperor?"

"And Stoic philosopher."

"Oh, a stoic." Dr. Torres's voice was gently mocking. "The kind of guy who thinks that if he pretends not to feel any pain, he won't actually feel it? Here's news for you: suppressing feelings doesn't mean you don't experience them."

"That's not what I'm talking about." Desmond wasn't inclined to share his personal thoughts with strangers, but he liked Torres. "People who say 'stoic' mean being unemotional. That's not what the philosophy is about. Stoicism doesn't mean you don't have feelings, but that you don't let those feelings control you."

"It still sounds like suppressing your emotions. That's not healthy."

"It's more like you feel them, but you let your better judgment guide you. Or you try to, anyway."

"I'm not sure why, but it's hard to picture you reading Marcus Aurelius."

He raised an eyebrow. "Are you stereotyping, Doctor?"

"No." She looked horrified. "I never meant that. I . . ."

"I know." He paused. "Tell you the truth, it's a struggle right now. My baby sister is dead. I'm going to have to bury her, and that is something I can't think about without getting emotional."

"I can only imagine." She handed him a folded piece of paper. "I wrote this up, in case it would be helpful."

Desmond opened the page. There was the name of a nearby funeral home and some other notes.

"I figured you'd want to take your sister home to be buried," Dr. Torres said. "Her body hasn't been released by the coroner yet. Depending on how long that takes, she may need to be embalmed before you bring her home. I know this is a lot to deal with right now, but if I can help, I'd like to."

"Thank you." He folded it up again and put it in his pocket. "Do I have to keep calling you Dr. Torres?"

"It's Willa."

"That's a pretty name."

"Thank you."

Now that the conversation had taken a vaguely flirtatious turn, Desmond didn't know what to do with it. His mood was about as far from romantic as it ever got. Desmond figured he'd have to be dead and buried and part of the ether before he stopped noticing attractive women, but he knew he wouldn't be acting on it.

"I want to talk with the cops again."

"They've already left. I can call them."

"I'd appreciate that."

Dr. Torres started to move down the hallway. "Don't think about going anywhere."

"I'm fine," he insisted.

"Well, I've got your laptop. If you want it back, you'll be spending the night in the hospital." She gave him a long look over her shoulder. "This isn't a negotiation."

22

Desmond couldn't get the cops to come back to the hospital on Saturday night. But that only gave him time to read and research and prepare. By the time he hunted Westergren down at a diner on Route 84 at nine o'clock Sunday morning, he was ready.

"They let you out of the hospital?" Westergren was clearly surprised to see Desmond, even though they'd spoken on the phone. The young cop hadn't sounded thrilled about getting together—to be fair, Sunday was his day off—but at least he'd agreed to it.

"Dr. Torres forced me to stay in for observation last night. That was enough."

Westergren nodded, as though that made sense. "I'm no good at lazing around, either. My partner, he'd be watching TV and hitting on the nurses."

"They've got some good-looking doctors at that hospital, too," Desmond commented. "But I've got a lot on my mind right now."

"That's what you said on the phone." Westergren's eyes were steady on his. He was a pleasant-looking kid with a boyish haircut that made him seem even younger than he actually was. His pale skin was flushed red, and there was a constellation of freckles over his nose. His prominent ears, which swung out like open doors on a car, gave him a faintly comic aspect. But Desmond realized the young man actually gave a damn about what had happened. In his estimation, that was more important than Westergren's youth and inexperience.

"What I need to know is this," Desmond said. "Is there any way that house could be a crime scene?"

Westergren's eyebrows rose. "You think this was foul play?"

"Yes. And at the hospital last night, I got the impression there's something that makes you think twice about this being an accident."

"Why're you asking me? I'm new on the job."

"You didn't say much at the hospital, and maybe I was a little out of it, but you were the one taking notes. A couple of times, when Tyson said something, you looked like you wanted to put your two cents in, but you held back."

"I've been here four months. This is my first real job in the field. I'm still learning." Westergren drank some coffee. "Tyson's gone over the scene and put together a working theory of what happened, and he's positive the deaths were an accident."

"What do you think?"

Westergren gave him an earnest look. "I think Tyson's decent at what he does, and his theory holds together. I mean, look at the facts. Your sister and her boyfriend came out to the house, which the boyfriend rented for them. They're having an affair and they want privacy. Maybe a car dropped them off—that part isn't clear right now. But we know they turned the furnace on, and it's faulty and it fills the house with carbon monoxide. Within a few hours, they're dead, and they probably never knew what hit them. It all hangs together."

"But?"

Westergren's eyes were wary. "But nothing. You probably think we're country mice who don't know how to do our jobs. Or we're too lazy to open a homicide investigation, so we're sticking with the accident."

"I don't think that." Desmond kept his voice even.

Westergren leaned forward. "The PMRPD is responsible for an

area over two hundred square miles. You know how many officers we have? Thirty-eight." He let that sink in. "It's a great force. Professional. Organized. But we're stretched thin. We have to ask for donations on our website."

"I'd be willing to donate," Desmond said. "How much?"

The young cop looked horrified. "No! I'm not trying to shake you down for money. I just want you to understand. We have seriously limited resources. We can't do what police in Pittsburgh or Philadelphia or New York would do."

Desmond thought about that. "To turn that around, if someone were planning a crime and they wanted to boost their chances of getting away with it, they might pick an area with a police force that's underfunded and shorthanded. Hard to go over a crime scene with a fine-toothed comb if you don't have the manpower."

"Why do you think it could be a crime scene?" Westergren leaned closer. As much as he claimed he didn't want to get involved, he seemed drawn to the idea that they were dealing with more than an accident.

"First of all, someone locked me in the basement. Given that the house was filled with carbon monoxide, I think he wanted to kill me."

Westergren shook his head. "I talked to a couple of doctors at the hospital. They said inhaling all that CO might've made you delusional. Maybe when you went down to the basement, the door shut and you panicked."

"That's not what happened." Desmond paused for a moment. "I broke through the door. Was the bolt still on when you saw it?"

"Part of it was torn off the wall when you broke down the door. The bolt was pointing down, like it had been shut, but could have been gravity. It just wasn't clear." He cocked his head. "Did you *see* anyone at the house besides your sister and her boyfriend?"

"I saw a car parked out front. . . ."

"There were tracks from a few different cars in front of the house," Westergren said. "Did you see another person in the house, or creeping around it?"

"No." Desmond reached into his coat pocket. "This was in my sister's hands when I found her body." He opened the crumpled tissue to reveal the two-inch-long nail. "I think there's blood on it. You could do a DNA analysis."

"You really shouldn't have taken that from the scene. It's going to make it pretty much impossible to process as evidence."

"I should've thought of that, but I didn't." Desmond set the nail in its frail white shroud on the table between them. "I wasn't thinking straight. When I realized my sister was dead, I . . . It was such a shock. I'd just talked to Dominique a few hours before. It still doesn't seem real."

"I don't think it ever does." Westergren sounded older than his years.

Desmond paused and weighed his words. In the hyperbaric chamber, and late Saturday night, he'd had time to think about what he wanted to say. "The thing you need to know is that my sister was scared."

"Scared of what?"

"There was a man named Max who drove them to the house. He took off, and he never came back. Now, maybe Max got into an accident. Maybe he got a call from home, saying he was needed. But don't you think it's strange that Max drove away from the house, never returned, and the two people he left behind ended up dead?"

A pen mysteriously appeared in Westergren's hand while Desmond was speaking. "Max," he wrote on a fresh page. "What do you know about him?"

"Dominique said there was something strange going on with

Gary, but she didn't know what. She said Max was at the house, and he was working for Gary, but he seemed like a thug."

"Did she describe what he looked like?"

"Not really." Desmond cursed himself for not asking Dominique to describe the man. He'd been so overwhelmed by the crazy story she spun on the phone that he hadn't even thought of it at the time. "Max showed up at Gary's house in the Hudson Valley. Dominique had no idea what was going on. Max was the one who drove Dominique and Gary to the house. It was in a white van, and the plate number was FAF-7-something."

Westergren almost dropped his pen. "How do you know the plate number?"

"Dominique believed something was wrong." Was it a mistake not to mention the mock kidnapping? Dominique had told him Gary set it up. Still, the couple had ended up dead, so maybe Max hadn't been playing the same game Gary was. "Look, what Dominique said was that it felt like a kidnapping. The guy showed up at Gary's house, put them in this van, and drove them for almost three hours into the middle of nowhere. Dominique only found out later that Gary set it up. She was pretty pissed off about it."

"This is incredible." Westergren made some rapid notes. "When did she last see him?"

"Dominique said Max drove off in the evening."

"So, Max stranded them at the house. They had no way out." Westergren shook his head as he wrote. "I *knew* something was screwy."

"You saw something strange in the house?"

"The fridge."

Desmond stared at Westergren, waiting for him to add something else. "What about the fridge?"

"Did you open it? The food in it was bought recently, but it rotted," Westergren said. "Here's the thing: there was nothing wrong with the fridge, and there was no power outage in the house. The lights were working and there were no fuses blown. You know why the food went bad? Somebody unplugged the fridge."

Desmond took a moment to process that. "It was unplugged when you went into the house?"

"Right. Think about it: somebody got the house ready for them coming over, right? But then someone unplugged the fridge?" Westergren got more animated as he spoke. His Adam's apple bobbed with excitement. "It was a guarantee they'd have no food, because they had no car and no way of getting out. I mean, they were basically trapped in that house. They had water and wine, and some chips and stuff, but no real food. Now, here's the thing." He leaned forward again. "I got the cell phone records. Gary Cowan's cell was used to make a bunch of calls."

"To who?"

"You, and a lady in Brooklyn named Sabrina Ogden—that call was less than a minute, so it might've gone to voice mail—and Trinity Lytton-Jones in Manhattan. You know, Gary Cowan's wife. Before that, there was a call to a Thomas Klepper, also in Manhattan. It went on for more than half an hour. He called Gary's phone a few times yesterday."

Tom Klepper. Dominique had mentioned him as Gary's partner in crime. Desmond couldn't wait to hear what that man had to say for himself. "You call him back?"

"No. Tyson says that's a waste of time." He grimaced. "There were no other calls on that phone," Westergren added. "Now, if you were at a house with no food, wouldn't you be calling somebody to rescue you?"

"Unless you had a guy who was going out to get food for you."

"Whoever unplugged the fridge did that days ago. That food wasn't just rotting for a few hours."

"Days," Desmond said, not so much to Westergren as to himself. He'd noticed the fridge but missed the significance, but this gawky kid who was still wet behind the ears had picked up on it. "What does your partner think?"

Westergren deflated a little. "Tyson says the plug probably fell out of the wall. He thinks because nobody's lived in the house for years, anything could happen there. To him, the key is that the deaths were obviously an accident."

"Were they?"

"There's no doubt about the cause of death. That was carbon monoxide exposure. The coroner doesn't even think an autopsy is necessary because it's so obvious. We don't exactly do a lot of autopsies around here, you know. But, if somebody drove them to that house and left them there, maybe that somebody knew the furnace was faulty."

"And that would be murder."

Westergren nodded. "Tough to prove anybody knew the furnace was faulty, though."

"What about the guy who rented them the house?"

"We talked to him. He was really upset when we told him what happened. He swears there was nothing wrong with the furnace when he leased the house."

Desmond's eyes narrowed. "I still find it hard to believe Gary rented that house. Did the agent ever meet him?"

"No. Everything was handled online." Westergren flipped back through his notes. "The payments were made on a corporate card registered to a company called Sardanapalus."

"Hold on. Sardanapalus." Desmond rubbed his forehead. His mind was still not working quite as well as he expected it to, but he knew he'd encountered that name as he's crawled the Internet into the small hours of the night at the hospital.

"Um, I already looked it up," Westergren said. "Gary Cowan is an honorary board member."

"Sardanapalus." Desmond's hand thumped against the table. "Of course. That's the holding company that belongs to his wife's family. Gary's the honorary board member who isn't even invited to board meetings. Dominique told me that." The picture in Desmond's mind was getting clearer. "So, either Gary made the transaction, or someone who worked for his wife did." He could still hear the urgency in Dominique's voice, her fear that Trinity Lytton-Jones was in danger. She couldn't have had any idea that Trin was really the hunter. Gary and Dominique had been the prey.

23

Okay, what are we actually looking for?" Westergren asked. He and Desmond stood in front of the old house together. The death house, as Desmond thought of it. The sun was shining, but that only made the decrepit old place look shabbier.

Westergren reminded Desmond of some young recruits he'd met when he joined the Army at eighteen. They sought direction, and they liked having someone to lead them. Desmond had been young and just as green, but he'd felt about a hundred years older, even then. He knew exactly why he was there, even if they didn't. *Waste no more time arguing about what a good man should be; be one,* as Marcus Aurelius wrote. That was almost, word for word, what his mother had told him when he was fourteen.

"Basically, we're mapping the scene," Desmond explained. "Taking pictures, looking for anything that seems strange or out of place. In CSI terms, it's a second walk-through." Desmond was making it up as he went along. His military experience flying helicopters in Afghanistan wasn't relevant here, but his soldierly bearing was. He could convince Westergren to follow his lead without revealing he was following crime scene investigation tips he'd picked up on television and online. "Remember, we want to make sure we don't add anything to the scene. That just confuses things later."

"Got it. Where do we start?"

Desmond felt the first stirrings of nausea whirling around him as he considered walking into the house again. "Let's walk the perimeter. That's what I did when I first arrived."

"Some of these windows are boarded up," Westergren observed. "Makes the place extra-creepy. You kind of wonder why your sister and her boyfriend didn't just turn around and go home."

"I wonder if they had a choice." Desmond stared into a window. "Somehow, I doubt it." The room he was peering into was one he'd seen the day before. Now that he knew there'd been someone else in the house, he wondered where that person had been when he entered. There wasn't much furniture to hide behind, but there were so many nooks and crannies.

He and Westergren continued to the back of the house. "That's a weird choice for a kitchen window," Westergren observed. "The thick glass makes it hard to see inside or out. Everything would be kind of warped."

What caught Desmond's eye was the caulking around the window. It was a pristine white, and it looked new. "Did you notice anything around those other windows?" Desmond asked. He took a few steps back and stared up at the house. Every window had that same thick white caulking around it.

Westergren moved to stand beside him. "The weatherproofing." He let out a low whistle. "Somebody sure went to a lot of trouble to make sure the windows were sealed. It looks weird. The caulking really stands out."

"Except at the front of the house, where it's boarded up." Desmond snapped some photos and Westergren followed suit. He pointed at one window, noticing it was broken. "Was it like that yesterday? I don't remember noticing any broken windows or a draft."

"Tyson did that," Westergren explained. "We had trouble airing the house, because none of the windows would open. We didn't want to risk anyone else getting carbon monoxide poisoning."

"I would've done that yesterday if I'd had the presence of mind."

Desmond took a deep breath, remembering how stuffy and hot the house had been when he walked in, and how despair had made him overlook that. "Let's take a look at those boards over the windows."

They circled around to the front. Desmond put his hand on one of the wooden planks. "Just so you know, this isn't exactly standard CSI. But we need to check this out."

He tugged at the board, and it gave way easily. Underneath was a perfectly fine window that had heavy sealant around its border.

"So, a perfectly good window was boarded up?" Westergren said.

"Makes the house look creepy, which might have been the point. But it also keeps anyone from wondering why there are rings of caulking around each window."

When they finally trooped inside, the first thing they checked was that the furnace was off. Desmond braced the front door so it would remain open, just in case. He wasn't taking any chances.

"We saw the broken railing." Westergren pointed to the staircase. "There are some splintery bits around, so it looks like it happened recently, but neither your sister or Gary had any bruising. Maybe it happened before they got here."

Desmond hadn't really noticed the railing before. The house was such a ramshackle, crumbling mess he'd assumed it was part of the eerie setting. Now, he regarded it with fresh eyes. "It looks like someone might have fallen near the top of the stairs, and they grabbed it. That would be quite a fall, though." He walked up the stairs. Westergren followed.

"We found a couple of guns," the young cop said. "They were both unloaded, and we didn't find any bullets. The big bedroom is kind of interesting."

The door was open and they entered, Desmond haltingly, the memory of his sister painfully fresh. This was where he'd found her. He knew that moment would haunt him in dreams for the rest of his life.

"There was a shirt with blood on it soaking in the sink in the bathroom." Westergren interrupted his thoughts. "It didn't look like a big deal yesterday, but . . ."

"Take note of everything. Maybe it was a nosebleed. But you never know." Desmond sniffed the air. "Roses. It smells kind of like my sister's place. She loves roses." He realized he'd used the present tense, but Westergren didn't correct him.

"That's partly why people think it was a romantic weekend away. There's all kinds of expensive stuff, like bath oil. Rose-scented everything."

They went from room to room, then down to the first floor, and finally to the basement. Aside from the obsessively weather-proofed windows that refused to open, there wasn't anything that seemed suspicious. Sure, it was odd that there were only a couple of habitable rooms, but that didn't make it a crime scene.

Westergren stopped to tie his shoe on the way out. "I'm glad we did this," he said. "Even if it didn't pan out, it'll put your mind at rest."

Desmond was still looking around, catching a faint glimmer at the edge of his peripheral vision. In the light, they didn't register, but in dark spaces, they became apparent. He thought of Dr. Torres's warning in the hospital about the fallout from CO poisoning, but he kept that to himself.

"You know what's strange?" Westergren asked.

"What?"

"This house is kind of disgusting and musty, right? I mean, aside from the nice rose-smelling stuff upstairs, it's pretty gross." He pointed to the stairs. "But these are sparkling clean. Not the ones at the top, but the others."

Desmond gazed up and down. The young cop had a point. The

stairs had been freshly polished. He remembered smelling a lemony cleanser when he'd walked into the house. "Look at the floor in the foyer. The part nearest the stairs has been scrubbed down."

"Why would somebody only clean that part of the house?" Westergren asked.

They both stared at the broken railing.

"I know you don't have a lot of resources, but you think someone can get their hands on any luminol?" Desmond asked. "I think I interrupted someone cleaning up a crime scene yesterday."

24

By the time a real CSI tech showed up to take samples, it was one o'clock Sunday afternoon, and Desmond was exhausted. He and Westergren had to wait outside. It was cold, but the sun was shining hard.

"Can I ask you something? If you wanted to be a pilot, how come you joined the Army instead of the Air Force?" Westergren asked.

"You have any idea how tough it is to get into the Air Force?"

Westergren shook his head.

"If you've already got four years of college under your belt and a pilot's license, the Air Force might take a look at you," Desmond explained. "They're flooded with applications. If there's any reason to turn you down, they'll find it. They've been known to reject recruits for hay fever."

"So they turned you down?"

"Yeah. They had a great time laughing at my application. Stupid inner-city kid who'd never even *been* on a plane wanted to fly." The memory still stung, but with less force than it used to. "I felt like a total fool. But one recruiter pointed me to the Army. They needed chopper pilots."

"It still sounds amazing."

"It was. I loved the service. Don't think I realized how hard it would be to retire from it."

"You're retired? But aren't you only forty?"

"You can retire after twenty years. I got in at eighteen, so I got out at thirty-eight. I figured I'd had enough of deployments. I was looking forward to civilian life."

Westergren cocked his head, his wide-set ears giving him a faintly comical appearance. "Now that you're out, how do you feel about it?"

"I miss the sense of purpose I had in the service," Desmond admitted. "You ever think about joining?"

"That was my dream. But my parents were terrified I'd get sent overseas and blown up. So I'm doing this." He sighed. "I thought I'd be making a difference. Catching bad guys and all that. But . . . well, things never turn out the way you think they will." Westergren had a strange habit of seeming very young at one moment, then transforming into an old soul, Desmond noted.

They were quiet for a while, pulling out phones and checking messages. Desmond found it hard to think about anything but the CSI tech inside the house, and what he was finding there.

"You said you were going to drive to New York tonight. What are you going to do there?" Westergren asked.

"There are some people I need to talk to. I think they might be able to shine a light on what happened here."

"You think this was planned by someone in New York? We can liaise with the NYPD if we need to."

Desmond gave him a sidelong look. "Don't take this the wrong way, but there are two dead bodies *here* and getting anyone to look at them is like pulling teeth. What are the odds the NYPD wants to question folks about two mysterious deaths that didn't happen in their jurisdiction?"

Westergren sighed. "Are you sure you're in any shape to drive?"

"I'd rather fly," Desmond admitted, "but I'll be okay driving."

"You look ready to fall over."

Desmond was sure it was an aftereffect of being in the death house. The more distance there was between himself and that hellhole, the better he would feel.

They were quiet until the tech came out of the house. He was a short, paunchy man in his late forties with a big mustache. "I've got bad news," he said. "Whoever cleaned this place up knew what they were doing."

"What does that mean?"

"Thanks to TV, most people think luminol can find blood even if the site has been cleaned with bleach."

"That's true, isn't it?" asked Westergren.

"Sometimes. But there's a type of cleanser that messes with luminol. It makes the whole area light up like it's washed in blood. It looks like that's what happened here. Otherwise, there was a bloodbath in there."

"It *was* a bloodbath," Desmond said, so softly the tech didn't understand.

"Nah," the tech said. "No matter how much blood there is, it doesn't go everywhere. There would be spots where it didn't hit. In this case, every clean surface looks like it had blood on it, but that stops abruptly where the floor hasn't been cleaned. There's a line of demarcation. It's the cleanser."

Desmond hung his head. It was hopeless.

"We found a nail inside the house," Westergren said, pulling the tissue out of his pocket and unfurling its corners. "It looks like it could have blood on it."

Desmond stared at him. Hadn't Westergren said, back at the diner, that it couldn't be used as evidence, since Desmond had removed it from the crime scene? There the young cop was, putting it into evidence himself.

The tech examined it. "Some specks on that. It's worth a try."

"Could you get DNA from it?" Desmond's mouth was dry.

"Possibly. We'll need to treat the samples with luminol reagent, but that's doable." He nodded at Westergren. "I'll let you know what

I find." He gave Desmond a polite nod, before turning and heading for his truck.

"I appreciate what you did. All of it. Thanks for coming out here with me." Desmond shook hands with Westergren.

"I . . . I haven't worked a case like this before, but I'm going to do everything I can," Westergren said. "We don't have much in the way of resources, but we have some good people. I'll be in touch."

After they parted ways in the middle of the afternoon, Desmond found the narrow ribbon of road that eventually curled back to the highway. He didn't mind driving, but he regretted not flying. He would have been so grateful to soar into the sky, leaving the dark, muddy earth of the Poconos for the clear promise of the darkening blue of the horizon. He was never disappointed when he abandoned the ground.

Instead, he was earthbound. He turned on Francis Johnson again, but the music didn't match his mood. The triumphant, uplifting notes of "Johnson's March" spiraled around him, and he couldn't keep up. Finally, he turned it off and drove in silence. What passed through his head, twisting around like a Möbius strip, was a faint echo of his mother's voice. *There's nothing you can do,* she said. *Let go.* The memory could bring him to tears if he allowed it. But his eyes remained dry and steady on the horizon. The uneasiness that dogged even his quietest days, brushing against his brain with the featherlight whisper of a breeze, was turning into a hurricane now. Deep down, he didn't trust the cops to do their job. Westergren was a good man, but he was a neophyte and could be smacked down quickly. Desmond's apprehension wasn't only about how the police would look at the case, but how a prosecutor would view it.

Anyone who wanted to play devil's advocate would have a field day with the facts. There were two dead victims, but no smoking gun. How did you prove that the killer knew about the defective furnace? That was an inspired choice as far as murder weapons went. He was glad Gary was rich and white, because that would mean the case couldn't just be swept into the gutter. Dominique was a celebrity in fashion circles, so there'd be media attention, but he expected gawkers who wanted to exploit a tragedy.

He parked his car at New Jersey's Newark Airport—he knew from experience driving into Manhattan was a hopeless, pointless task—then hopped a train to New York. When he checked his voice mail at home, there was message from Dominique's best friend, Sabrina. "Hey, Desmond, I'm sorry to bother you, but I've been trying to reach Dominique since yesterday morning. I don't want to be a worrywart, but she went away for the weekend with Gary, and I . . . I'm just a little concerned. Can you let me know if you hear from her? Thanks."

He knew he had to tell her the awful news, but he wasn't ready to do that. While he wrestled with his impulses, he received a text from Westergren. *We found the van.* He dialed the cop with a steady hand that belied his emotions. Westergren hadn't said anything about finding the mysterious Max, only the vehicle.

"You got my message?" Westergren was as excitable as a puppy.

Desmond could picture the young man as he spoke. His enthusiasm crackled through the line. "Where was it?"

"A campground a few miles from the house. Get this: the whole thing wreaks of bleach."

"He scrubbed it out?"

"Yeah. We're going to check it for prints and stuff, but I don't know how much there is left to find." Westergren paused. "This Max guy did a pretty good job of cleaning up."

He did, Desmond agreed mentally. Whatever else Max was, he was a professional.

25

By the time Desmond arrived at Penn Station at six Sunday evening, he had a hotel reservation set up and a line on Thomas Klepper. If Dominique had been beside him, she would've teased him about his ruthless efficiency. *You don't care about looking at the sunset unless you're flying toward it,* she'd once claimed. She wasn't wrong. It was a character flaw he acknowledged. He couldn't sit calmly and appreciate a thing for what it was. He needed to know its purpose and its trajectory. In the cockpit, whether you were flying on instruments or visual flight rules, you were watchful every moment. In the air, that made sense. On the ground, it worked against him.

Tom Klepper hadn't been hard to find. Thanks to Google, Desmond even had a photo of the man. Klepper resembled a bullfrog with a low brow, eyes that popped out of their sockets, and a broad, mushy jawline. He was an attorney with an office in the Empire State Building, which Desmond knew sounded fancier than it actually was. Gary Cowan had spent half an hour on the phone with Tom Klepper on the day he died. Desmond wanted to know about that conversation.

He walked from Penn Station to Grand Central, zigzagging up from west Thirty-fourth Street to East Forty-second, casting suspicious glances at the Empire State Building on the way. The Grand Hyatt Hotel was, to Desmond, a place that resembled Tartarus, the Roman version of hell, teeming with lost souls, each one a mini-Sisyphus weighted down by giant shopping bags. But he had one positive association with the place: it was where he and Dominique had stayed when he brought her to the city to launch her modeling career. Desmond had disapproved of every part of his sister's plan, arguing that with her excellent grades and drive to succeed, she belonged in college. But she'd made up her mind. She wanted to be at the center of the universe, which meant Forty-second Street to her. The hotel rose above the specter of Grand Central Terminal, much to Desmond's dismay and Dominique's delight.

After he checked in, he took an elevator up to the eighteenth floor. His cramped cell boasted a king-size bed, which he was glad to see, even if he was certain his six-foot-three frame wouldn't fit comfortably if he tried sitting at the tiny desk. He washed his face and changed his shirt. He'd packed an overnight bag before he left Hammond, but that wouldn't keep him going for long. He was going to need some clothes if he planned to stay more than a couple of days, he realized, dropping his shirt in a laundry bag and hanging it outside the door of his room. The thought horrified him, especially the image of himself lugging a shopping bag through the hotel lobby. Dominique would have laughed her head off at him.

Dominique. Just thinking of his sister squeezed his chest tight.

He switched his focus to practical matters. At least he didn't have to worry about work. He'd sent a message to the owner of the company he freelanced for, and she'd already responded offering condolences, promising as much time off as he needed, and asking where she could make a donation in his sister's memory. He considered calling Sabrina, but explaining the truth to her was too painful to imagine. Deep down, he hoped she would see the news when it broke on Monday, as it was sure to. After that, they could talk. He dialed Tom Klepper's office number, left a terse message, and hung up. What was he supposed to do now? It was a Sunday night, so there was only so much he could accomplish. He wanted to hunt down Trin Lytton-Jones, but only after he talked to the others on his list. He needed to be prepared for that encounter.

While he was working out his next move, his cell phone rang. Desmond answered on the first ring.

"Stop playing games with me, you S.O.B." The voice was a man's, but wound so tight there was a squeak in the back of his throat.

Desmond glanced at the screen, but didn't recognize the number. "Who the hell is this?"

"You just called me!"

"Ah." All Desmond had said on Tom Klepper's voice mail was, *This is Desmond Edgars. I'm calling about Gary Cowan.* That, and a phone number. The man's reaction was baffling. "That was fast."

"Can it, you schmuck. Is he okay or not?"

"No."

The other man spluttered. "What do you mean?"

"You don't even know who this is, do you?" Desmond asked.

"You're a piece of garbage who works with Max."

There it was. *Max.*

"Funny you mention Max," Desmond said, "because I want to talk with him."

There was stunned silence on the other end. "Who . . . who is this?" Klepper croaked.

"I told you when I called. Desmond Edgars."

There was silence on the other end of the line, but Desmond could sense the gears turning in Klepper's brain. "Edgars . . . wait, I've heard that name before. You're the Glamazon's brother, aren't you?"

"If by Glamazon, you mean Dominique Monaghan, yes."

"Why are you calling me? What do you want?" The tension left Klepper's voice with the suddenness of a balloon pop. His taut, strained interest dropped precipitously, but picked up again. "Wait, did Dominique call you? Because I haven't been able to reach Gary. I never thought of calling her."

"Yes, Dominique called. She filled me in on what was going on this weekend, including Gary's little scheme."

"His *scheme*? What's that, exactly?"

"Gary arranged to have himself kidnapped this weekend."

"That's crazy!" Klepper sounded outraged.

"Gary spilled everything to Dominique, you know."

"Oh. In that case . . ." Klepper sounded completely deflated. "You know you can't tape this call, right? That's illegal in the state of New York. It's not admissible in court, and you'd go to jail for taping me against my will."

Desmond rolled his eyes to the ceiling. Marcus Aurelius had plenty of advice for dealing with fools—clearly, they were as plentiful in ancient Rome as they were today—but he figured the Stoic philosopher would be hard-pressed not to lose his temper with Tom Klepper.

"You helped him out with his kidnapping plan."

"You can't kidnap yourself," Klepper corrected.

"You hooked him up with Max."

Even though he couldn't see the man, he was sure Klepper got pale. "I—I—I only wanted to help Gary." Klepper drew in a sharp breath. "That's all I care about."

"Well, all I care about is finding Max."

"I want that, too," Klepper admitted. "He won't let me contact Gary. For all intents and purposes, he's holding Gary hostage."

"Are you sure about that?" Desmond wasn't ready to tell him that Gary was dead. He wanted to see his reaction in person. The demand for a ransom was hard to believe. Had Max killed Gary and then demanded a payoff for him? Quite the set of brass balls on Max if that were true.

"Max called me late last night," Klepper said. "He said he'd been thinking, and since Gary wanted to be kidnapped, he might as well do a good job of it. He told me I had to pay a substantial fee if I wanted Gary to live through this."

26

Desmond chose Fifth Avenue as his conduit to Tom Klepper's office. That route took him past the grand edifice of the New York Public Library and its guardian lions, and into a throng of tourists. At almost eight o'clock on a cold, dark night, the streets were packed. He didn't enjoy crowds, but he welcomed the sight of the marble jungle cats. Patience and Fortitude, he could never remember which was which, only that Dominique had told him the lions' names that first time they'd visited New York. She cared about details. She always wanted to know more.

He resisted the urge to gaze up at the Empire State Building as he made his way down to Thirty-fourth Street. He didn't want to be marked as a tourist. He was a man with a mission. Moreover, he didn't understand how people could be bowled over by the sight of tall buildings. Had they never been up in the air, looking down? From that perspective, even the tallest building was just part of the landscape.

Security was tight, which he'd expected. He handed his driver's license to one of the uniformed guards at a desk, waited for him to peck-type his information into a computer, then stood still, stone-faced, as they took his picture. After that, the guard called Klepper's office, gave Desmond a badge, and told him to go on up to the twenty-eighth floor.

Tom Klepper answered the door of the suite himself, cell phone in hand. "Come in," he squeaked, locking up behind Desmond. Up close, the lawyer was even more like a bullfrog than he had appeared in his photo, with pale, protuberant eyes permanently at half-mast. He was bald but for a few stringy strands pulled across his pate; they drooped forlornly as if aware of their failure. He had the leathery hide of a creature who spent too much time in the sun, and the deep lines baked into it resembled a road map. His suit looked as if it had been hitchhiking cross-country on its lonesome.

"This way," Klepper said, leading Desmond through a corridor lit by a fluorescent bulb, which bled into sepia tones along the hallway. He stopped in front of a door marked with a brass plate etched with THOMAS W. KLEPPER, JURIS DOCTOR, HARVARD, and ushered Desmond inside.

"I have donuts," Klepper said. "Want one?"

"No, thanks."

Klepper wasn't a tall man, but he was puffy and wide, which made him seem big. His flesh quivered as if he were jelly-filled. His fingers narrowed at the joints, then swelled like sausage links. Dropping into his seat with the force of a boulder, he opened the box, clenched a donut, and devoured it in two bites.

"I'm an emotional eater," Klepper explained as he chewed. "If I'm under a lot of stress, I have to eat. And I'm under a hell of a lot of stress right now." He grabbed another donut and looked Desmond over while he bit into it. "You don't look much like Dominique," he opined, chewing with his mouth full. "You're a lot darker."

Desmond wasn't in the business of handing out explanations to people. Even if he'd been in the mood to satisfy Klepper's curiosity, he didn't accept the term "half-sister." What did that even mean? Dominique was his flesh and blood. The fact they had different fathers was irrelevant. It always had been.

"Who else knows about Gary Cowan's kidnapping plan?" Desmond asked.

"No one. He thought about telling the Glamazon in advance, but decided it was too risky. She spills everything to her buddy Sabrina, who puts everything on Twitter. Gary only told me."

"And Max," Desmond pointed out. "Obviously."

"Sure, yeah. He hired Max."

"Gary found Max through you." Desmond's tone brooked no argument.

"Me? What do I have to do with it? Hey, man, you're stressing me out with your pacing. Can you sit down?" Klepper's face crunched in disapproval.

Desmond ignored that. "Gary told Dominique *you* found Max. You saying that's not true?"

Klepper stopped chewing on his donut. "It's not like he said, 'Hey, do you know a goon who can kidnap me?' okay? I didn't know what he was up to for a while. He wanted to know if I knew any tough guys who could keep their mouths shut. That was Max."

"How do *you* know Max?"

"He's just a guy, you know?" Klepper gestured at the walls, which groaned under the weight of framed photographs of champion boxers. "I'm a manager as well as a lawyer. I meet a lot of guys."

Desmond stared at the pictures. "Are any of these Max?"

Klepper snickered. "Hell, no."

"Well, it's going to be interesting watching the cops rip into each and every one of these guy's lives. I hope they've got nothing to hide."

That unsettled Klepper. "This has nothing to do with any of my fighters. Leave them out of it."

"It's a natural angle to follow. You're not going to try telling me you met Max at church, right?"

Klepper dropped his gaze. "Max is a drug dealer." He glanced at Desmond and looked down again. "I buy pot off him."

"That's your big criminal connection?"

"He has other stuff, too. Coke, pills, Ecstasy. Whatever you want, Max can get it for you." Klepper raised his eyes again. "I don't do that shit anymore. I've got a girlfriend now."

"Good for you. Look, if this guy was your dealer, you obviously know how to get in touch with him."

"Believe me, I've tried! But he's always been really careful. Burner phones, that kind of thing. He won't use email because he says the government is tracking everything. I'm not even sure what his last name is."

"His other clients must be pissed if they can't reach him," Desmond pointed out.

"I guess. But unless you've got another solid source, you've got no choice but to wait. One thing I'll say for Max, his drugs are good. He doesn't cut coke with levamisole or anything like that." His eyes opened wider. "If you've ever had that happen, you're patient with a dealer who delivers the goods."

"Do the other lawyers at your firm buy from him?" Desmond asked. He remembered when Dominique was dating a creep who worked on Wall Street. She'd told stories of a certain white-shoe firm that had regular deliveries of blow.

"This isn't a law firm. I just rent an office in a suite of lawyers," Klepper explained. "Everyone just kind of keeps to themselves. The receptionists totally hate me. I like to work from home. Mostly, I come here if I have a client meeting. Everyone's super-impressed by the Empire State Building."

Desmond looked around the shabby office, doubting that it had bowled anyone over in a while. It reeked of fried pork and dumplings, and there was powdered sugar settling on the desk. The furniture had probably been attractive once, but there were stains and small tears in the upholstery. "The only thing impressing anyone is that you . . ." Desmond's voice trailed off. He scanned the walls, looking for Klepper's law degree, but he couldn't find it. "Doesn't it say on your door you're a Harvard grad?"

Klepper's eyes popped a little, as if the question were somehow improper. "Yes, I attended Harvard."

That was the moment when Desmond saw how slippery this character really was. Klepper was the kind of lowlife who thought he could stretch reality in convenient directions and still call it truth. "Where's your law degree actually from?"

"I don't see how any of this matters, unless you're thinking of hiring a lawyer?" Klepper threw that out like a challenge, but there was just a tiny glimmer of hope in his tone, which depressed Desmond. He was starting to think the man's law degree came from a Cracker Jack box.

"Are you Gary Cowan's lawyer?" Desmond asked, careful to keep things in the present tense.

"He's my client as well as my friend." Klepper beamed, revealing perfect white teeth clogged with pastry residue.

"You have other clients?"

"Of course I do." The attorney's mood took a nosedive. He reached for another donut. Before Desmond could ask another question, Klepper's cell phone rang. "Hello? Who's this?" There was a pause. Then he mouthed a single syllable at Desmond. *Max.*

s Gary okay? Put him on the phone!" Klepper demanded.

"Put him on speakerphone," Desmond whispered.

Klepper shook his head. "Why not? Where is he?"

Desmond wrestled with the urge to knock Klepper down and take his phone. But what would that accomplish? Max would hang up and he'd gain nothing. Better to figure out what kind of game the man was playing with the lawyer.

"Well, I'm not paying you a nickel if I can't talk to him!" Klepper yelled. "Forget it!"

His defiance was short-lived.

"No, no, don't do that. Please," Klepper begged, turning pale under his weather-beaten skin. "No, seriously, man. Be cool, okay? I've got your money, okay? It's not a problem. When are you coming over to pick it up?"

It was excruciating for Desmond, but it looked like his patience would pay off. Then Klepper said, "Where's Lighthouse Park?" There was a dumbfounded silence from Klepper. "How am I supposed to get to Roosevelt Island?"

Desmond could picture that slender slip of land in the East River between Manhattan and Queens. He'd never set foot on it, but he'd admired it from the air.

"Hold on. I need to write this down," Klepper panted, but he didn't pick up a pen. "Okay, say that again. A red, horseshoe-shaped railing in front of Lighthouse Park. Okay. It's on the where? The edge of the grass. And you want the bag with the money on which side? The left, at the end next to the lamppost. Wait, hold on, which is left? Facing which way? I mean, the Queens side or the . . . okay, the Manhattan side. Why didn't you just say that in the first place?"

Desmond passed one hand over his eyes. He'd barely slept at the hospital on Saturday night, and Sunday was turning out to be one hell of a long day. Weariness tugged at his consciousness like an animal begging for attention. Between Klepper and the kidnapper, his nerves were fraying.

"Obviously I'll come alone. Who would I bring, anyway?" Klepper rolled his eyes, looking like nothing so much as an overgrown frog watching a fly. He lowered his voice. "You don't have to do that, man. Don't threaten her. Leave her out of it, man."

Desmond noticed Klepper's hand shaking. Sweat trickled down his temples.

"Nobody wants that. I'm not kidding. . . ." Klepper's voice trailed off. He pulled the phone away from his ear and glared at the screen. "He hung up on me." He set the phone down and rubbed his temples. "He said I'll never see Gary again if I don't pay him."

"It sounded like he was threatening Dominique, too."

Klepper looked up and frowned. "What?"

"You said to leave her out of it."

"Yeah." Klepper nodded. "Right. It's just . . . I'm more worried about what he'll do to Gary. Max is a psycho."

"How do you get to Roosevelt Island?" Desmond asked.

"Damned if I know. There's a subway, and a bridge, or something. Lemme see." Klepper's balloon fingers tapped away on the laptop on his desk. "Okay, Roosevelt Island is a pain in the ass to get to. There's a tram from Fifty-ninth Street. There's the subway, but only the F train stops there."

"What about by car?" Desmond asked.

"Ha, that's a good one. According to this, from Manhattan you have to take the Fifty-ninth Street Bridge over to Queens, drive up to Thirty-sixth Avenue, and drive over *that* bridge. It's the only bridge that connects the island by car, can you believe it?"

Desmond didn't have much trouble believing anything about New York City, which was one reason he stayed away from the place. "This city doesn't make any sense," he murmured.

"I wonder why he picked that spot," Klepper mused. "It's kind of a weird choice."

"Who is Max working with?"

Klepper's eyes popped in surprise. "Working with?" His jaw fell open, just a little, and he rushed to stuff another donut into his mouth.

"Gary told Dominique that someone was going to kill his wife. Max was supposed to have a partner."

"I don't believe that for a second," Klepper's voice went up an octave.

"How's that?"

"That's a lie about Gary wanting to kill his wife." He looked Desmond over. "Are you wearing a wire?"

"Gary wanted to be kidnapped so he'd have a solid alibi when his wife was found dead."

"No. You don't understand." Klepper sighed. "Gary kidnapped himself once before, in Mexico. He did it for the ransom." In response to Desmond's skeptical expression, he went on. "Look, his wife and her family keep him on a short leash financially. He got desperate, you know? Gary loves the good life. He likes to have the best of everything. He's earned it. He grew up poor, and he got out with his fists. He hasn't had an easy ride, you know."

Desmond had never considered Gary that way. He'd thought of him as a spoiled, rich knucklehead with manicured nails. It hadn't occurred to him that there'd been some grit under that smooth front he put up. It didn't make him like Gary, but it made him more sympathetic.

"Even if what you're saying is true, it doesn't fit this scenario," Desmond said. "Gary must've had other reasons for doing what he did." He sighed. "Look . . . I'm sorry to have to tell you this, but Gary is dead."

Klepper's round eyes stared at him, and his lumpy body quivered. "No way. That's not possible."

"Listen to me. I saw him with my own eyes. He's dead."

"No. He's being held for ransom."

"Gary and Dominique were found in an old house in Pennsylvania yesterday. They died of carbon monoxide poisoning."

"You're a liar." Klepper made a wet sound that was a mix of a gasp and a sob. "I talked to Gary on Friday evening. Everything was going the way it was supposed to."

"Here's how it played out. Max abducted Dominique and Gary, and he drove them to an old house in the Poconos. Max left, and he never came back. There was something wrong with the furnace. That's how they died."

"Gary wanted an alibi." Klepper's whisper was as rough as sandpaper. "He didn't say anything about his wife. Just that he needed an alibi." He stared up at Desmond, and his round eyes were pleading. "Are you absolutely sure he's dead?"

"I'm positive. You can talk to the cops if you don't believe me."

"But there hasn't been anything on the news about it." Klepper's voice had the plaintive whine of a small child learning there's no Santa Claus. "Gary's famous. If he were dead, it would be all over the news."

"They died in rural Pennsylvania. The cops haven't been able to reach Gary's wife, who's technically his next of kin. I don't think the state troopers were calling gossip sites. It'll probably be in the news tomorrow."

Klepper's eyes were full of tears, and his nose was running. He wiped it with the back of his sleeve, then ambled to his feet, making little gasping sounds. "I'm going . . . to hit the . . . men's room," he mumbled, grabbing his leather satchel before rushing out of the room.

Desmond had wanted to see Klepper's reaction to Gary's death, but now that he had, he almost regretted it. The lawyer was dirty, but Desmond didn't believe he'd known Gary was dead. The man was a sleazeball, not a murderer.

While Klepper was gone, Desmond pulled up a map of Roosevelt Island and Lighthouse Park on his phone. He zeroed in on the area, taking a look at a satellite view and a topographical one. It wasn't much of a park, just a few blades of grass and a panoramic view, from the look of things. He straightened up, tapping his fingers idly on the desk. It showed an incredible amount of nerve on Max's part to actually kidnap Gary and then charge his friend a ransom. Was this just crass opportunism on Max's part? Was it possible that he'd driven away from the house, unaware that he was leaving Dominique and Gary to die there? No, more likely, Max knew Gary was dead and was trying to capitalize on the fact that the information wasn't public yet. Catching him while he picked up the ransom that evening might be the only chance to grab him before he ran.

Klepper had left his computer open, and Desmond couldn't resist the opportunity to take a closer look. He didn't think the lawyer was lying, exactly; more likely, he was omitting certain facts that could send him to jail. His email inbox looked like a junk mail folder, full of Fresh Direct orders and promos from jewelers and Facebook notifications. According to Gmail, Klepper had more than thirty-five thousand unread messages. If there was such a thing as an email hoarder, Desmond had found him.

He decided to focus, searching for emails from anyone named Max. There were a bunch, but a scan of the subject lines looked distinctly unpromising. Next, he tried Gary Cowan. There were hundreds. One from a month back caught Desmond's eye. It was from Gary, with the subject heading "Look at this. More fraud!!!" Desmond clicked on it.

> *Found more of Trin's papers. They don't match up with the corp's public filings. Not sure what kind of a scam she's pulling. Can you figure it out? Can she be sued / dragged into court with this??? Can I use it to threaten her?*

There was an attachment filled with numbers. Klepper's response wasn't very helpful.

> *Hi Gary,*
>   *I looked into this. The discrepancies are because the Sardanapalus Corporation isn't publicly traded, so they don't have to release a lot of these numbers. The bottom line is that they don't have to tell regulators or the public this stuff.*
>   *Are you free for dinner next week? I met someone and it would be great if you could meet her!*
>   *Tom*

Desmond was disgusted with himself. He hated people prying into his business, so it felt all wrong for him to do that to anyone else. He closed the mail program, and as it shut down, he saw a photograph open on the screen. It was a white girl wearing a low-cut black dress and a very aggressive push-up bra. She was pretty in a trashy way, with very light blond hair and ghostly pale skin caked with makeup thick as what Dominique used to wear in fashion shows. Her eyes were ringed with raccoonlike black kohl. She was sitting in a restaurant between Tom Klepper and Gary Cowan, her red lips parted, smiling widely. Her head rested on Gary's shoulder.

Curious, Desmond clicked through to the next shot. The same woman was sitting in a dimly lit restaurant, looking at someone off-camera and holding up a water glass. Her wrists were so thin they might've snapped like twigs after the shot was taken. The girl wasn't posing for the camera. She looked engrossed by whomever she was with, but he was off-camera. Desmond wondered if she even knew the photographer was there.

Klepper came back into the room, snuffling. He had a ball of wadded-up tissues in one hand. "What are you doing?"

"I wanted to look up Roosevelt Island," Desmond said.

"Oh!" Klepper yelped when he saw the girl on the screen. "I shouldn't have left that open."

"Why? You stalking this girl?"

"Of course not." Klepper's tone was way too bright. Desmond had a feeling he knew what was in the satchel, and that Klepper hadn't been telling the truth about being off cocaine. "That's my girlfriend."

"She looks kind of young for you."

"Age has nothing to do with attraction. When two people are in love, age doesn't matter, okay?"

Desmond suspected that the blonde wasn't Klepper's girlfriend. Not any more than the sloe-eyed beauty Desmond spent time with now and then was *his* girlfriend. Cash was passing hands, but that wasn't really any of his business, and he was in no position to judge. He had more pressing concerns. "Have you talked to the cops yet?"

"Don't be ridiculous!" Klepper's confidence had been restored by whatever he'd inhaled. "How could I go to the cops?" His shoulders slumped. No drug could keep him buoyant for long. "Anyway, what does it matter if Gary's dead?"

"Do you want the police to catch his killer?"

"You said they're already on it." Klepper's high-pitched voice was getting whinier.

"Yeah, and it's going to look a lot better for you if you go to them now and tell them Max is trying to extort cash from you."

"I can't! It's nine o'clock," Klepper pointed out. "I'm supposed to be at the park in an hour. It's going to take almost that long to get there."

"I'll go to the park," Desmond answered. "You talk to the cops."

"Okay." Klepper picked up a black duffle bag, started to hand it to Desmond, then jerked it back. "Hold on. I'm not sending the money with you now that Gary's dead."

"Just give me the bag. You got any newspaper around?"

"What's your plan?" Klepper croaked.

"That depends on who comes to pick up the money."

28

It was freezing out by the water on Roosevelt Island, so cold that Desmond could feel his face hardening in a grimace. Max's instructions had been clear: drop the bag near the lamppost on the left and leave. Desmond had no plan to follow that through, and after he put the bag in place, he did a quick walkabout, checking to see if anyone was hiding in the lighthouse. The gray stone structure towered over the park, and its vaguely medieval appearance—the narrow, rectangular windows would've been perfect for archers to defend—was ominous in the dark. It was the only possible hiding spot, Desmond thought, but no one was in it. The small park was so flat and empty he had to pull well back from the spot where he left the bag. He knew he'd be able to see anyone coming, but the only people who came was a man with a small boy. That would be a hell of a disguise, Desmond thought, but they went nowhere near the bags.

Within five minutes, a woman came into the park. She had a gorgeous chocolate lab that reminded Desmond of a dog he'd had as a boy, after his dad died and it was just him and his mom. The woman and the man greeted each other. They were obviously neighbors. She glanced over at Desmond and let her dog off his leash.

"Hershey!" the boy squealed. "Run this way!"

The boy and the dog chased each other for quite a while. When Desmond looked at the woman again, he found her staring back with obvious disapproval. He knew, in that moment, that she thought he was a predator. It was something he'd encountered before, though, to be fair to this woman, she might have suspected he was showing an unhealthy interest in the boy. Usually, kids had nothing to do with it. Some women turned brittle and fearful when they caught sight of a tall, athletic black man. It wasn't a daytime phenomenon, unless you counted the occasional little old lady, hair permed corkscrew-tight, thin lips pressed into a line, who clutched her purse to her side like a football whenever she caught sight of him. No, it was only after sunset that women started casting those nervous glances. He knew they were trying to calculate what his intentions were based on his proximity, the speed of his step, what was in his hands. The really skittish ones sometimes reached into their bags, presumably grabbing pepper spray or Mace or whatever else they carried to defend themselves. Sometimes he crossed the street to give them peace of mind. Sometimes it made him sick inside. Why was it his job to allay their fears? But another part of him understood. It had been a long time since he'd had to kill a man, but that didn't mean he wasn't ready to if the need arose. When he'd joined the Army at eighteen, preparedness had been drilled into him at basic combat training. *You never know when you'll be called on to defend yourself or your fellow soldiers,* his drill sergeant told them. Desmond knew that was true. You never knew when the moment would come until you found yourself in it.

Finally, everyone left—the woman shot him one last suspicious look on her way out—and Desmond was again alone in the park. It was close to eleven, and he wondered how much longer he'd have to wait. He'd told Klepper that all he'd do was drop off the bag, but since he was there, he couldn't resist the impulse to see what happened next. More than that: he wanted to snap Max's neck.

At midnight, he called Tom Klepper's cell. Getting no answer, he tried the office line. Klepper was supposed to contact him after finishing with the police. It wasn't impossible that he was still at the station, maybe going through mug shots. Gary and Dominique couldn't identify Max, which meant that Klepper was their only hope. That left Desmond uneasy. He'd watched Klepper get into a cab in front of the Empire State Building, giving the driver the address of the nearest precinct, but what proved that the crooked Klepper didn't change his mind after Desmond walked away?

He thought about Dominique, and how terrified she'd been for Gary's wife. She'd sacrificed herself because of it. It meant more to her to save that woman's life than it did to get out of the trap she was in. It hit him suddenly that Max might be playing some kind of game with the new widow, too. He gave his head a shake. No. The likeliest thing was that Max was working for Gary's wife. She was the one who benefitted from his death. Not financially, of course, but, if anything Gary ever told Dominique was true, she'd managed to slough off the husband she despised.

Just after midnight, he got a text from Westergren. *We found the car.* Desmond stared at it, wondering if Westergren had forgotten that they'd already talked about the white van late that afternoon. Or maybe his phone repeated the message? No, the first one said *van,* the second one *car.* Desmond dialed his number.

"I hope it's not too late to call, but I just got your text," he said.

"No problem! I'm a night owl."

"What's this about a car being discovered?"

"Sorry, I should've explained better. We found Gary Cowan's car."

"Where?"

"It was in a camping lot not far from the house," Westergren said. "But by *not far,* I mean a half-hour hike. Who would stay at a house in the middle of a wilderness and park so far away? It makes no sense."

"Well, there's one way it does," Desmond said. "If somebody was waiting to park the car in front of the house once he was sure the people inside were dead. Only, he had to clean some things up first. I think I interrupted him before he could take care of that detail."

29

It was almost three in the morning when Desmond let himself into his room at the Grand Hyatt. He'd waited at Lighthouse Park, feeling more like a frozen fool with every minute that passed. *Just a little bit longer, just a little more,* he'd told himself. He hated giving up. What had it gotten him? Nothing, except frostbite and the suspicion that Tom Klepper was playing him. Annoyed, he'd hefted the bag—it may have been filled with recycled newsprint, but it wasn't as if it had a tracker inside—and he'd walked the long, lonely hike back to Roosevelt Island's sole subway station. The F train had been virtually empty, except for some homeless folks looking to keep warm on a brutal night. It snaked through Manhattan, finally spitting him out at Bryant Park, right beside the great library with the magnificent lions. The milky marble glowed at night, he discovered. It was the one good thing he'd seen so far, and he wished Dominique was beside him to share it.

He brushed his teeth and washed his face, then collapsed into bed. There were a million thoughts crowding into his head, just like people cramming into Grand Central at rush hour. Autopsy. DNA. Funeral. Strangle Tom Klepper for being the freaky little bullfrog he was. Desmond had mistakenly given the man too much of his trust. He wouldn't make that error again.

When sleep finally descended, it was fitful and strained. He dreamed Dominique was a little girl again, arms outstretched, waiting for him. *Where's Daddy?* she asked, and his heart sank down to the toes of his running shoes.

He got hurt, he told her. *He can't come back.*

I don't believe you, Dominique pouted, and she turned from him and ran.

Go after her. That was his grandmother's voice, commanding and confident. That woman never doubted she was right. *She needs you to be her daddy now.*

Desmond didn't argue. Instead, he chased after the tiny girl. No matter how fast he ran, she was always just out of reach.

Dominique! he called. *Stop!*

She wouldn't.

"Dominique!" He sat up in bed, suddenly aware he'd been shouting her name. The clock on the bedside table said it was five-thirty-one. He crashed back on the pillow, groaning. The military had crushed his nocturnal ways and made an early riser out of him. It didn't matter how late he went to bed, his body was determined to be up for reveille.

He lay there, forearms crossed over his face, but sleep had already parted ways with him. "Fine," he muttered, pushing the covers back with resentment.

After he showered and dressed, he went downstairs. From the hotel's lobby, he followed a quiet passageway into the hubbub of Grand Central Terminal. He bought a bagel with lox, devoured it in sixty seconds flat, and got another. That brought to mind Tom Klepper inhaling donuts. He'd deal with the bullfrog soon, but it was only seven in the morning, so that would have to wait. At that hour, there was one task that came to mind: going to his sister's apartment. He had her keys in his pocket. It was the last thing he wanted to do, but his feelings didn't count.

He walked down the wide boulevard of Park Avenue, past the viaduct and down to Twenty-eighth Street. Dominique had been subletting a condo that faced onto Park Avenue South. It was a nice enough building in a decent area, but Desmond remembered the glamorous condo with the high ceilings and crown moldings she'd called home when she was with Gary. It was on Fifty-ninth Street, right at the foot of Central Park. She'd loved it there, and the memory of her fragile happiness made it hard to breathe for a moment.

Desmond let himself into the building. There was no doorman, and that was cutting too many corners, in Desmond's view. Even though the issue had nothing to do with his sister's death, it troubled him, as if she'd been unwittingly courting danger. On the elevator ride up, he wondered if she'd been short on funds. She had a job she loved, but New York was a crazily expensive city. She never asked him for financial help, not after those early days when she was eighteen and he'd gotten her settled into the city. Now, he felt guilty for not offering. He'd showered presents on his baby sister—so many that his ex-wife had nursed a grudge over the issue—but he should've made sure Dominique was more secure.

He took a deep breath as he unlocked her door, expecting to be hit full force by the scent of roses and by a wave of memories he couldn't suppress. Instead, he stared around his sister's living room, realizing that someone had broken in.

30

The ransacking of Dominique's apartment might not have been obvious to anyone who didn't know her as well as Desmond did. His sister had no problem kicking her stiletto heels deep into a corner when she came home at the end of the day, letting them lie like weary soldiers. But she believed that even the smallest bit of paper had to be in place. That was one way she'd taken after their grandmother, who regarded an ill-placed Post-It note as a signpost to hell.

Dominique's apartment was clean enough, but it wasn't orderly. Opened mail spilled over the coffee table, pooling on the floor-boards. A short file cabinet yawned open a foot, which would have driven his sister crazy. Presumably, her laptop had been on the kitchen table, because the power cord lay there, still clinging to the outlet. The computer hadn't been with her in Pennsylvania, and because the power supply was sitting in front of him, Desmond was sure she'd left it behind. That meant it was in the hands of whoever had broken into her home.

The kitchen seemed undisturbed, but the bedroom was a minor disaster. An entire shelf on the bookcase next to her bed was empty, and Desmond stared at it for a full moment before realizing what had been there. Dominique always kept diaries, and they were gone—not just the last year's notes, but all of them. That realization brought bile into his throat. He had no intention of invading his sister's privacy, even postmortem. But he had a duty to protect them, or even destroy them. The knowledge that they were in a stranger's hands was agonizing.

The air was heavy with the scent of roses, and it enveloped him. Dominique would never walk through that door again. Her quick smile and easy laugh were gone, and he was going to have to live with that.

The invader had gone through his sister's jewelry box, not even caring enough to reseal it. Desmond took stock of what was there, but he had no idea what was missing. The family pieces that he remembered—a gold locket that had once hung around their mother's throat, a pearl ring that once shone on their grandmother's right hand when she went to church—were still there. More than that, a heavy gold chain lay entwined with a pink pearl necklace, turquoise beads, and dozens of pairs of gold earrings. That told him the thief had been very selective, and had combed through the apartment with a specific objective. It seemed to Desmond that any information that might shed light on his sister's life—and especially her recent associations—had vanished. That part of her had been whisked away.

He was surrounded by Dominique's things, signs and signifiers of her young life, but Desmond was the one who felt like a ghost.

He knew he had no choice now but to call the police. That had been the second item on his to-do list for the day, right after making the sorrowful pilgrimage to Dominique's home. He'd needed to see it with his own eyes, but he'd also wondered if his sister had left anything incriminating lying around. But if there had been a clue that revealed her plan to humiliate Gary, it was AWOL.

He spent some time taking whatever inventory he could of the place. He took some photographs with his phone, and he recorded every number that had dialed in or been called from Dominique's land line. He was afraid of touching things. The apartment would need to be fingerprinted. Of course, if the man who'd bleached the stairs at the death house had sifted through the apartment, that wouldn't accomplish much.

When he went to call the cops, he discovered he'd missed a call from Dominique's friend Sabrina. She was sobbing so hard on the message, it was hard to make out words, but clearly she'd just heard the awful news. He knew Sabrina loved his sister, but that made the thought of a conversation all the more daunting. Feeling furtive and guilty, he sent back a text message. *I just don't have any words right now. I'll be in touch later.*

He knew he wouldn't be able to keep his reserve up if he got on the phone with her. Whenever he saw Sabrina, she had a way of gently prodding him to reveal things he never imagined disclosing. It was as if these thoughts were bubbling under the surface, and she guided them to daylight. It was an appealing trait, but a dangerous one. He knew that if he spoke to Sabrina that day, he would break down weeping in guilt and shame and sadness, and he wanted to avoid that at all costs. There would be a time to mourn Dominique later. Before he could do that, he had to get justice for his sister.

Desmond couldn't have explained exactly what reaction he'd expected from the NYPD, but the pair of uniformed cops that arrived at Dominique's door didn't fit his expectations. One was a young Latino man whose eyes spun in his head when he saw Dominique's photograph. "I know her!" he said excitedly. "I used to have her calendar when I was in high school!"

Desmond understood that a ridiculously large percentage of men in their twenties had once owned a calendar featuring Dominique. Unlike many top models, his sister refused to pose nude, but that didn't mean she was a prude. Her swimsuit calendar made Desmond's face get hot whenever he remembered it.

"Did she die?" his partner asked. She was a sleepy-eyed woman in her midtwenties with straightened hair and a mouth full of gum. "I swear, I think I heard that on the radio this morning."

Desmond cleared his throat. "She died at a house out in rural Pennsylvania." His voice was reined in, his tone as close to neutral as he could manage. "She and her boyfriend were murdered."

The uniformed cops looked at each other and back at him. "For real?"

"The police in Pennsylvania were supposed to call the NYPD." Desmond looked from one to the other. "You have no idea what I'm talking about, do you?"

"No, but we can call over to get a detective over here," the female cop offered.

"Or maybe you want to go to the station? Talk to people there?" her counterpart asked.

Voluntarily walking into a police station ranked somewhere on Desmond's wish list between crashing his helicopter and getting rabies. "Sure," he said. "Let's go."

31

"S o your sister was this boxer's mistress?"

Desmond stared at the NYPD detective in front of him. They were in an interview room at Manhattan's Thirteenth Precinct on East Twenty-first Street. Reich had been the name given while a vise of a handshake was administered. The man was white, with hair the color of a dirty bristle brush cut into short spikes. He reclined in a chair with his chest puffed out under a shiny blue dress shirt that surely had a disco somewhere worried about its absence. His arms were spread wide, making the shirt seem tight and showcasing his dedication to the gym.

Desmond looked at the man for a long time without speaking. *Fangs out* was the way he'd have described him in the service. This was exactly the type of situation he needed Marcus Aurelius for. *Take care not to feel toward the inhuman as they feel toward men.* Stoic philosophy or not, it wouldn't take much more of a push to beat Reich until his shirt turned purple. Marcus Aurelius was all about subduing anger, which was part of the reason Desmond had connected with him in the first place. He'd discovered him almost by accident, after his mother had gone to prison and his grandmother had forced him to attend a Jesuit-run school. They weren't Catholic; it was just the strictest school she could find. His Latin teacher had assigned each student a different chapter of the *Meditations* to translate, and Desmond had been captivated. Through the calmness Marcus Aurelius preached, he could tell that the philosopher was a man full of anger and passion, much like Desmond himself. The philosopher had had to rein himself in because failing to do so would've cracked his heart and soul apart. Desmond understood all too well. Stoic philosophy didn't answer everything for him, but it made him feel that, whenever he found himself in the dark, he knew how to reach for the light.

"That's not what I said," he finally answered Reich.

The detective cricked his head to the side, as if his neck were cramping under the pressure of all that muscle. "She was dating a married man, so . . ."

"Let's move on," his partner interjected. Detective Iorio wasn't pretty, but she was striking: tall, athletic, brown-haired, and olive-skinned. She didn't seem any more amused by Reich than Desmond was. "We need to talk to the state troopers who found her, but it would be helpful if you could fill in some background for us."

"You can talk to a cop named Westergren," Desmond said. "There's a CSI tech who's already collected samples from the house in the Poconos. Westergren can put you in touch with him, too." He leaned back. "What kind of background do you need?"

"Well, you said your sister and her boyfriend were murdered, that the carbon monoxide poisoning wasn't an accident. You have any proof of that?"

"The cops in the Poconos are working on the crime scene, so they'll fill you in on that part. What I can tell you is this: someone else was in that house when I walked in. There was a car parked at the front, a black Honda. Whoever was driving it locked me in the basement. I had to break through the cellar door to get out. The house was filled with carbon monoxide at that point. That person tried to kill me."

Reich started to say something, but Desmond put up his hand. "The police already found that someone recently sealed all the windows in the house. The caulking is still fresh. So someone wanted to make sure the poison in the air didn't escape. The house was a death trap."

"Who would have motive? Has anyone threatened your sister, to your knowledge?"

"No." Desmond blinked. That question hadn't occurred to him. It was obvious to him that Dominique died because she was ensnared in Gary's plans, not because she was a target. "I don't know anyone who'd want to hurt her, except maybe Gary's wife." He felt slightly cruel casting aspersions on a woman he didn't know. Maybe Gary had other enemies, but it didn't hurt to start with the one at home.

"Was Dominique ever married?"

"No."

"Then how come you have different last names?" Iorio asked.

"Our mother was married twice. My father was in the Army. He died when I was three. My mother took me back to Chicago after that. When I was nine, she remarried. That man's name was Mr. Monaghan." The name popped out of his mouth reflexively. *Mr. Monaghan.* He could see how strange that sounded to the cops. "Eli Monaghan, I mean. Dominique was born a year after that."

"Is her father still alive?"

"No."

An almost electric current passed between Iorio and Reich. "When did he die?"

"Look, this is going to come up in your investigation sooner or later, so you might as well know it up front." Desmond took a deep breath. "My mother went to prison for shooting Dominique's father. He died when my sister was four."

That caught both detectives by surprise. "Was it an abuse situation?" Reich asked.

Part of Desmond's memory flickered to life, and he struggled to put it back in the compartment he usually housed it in. "That's not an unfair description."

"So, who raised Dominique? And you, because you would have been, what, fourteen?" Iorio could do math.

"Our grandmother. My mother's mother, I mean. She took us in."

"Did you have to move?"

"Not far. She lived just a few blocks away. We'd always spent a lot of time with her, anyway." That wasn't wholly true. Desmond had passed endless hours with his grandmother when he was young, and especially after his mother married Mr. Monaghan. But as he got a little older, he'd pulled away. At the time his mother was taken to jail, he hadn't seen his grandmother in a couple of months.

"So, your mother went to prison for killing her husband," Iorio said. "That's tragic. It must have been a heavy burden for you and your sister."

Desmond stared at her. He couldn't stand anyone defaming his mother. *Everything we hear is an opinion, not a fact. Everything we see is a perspective, not the truth.* There was Marcus Aurelius again, backing him up. His grandmother didn't like him quoting a Roman emperor. *Godless heathen,* his grandmother called the Stoic. It was ironic, given that her quotes from the Bible and Desmond's from Marcus Aurelius's *Meditations* weren't worlds apart.

"The tragedy is my mother died in prison," Desmond said. "The tragedy is she had ovarian cancer that wasn't found in time or treated properly. The tragedy was that she never got to clear her name."

There was more crackling energy between Reich and Iorio as they took that in. This was what Desmond had feared: the NYPD was more interested in rehashing gossip from the past than investigating a crime disguised as an accident.

"What I need to tell you about is the call my sister made to me from the house where she died." Desmond realized he needed to take charge of this interview, instead of answering questions that didn't have anything to do with Dominique's death. "She thought she and Gary were being kidnapped on Friday, but it turned out to be something Gary staged."

"Staged?"

"He hired a man named Max to kidnap them." He turned his palms up and shrugged. "Don't ask me. I didn't know Gary well. I can tell you Dominique was really upset about it, though. She was also worried about Gary's wife. She thought that woman was in danger."

"Gary sounds like a piece of work," Iorio observed.

"He was a damn fine boxer in his day," her partner threw in. "At least until that mess he got himself into."

Iorio gave him an exasperated look. "Please don't talk sports. I hate it when you do that."

Desmond was getting bored with the back-and-forth between the cops. He got the sense that they'd rather he weren't in the room. "Gary's friend Tom Klepper set him up with Max. He's also Gary's lawyer. I talked to Klepper last night. I was with him at his office when he got a call from Max demanding a ransom for Gary. He was told to go to Lighthouse Park on Roosevelt Island to deliver the cash. I went instead. I waited a long time, but no one showed up."

"You still have the cash?" Reich asked, suddenly interested.

"I never had the cash. Tom Klepper gave me a bag of newspaper."

"Some friend." Iorio made a face.

Desmond passed a slip of paper with the phone numbers he had for Klepper across the table to Iorio. She didn't pick it up. "Klepper says Max uses burner phones, but you might want to check on that. The call last night came in around eight-thirty."

"Thanks for telling us how to do our jobs," Iorio said drily. "You have any other crime-solving tips?"

Desmond pretended not to bristle at her dismissive attitude. "Someone's got to find Gary's wife. The cops in the Poconos tried, but she was gone. Her doorman said she left in a hurry on Friday night."

The cops looked at each other, and Desmond could see they were done listening to him.

"Mr. Edgars, you need to understand something," Iorio said. "Obviously, you're grieving the loss of your sister. We get that, and we're sorry for it. But sometimes, people want to see an accident as a crime. They want to find a bad guy behind it, someone they can blame."

"This is not my overactive imagination at work," Desmond seethed. "Dominique was murdered. Gary was murdered. Someone tried to kill me."

"Not in New York City," Reich shot back.

"Someone was trying to shake Tom Klepper down for cash right here in Manhattan," Desmond answered. "That's in *your* jurisdiction."

"Maybe the guy made up a story to get away from you," Reich snarked back. "Because he thought you were unhinged."

"If the police force in the Poconos asks for help, obviously we'll assist them," Iorio said. "But, at this time, the best thing you can do is leave everything in their hands."

Desmond felt sick to his stomach, but he stood. It had been a mistake to talk to these people. He'd owed it to Dominique to do it, against his gut instinct. But these strangers didn't give a damn about finding out what really happened. The only way his sister would have any justice was if Desmond obtained it himself.

32

It was ten-thirty in the morning when Desmond left the police station, heading north along Third Avenue. He dropped Iorio's business card in the first trash bin he passed. That had been a first-class exercise in pointlessness. It didn't matter, though, because he had questions for Tom Klepper and he was going to get answers.

His route to the Empire State Building let him keep a wide berth from his sister's apartment. The security guard who'd signed him in on Sunday evening was still at his post, which made Desmond wonder what hours the man was working. There was no ring on his finger, but he had the haggard, put-upon look of a man with too many mouths to feed.

The guard called upstairs and sent him up. There was a receptionist answering the door today, a tall, heavyset woman with arresting curves. Her hair was a startling mix of unnatural colors.

"I'm here to see Tom Klepper."

"Sure," she answered, obviously unconcerned. "His office is back that way. Want me to call him?"

"That's okay. I know my way back."

He strolled down the corridor. Klepper's door was locked shut. Desmond knocked lightly on it, then pressed his ear to the door. There was no sound, and the space under the door revealed no light.

Watching the empty hallway, he lifted his keychain out of his pocket and tried the lock. He kept a few skeleton keys, because you never knew when you might need them at a tiny regional airport with no staff around. When he was almost a teenager, he'd shown a startling aptitude for breaking into houses. It was penny-ante stuff, and the trespassing was more exciting to him than sifting through the detritus of people's lives. It wasn't a skill set he'd bragged about to anyone since he was a kid.

He found one key that slid in easily, and he gave the lock a swift, hard rap. The tumblers spun on cue and it opened wide. *Nothing to it,* he thought, but the words were ringed by an echo of shame. He remembered being dragged home one night in the back of a Chicago PD squad car. His terrified mother and furious stepfather were waiting. *You're nothing but common trash,* his stepfather had said. *You don't belong in this family.*

That recollection made him shut the door of Klepper's office with more force than was strictly necessary.

Klepper's laptop wasn't there, but the office was otherwise the same, right down to the donut box, still bleeding powdered sugar on the desk. Desmond made a quick search of the room, but what turned up seemed like junk. The mess inside the top desk drawers suggested pathological hoarding. Desmond didn't think he'd seen so many sugar, salt, and soy sauce packets outside an airport food court. There was a leather-bound calendar, but all that Klepper had scrawled into it was "Lunch at the Harvard Club" every two months or so. That left Desmond wondering how he got in, given that he wasn't a graduate. How obsessed could one grown man be with a college?

Desmond's biggest find was a series of scrapbooks and notebooks that detailed Gary Cowan's career. Klepper seemed less of a friend and more like a starry-eyed fan. Toward the end of one scrapbook, there was an article that used the phrase *disgraced fighter Gary Cowan.* Disgraced? What had he done? He made a mental note to check on that later.

At the bottom of one drawer was a framed diploma from Loyola in Los Angeles. Desmond shook his head. He didn't know much about law school rankings, but that was the law school Johnnie Cochran had graduated from. Even if it wasn't a household name, it was a damn fine school and Klepper was a fool not to see that.

Before he left, he checked Klepper's desk phone. Lots of calls to Gary. Some calls from random numbers with varied area codes. Nothing jumped out at him as suspicious, but he jotted it all down to check out later.

On his way out of the office, he stopped by the receptionist's desk. "Tom Klepper isn't in his office. Is there somewhere else he might be in the building?"

"He doesn't come in all that often," she answered. "He's probably working from home. Or, you know, *working*." She lifted her hands and made air quotes around the last word.

"He's not exactly in demand?"

"Honey, you are the first person who's asked for him in a donkey's age." She looked him up and down with her soft brown eyes, pleasantly plain next to her varicolored hair. "You're not here because you want to hire him, are you? He owe you money?"

"More like an explanation."

She nodded. "Good luck getting that."

Desmond raised his eyebrows. "You ever meet his client Gary Cowan?"

The woman's eyes lit up. "The fighter? Sure, he's been in here a few times. Always so charming. He's a gentleman."

"I was kind of surprised he's a client of Tom's."

The receptionist nodded. "That's his *only* client, far as I know. He used to represent a lot of boxers and boxing promoters. I think he might even know a thing or two about sports law. But that all fell apart for him awhile back."

"What happened?"

"I don't really know. But that poor man should have a lawyer protecting him from his lawyer," she said. "Because Tom Klepper is nothing but a leech."

On the elevator ride down, Desmond plugged the various phone numbers he had for Tom Klepper into a reverse lookup directory and turned up a residential address on East Thirty-seventh Street. Klepper's home was a short walk away, but long enough for Desmond to get increasingly annoyed with that amphibious excuse for a man. Why hadn't he talked to the cops like he promised? Did Klepper have such a huge drug problem he wasn't willing to turn in his dealer until he lined up another source?

On the walk over, he texted Sabrina while he waited to cross a light. *Got your message. So hard to talk right now.* He planned to leave it at that, but she responded almost instantly.

My heart is broken. I can't believe it. So very sorry.

Thank you. He couldn't think of anything else to say.

Are you coming to NYC?

I'm in now, he answered.

Do you need a place to crash?

Already at the Hyatt, but thanks.

We need to talk, she texted back. *Do you know what happened?*

He didn't answer that. He knew too much, and yet not nearly enough.

When he arrived at the brownstone, he found Klepper's name next to a buzzer. No one answered it. Desmond pressed it for half a minute and heard the noise reverberating almost under his feet. He glanced down, realizing Klepper's home was the street-level apartment. He took the stairs down and let himself in through a black wrought-iron gate. He knocked on the door and then tried to peer through the window, but the blinds were shut. Desmond was studying the multiple locks considering how much trouble it would be to open the door when a head popped over the side of the railing above him.

"Hey! You, there. What you doing with that door?" barked a white-haired man in his early sixties. He had a strong Puerto Rican accent.

"Looking for Tom Klepper." Desmond feigned innocence. "You seen him around?"

The man gave him the evil eye. Desmond was fairly certain the attorney had hightailed it with his stack of cash. He felt like a fool for believing Klepper would go to the police.

"Do you know where he is?" Desmond asked again.

"Who wants to know?"

"I'm a friend of his." Desmond knew he didn't sound convincing. "You know where I can reach him?"

The man only glared. Desmond conceded it was a lost cause, backing off and moving away from the brownstone. Halfway down the block, he looked back and saw the man staring after him. He hoped the cops would be as frustrated as he was whenever they finally tried to question Klepper. By then, the man's trail would be stone cold.

33

Desmond didn't know where to turn next, not without more direction from Westergren in Pennsylvania. But he was compelled to keep busy—no knowing where his brain would lead him if he let it rest—so he turned his attention to Dominique's burial arrangements. That was tougher than he expected. He walked out of one funeral home after its director aggressively recommended cremation. He didn't want his baby sister's remains scattered to the four winds. She needed to have a final resting place where he could visit her. He could accept that it would be in New York—Dominique loved that city, after all—but he couldn't cope with the notion of ashes in an urn.

When he got back to the Hyatt, he was planning to head upstairs and shower, but he halted in his tracks when he recognized Sabrina Ogden. She was perched on a sofa, waiting for him.

The sight of Dominique's best friend made his heart lighter for a fraction of a moment. Looking at her, he forgot, just for a split second, what he was doing there. Then it rushed back, and he felt as if he were dropping through the sky in what pilots called a nylon letdown—when you ejected from a plane and sailed back to the earth on a parachute. Only, in this case, his chute wouldn't open.

Sabrina had spotted him first, and she stood and walked toward him, looking as lovely as ever. Her blond hair was cut into a bob now, which emphasized how pretty and delicate her features were. She wore slim-fitting jeans and a pale green sweater, and her coat was open. The only thing out of place was the redness of her eyes and the swelling around them.

"I couldn't help myself," Sabrina said. "I decided to hunt you down."

"I'm glad you did."

She put her arms around him and they hugged for a long time.

"I can't believe she's gone," Sabrina whispered. As she pulled away, there were tears standing in her blue eyes.

It was deeply unsettling to see her. He'd known Sabrina for some time; she was one of the first people Dominique met in New York, and they had been roommates for years. He felt like a heel for not calling her, especially because he knew exactly why he'd avoided it: he was genuinely afraid of what she would see in him. Sabrina could read things anyone else would miss. A year ago, after his divorce was final, Dominique had set Desmond up on a date with Sabrina. His sister didn't call it that, but he knew a setup when he saw one. It had gone well. Too well. Desmond remembered that he'd never had such an easy time talking to anyone in his life. Afterward, there had been a few weeks where he and Sabrina were chatting every day, sometimes more than once. But then he'd realized he was on the edge of revealing things to her that he'd never told anyone, and he pulled away. He'd made a fool of himself explaining that he wasn't ready to date, but that was just a sorry lie. He was terrified of what those searching eyes would lure out of him.

"I know. I keep turning around and thinking she's there," Desmond said.

"She is there. You don't have to worry about that. It's just hard for us because we're left behind."

He knew that Sabrina had strong religious beliefs. His own weren't so powerful or clearly formed, but that didn't mean he couldn't take comfort in the idea that his sister was somewhere close by, aware of what they were doing even though they couldn't reach her. He'd held that notion in his heart when his mother died, too.

"Let's sit down somewhere," Desmond said. "Do you have time for dinner?" He glanced at his watch; it wasn't quite four o'clock.

"I wish. I have to get home soon. It's a long story." She grimaced. "But the short version is that Copper is sick, and I have to pick him up from the vet."

He remembered that Copper was her dog. Sabrina doted on the creature like a child. He didn't doubt that she was telling the truth, but he wondered if the pup hadn't been ill, what her excuse would've been. "I'm sorry. You want to get some coffee?"

"Yes, even though I don't drink caffeine." She smiled. "Though I do make an exception for Mountain Dew."

"I almost forgot you're the one girl who made my sister look hedonistic."

They left the hubbub of the hotel lobby for the nonstop commotion of Grand Central Terminal, sweeping up one of its grand staircases to Cipriani Dolci. They found a table overlooking the melee below. Desmond told her about going to the house and finding Dominique.

"I can't believe this is real. It's like a horror novel," Sabrina said. "How could it happen?"

Desmond's eyes met hers. "I need you to level with me completely. I talked with Dominique on Friday night. She told me she had a plan to blackmail Gary. What was going on with her?"

"She swore me to secrecy, but I don't think that applies now, does it?" Sabrina sighed. "The only reason she met up with Gary and went to his country house was to get Gary to confess."

"Confess to what?"

"Did Dominique ever tell you why Gary could never got divorced?" She took a small bite of her cupcake.

"I remember excuses, not an explanation."

"There was a complicated legal situation. Gary signed some kind of crazy agreement with Trinity's father. Gary got money out of the deal, but the family basically had him trapped like a rat. He couldn't divorce Trinity, and he couldn't talk to anyone about the agreement he'd signed. There was some kind of huge legal penalty for that." She gave him a sad little smile. "Of course, he talked about it to Dominique."

"And Dominique told you."

"Right. And Dominique was going to get him to talk about it again over the weekend, only this time, it was going to be on tape. A man named Zachary Amberson was going to pay her a lot of money for it."

The name rang a bell in Desmond's head. "Who's he?"

"He's a lawyer who was best friends with Trinity's father. The father didn't trust his kids not to run wild with the family money, so he left things in trust and Amberson administers all that." Sabrina looked down at the crowd. "I think Trinity was desperate to divorce Gary. She really hated him. The problem was, she had to get married again within thirty days."

"Do you know who Trinity was planning to marry?"

Sabrina shook her head. "No idea. I said to Dominique, maybe it would be Zachary Amberson himself, since that would give him total control over the family fortune, but Dominique said he's already married. Apparently, he has a thing for Las Vegas showgirls. He gets a new one every eight to ten years. Dominique says the current one has breasts as large as a human head." She smiled, but its wattage dimmed quickly. "*Said*, I mean. Not says."

"I've been doing that a lot."

"There's something I have to tell you. Don't hate me," Sabrina said, "but I gave Dominique some muscle relaxant that was prescribed for me. I was having lupus-related jaw problems and . . . oh, it doesn't matter why. I know it sounds horrible, but I wanted her to be able to get back at Gary for what he did to her. She was going to mix the relaxant into a drink for him. It wasn't enough to knock him out or anything, but it would make him relaxed enough to say awful things about his wife and the agreement he signed."

"What did Gary do to make my sister hate him so much?"

Sabrina looked worried. "I don't think I can tell you this part. Dominique would kill me."

"It's not going to hurt her now."

"She never would've sold Gary out, not in a million years," Sabrina said. "But Gary cheated on her."

"A creep who cheated on his wife stepped out on his girlfriend?" Desmond shook his head. "I hate to say it, but what's the surprise?"

"You don't understand. It broke her heart. Dominique really, really loved him. He convinced her his marriage wasn't real, and I don't think he was lying about that." She took another small bite. "But then she found out he was sleeping with some blond cheerleader."

"A *cheerleader*?"

"That's just what Dominique called her. She showed me the photos. In some of them, the woman looked like a high-priced call girl, but in others, was wasn't wearing much makeup and she seemed really young."

Desmond was trying to wrap his mind around the story. "How did she find out about the cheerleader?"

"Someone mailed her photos. Anonymously, of course. She showed them to me. They were pretty bad."

"Someone anonymously sent photos to Dominique? What were they, nude shots?"

Sabrina's hand fluttered to her mouth. Her face had flushed red.

"I didn't mean it like that! No one was naked in the shots I saw. It was just that Gary and this girl were in Central Park with their arms wrapped around each other, for example. There were a bunch of photos from Gary's condo, after Dominique moved out. That made her angrier than anything." She stared at Desmond. "Dominique didn't tell you any of it?"

"She knew I didn't like her dating a married man, so she avoided talking about her relationship with Gary most of the time."

"I wouldn't normally be a fan of that, either, but Gary wasn't really married. I mean, he never had sex with his wife. His wife never wanted to get married. It's not because she was in love with anyone else, or because she's gay. She's just asexual. She's never had a boyfriend—or a girlfriend—in her life."

"But she's, what, thirty-five years old? No one can survive like that."

Sabrina gave him a bemused look. "Do you know who Edward Gorey was?"

"It doesn't ring a bell."

"He was a genius illustrator. You have to read *The Gashlycrumb Tinies*. It's the best thing ever." She gave him a guilty smile. "Anyway, Gorey was supposed to be asexual. So was Sir Isaac Newton."

"Seriously?"

"What's Google for, if not to look up things like that?" She took her last bite of cupcake and chewed thoughtfully. "I'm—I mean, I was—probably a bad influence on Dominique. I Google everything. You have to read about Trinity's family. Her father made up their last name, you know. He was married four times, and after he divorced Trinity's mother, she never saw her again. And all three of Trinity's brothers are dead."

That caught Desmond's interest. "Do you know anything about how they died?"

"Byron Lytton-Jones died of a drug overdose. Shelley died in a car accident. Keats died somewhere in South America."

"Those were really their names?"

"They were all named for English Romantic poets," Sabrina said. "Trinity was named for Trinity College at Oxford. The father was an obsessive Anglophile. I can't explain it any better than that."

"Her brothers didn't leave behind any kids, I take it."

"No. Actually, I think Keats died just after he got married. That was part of the reason Trinity's father was obsessed with getting her married off. His sons died without leaving heirs. The father told Gary that Trinity was his last hope. He thought he was creating this dynasty."

"Until Trinity had them killed."

It was Sabrina's turn to look stunned. "The deaths were accidents. I never read anything suggesting they weren't."

"The police in Pennsylvania were ready to write off Dominique's and Gary's deaths as accidents," Desmond said. "Carbon monoxide poisoning isn't uncommon. The only reason I knew it was foul play is because Dominique called me."

"You think Trinity arranged for her brothers to die?"

Desmond considered that. "Who else benefitted from their deaths? She went from sharing a multibillion-dollar fortune to having it all to herself."

34

After Sabrina left, Desmond rushed out of Grand Central, heading north. He hoped his head would clear by the time he reached Zachary Amberson's office on Park Avenue. Desmond hated lawyers, as a rule. If his own experience with them, and his mother's, had taught him anything, it was that when the chips were down, all a lawyer cared about was saving his own ass. It didn't matter where they went to school, though he reserved an extra dose of contempt for the ones with Ivy League degrees on their walls and cushy Italian shoes on their feet. He'd had one of those once, when he was fourteen and he'd gotten into serious trouble. He'd been caught holding drugs for a dealer, and his court-appointed attorney was a shark in a slick suit who was doing some pro bono work in the war zone of Chicago's South Side. It only occurred to Desmond later that the man was probably being punished for some transgression of his own, and that was why he listened to Desmond's mother talk with his eyes glazed over. *All the boy has to do is roll over on the dealer,* the lawyer explained in his oily voice. *It's that simple. The prosecutor doesn't give a rat's ass about him. He'll get some community service and you'll be done.*

Until someone firebombs our house, his mother pointed out.

In the end, Desmond got lucky. The dealer turned rat, and Desmond was mostly off the hook, since no one needed his testimony anymore. When he looked back, he wondered what was going on inside his childish head then. How could he have put his mother through the things he did? But then he remembered what happened the day that the court lost interest in him. Once his stepfather realized the boy didn't need to show up for any more interviews, he took his old leather belt and beat Desmond with it for a half-hour. He didn't stop until long after Desmond started bleeding.

The best revenge is to be unlike him who performed the injury. That was Marcus Aurelius. Desmond focused on the words until the past receded and he was fully in the present again.

Amberson's office was at a predictably expensive address in Midtown. The building looked like a movie set. In the lobby there was some weird, twisty sculpture that probably cost a million bucks. The place reeked of money.

"I'm here to see Zachary Amberson," he told one of the uniformed guards at the security desk, an elderly man who looked like he'd rather be elsewhere.

"You have ID?" The guard's eyes were dark, almost as brown as his skin.

"Yes." He fished into his pocket for his wallet and pulled out his driver's license.

"Hammond, Indiana?" the guard read aloud. "Never heard of it."

"It's a suburb of Chicago."

He typed Desmond's name into a computer. "You have an appointment?" He sounded dubious.

"No."

"That lawyer don't see nobody without an appointment."

"He's going to want to see me."

The guard's eyes were flat. "We'll see," he muttered, picking up the phone and tapping in a code. "Hello. We've got a Desmond Edgars here to see Zachary Amberson." The guard listened for a moment, glancing up at Desmond. "She says you don't have an appointment."

"Tell her it's about Dominique Monaghan."

The guard repeated this into the receiver. "She still says you don't have an appointment."

"It's also about Gary Cowan."

The guard's eyebrows crawled up his creased forehead, and he dropped his head forward in obvious disbelief at Desmond's obtuseness. Still, he passed the message along. Then he rolled his eyes and hung up the phone. "She hung up," he told Desmond.

"But how do I get up there to see him?"

"You don't." The guard picked up Desmond's ID and started to hand it back, but he glanced at it again and his expression softened slightly. "You were in the service?" The Indiana driver's license made that fact hard to miss, with its *Veteran* designation.

"Combat Aviation Brigade, Fourth Infantry Division."

"Iron Eagles." The guard nodded at him. "What'd you fly?"

"Apaches and Black Hawks."

"My father was one of the original Red Tail Angels. You know about them?"

"The Tuskegee Airmen? Of course!" Desmond didn't have much regard for actors or sports stars, but he revered the Tuskegee Airmen. They were the first African-American aviators in the armed forces, serving with supreme distinction in the Second World War. He fought the urge to tell the guard that the fire-breathing panther on his left deltoid was based on their unofficial emblem, and it was in their honor.

The guard smiled at his boyish enthusiasm and handed back his license. "Don't take it personal. They don't see nobody up there. Amberson's secretary, Marina, is like a pit bull. Got a lot of mileage on her, but she's not slowing down. She wouldn't let the Pope up there." He hesitated slightly. "That lady you mentioned, she a relative of yours?"

"My sister."

"She's been in here a couple of times. She's a model, ain't she?"

"She was a model. About three years back, she became a stylist. But she still looked like a model."

"You couldn't miss her," the guard said. "Or forget her. Nice girl, too. Raised right. She doing okay?"

"She died over the weekend." There was a catch in Desmond's throat as he said the words.

Something shifted in the guard's face. "She was in an accident?"

"Carbon monoxide poisoning."

The guard shook his head slowly. "What a tragedy. I am sorry."

Desmond nodded dumbly before he found his voice. "Do you remember when she came in?"

"First time was a month ago. October, definitely, because I was just back from visiting my son. He and his wife just had their first baby. Then she came in again last week. Most folks wouldn't spit on you if you was on fire, but she asked after my son and his family. Definitely raised right."

"Last week? Did she say anything about why she was visiting Zachary Amberson?"

"No, nothing like that." The guard shrugged. "All I can tell you is, she had an appointment. Both times she was here."

35

Can you come into the station?" Detective Iorio's voice crackled over the phone line. Desmond was astonished to hear it at all. That morning, he hadn't expected to hear from her again. "We've found something important."

"What is it?" It was after seven, and Desmond would've sworn someone had crushed his heart and soul in a vise that day when he wasn't looking.

"I can't talk about that over the phone."

"Did the cops in the Poconos call you?" Desmond asked. "Did they find something else in the house?"

"Sorry, I can't say. You need to come down to the station."

"Fine. I'll be there in a few minutes."

He took a cab straight down Lexington Avenue to where it ended at Gramercy Park. He walked the last half-block stretch over to Third Avenue, since the cab couldn't turn that way. When he looked at the sky, he missed the stars. With all the light pollution from the city, that was probably as good a the view of the heavens as a New Yorker ever got. *Dwell on the beauty of life. Watch the stars, and see yourself running with them,* he thought. Those words filled him with sadness. That was the last thing he'd said to Dominique before she died.

"Thanks for coming in," Reich said when he got to the precinct. Desmond thought it strange that the detective was waiting downstairs for him, but he didn't mention it.

"What's going on?" he asked instead.

"Let's go sit down." Reich led him upstairs. "My partner has an interview room waiting for us. How are you holding up?"

"Okay. What did you find?"

"Let's wait until my partner is in the room. Then we don't have to go over everything twice."

Desmond was suspicious. Reich being solicitous didn't track. There was something afoot, but he couldn't figure out what.

"Can I ask you something about Gary Cowan?" Desmond decided to go in a different direction. "This morning, you said something about him being a great boxer, until he got himself in some kind of jam. What was that?"

"Boxing's kind of a shady sport. You know, like Jake LaMotta throwing his match with Billy Fox. Lotta fight-fixing, that kind of thing."

"By *fixing,* you mean rigging?"

"That's the idea."

Desmond let out a low whistle. "Gary Cowan was into that?"

"I don't know if it was a regular thing, but he threw one fight and screwed it up bad. It was all over YouTube. The other fighter threw a punch that barely grazed the top of his head, but Cowan went down for the count. Never heard a crowd boo so loudly in my life."

When they got upstairs, Iorio was standing in the same interview room they'd spoken in that morning. "Thanks for coming in." She didn't sound thankful.

"Sure. What did you find?"

"Please sit down." She indicated a chair. When he took it, she sat next to him. "So, this morning you mentioned a man named Thomas Klepper. How do you know him?"

"I met him yesterday. He was friends with Gary Cowan. He was also Gary's lawyer."

"*Was* friends? *Was* his lawyer? Interesting use of the past tense," Reich interjected.

Desmond stared at him. "Gary's dead. How else would you put it?"

Reich blinked. "Oh, right."

But that slip was enough for Desmond to realize that something bad had befallen Tom Klepper. He kept his body relaxed, but his guard went up. They'd tricked him into coming in. This wasn't about his sister. The cops had their own agenda. He should have known better.

"This morning, you told us you met with Thomas Klepper on Sunday evening." Iorio took the reins again. "What time was that?"

"About eight o'clock. I called him, he phoned me back, and then we met at his office in the Empire State Building."

"Is that the last time you saw him?"

"Yes. What's going on?"

She frowned, formulating her next question. "You called Thomas Klepper something like thirty times last night and today. What's that about?"

Desmond took a breath, remembering what he'd already said to the cops. He wasn't going to tag on any new details for them to chew on. "I told you this morning. A man named Max was trying to extort money out of Klepper, telling him Gary had been abducted and he had to pay a ransom. Klepper didn't know Gary was dead until I told him. After that, we agreed he'd go to the police while I went out to Lighthouse Park with the bag." He looked from one to the other. "As far as I can tell, he never went to the police."

Iorio sat back, her skeptical expression hardening as she watched him. "So, you contend that you and Tom Klepper were working together?"

He stared right back. "I don't *contend* anything. You called me, saying you had found something about my sister's death. Was that a lie, detective?" He stood. *Never talk to cops* had been the rule where he grew up. As far as he was concerned, that South Side wisdom still applied. "Unless you've got news you want to share with me, we're done."

"Thomas Klepper is dead." It was Reich who blurted the words out. Iorio didn't look happy about it.

"What?"

"He died in his apartment," Reich answered. "He was strangled."

36

We don't have the forensics yet but there's bruising on his throat and marks from the cord his attacker used," Reich said. "There was an open wall safe, so the scene is set up like a robbery. Not clear that's what it actually was, though. Lividity and decomp place his death late Sunday night or early this morning."

Desmond closed his eyes and shook his head. On Sunday night, Klepper had sat across from him, polishing off one donut after another. That morning, when he tracked Klepper down in his brownstone apartment, the man was lying inside, dead.

"What can you tell us about Thomas Klepper?" asked Iorio.

"All we really talked about was Gary. He . . . I don't think he cared that my sister died, but he cared about Gary." Desmond had recovered from his shock enough to speak. He hadn't liked Tom Klepper. The bullfrog face, the croaky voice, the soft hands, the sense of entitlement had all conspired to make him feel Klepper was a creep. But the shady attorney was the closest thing to a professional ally he had in New York; at least the man understood that Dominique's and Gary's deaths were by design, not an accident.

"My sister and her boyfriend were murdered," Desmond said slowly. "Now, suddenly Gary's best friend is dead. It's obvious there's a connection."

"Or someone wants us to *think* there's a connection," Reich said. "I don't believe in coincidences."

Iorio shot him a tight-lipped look.

"Nor do I," Desmond answered. He caught the look, and he understood the significance of it.

Soon, very soon, you will be ashes or a skeleton, and either a name or not even a name; but name is sound and echo. But Marcus Aurelius was no help to him now. Stoics were supposed to make themselves comfortable with their impending death, since getting riled about it was nothing but a waste of a mind. But Desmond couldn't accept Tom Klepper's passing with the same equanimity. It severed the last link to Max.

"Who found him?" Desmond asked.

"His superintendent. He was concerned because there was a man lurking around Thomas Klepper's apartment."

"A black man about six foot three, between the ages of thirty-five and forty-two," Reich added.

"The superintendent called Klepper's office to let him know and found out Klepper hadn't gone in. So he let himself in and found the body." Iorio's voice was soft, almost as if she were talking to herself. "It's really sad. He's got a couple of kids by his first wife. They're teenagers."

"The man the superintendent saw was me. I went over there today," Desmond explained. "I wanted to find out why he was ducking me."

"Did you go to his place last night, maybe on your way back from Roosevelt Island?" Reich asked.

"No." The Lighthouse Park setup might have been nothing but a cheap ruse. Had Max wanted Klepper out of his apartment so he could break in and wait for him to come home? He wondered if Klepper had actually intended to go to the cops, after he'd come down from his cocaine-induced high. He'd never know.

"Did anyone actually *see* you on Roosevelt Island?" Iorio's voice was sly.

From the moment he realized something had happened to Klepper, Desmond saw that Iorio and Reich were measuring him up for the crime. What did he expect from two white cops?

"Yes," he answered, without elaborating. "Here's the key thing: Tom Klepper knew Max." He tried to speak patiently. "He told me he'd bought drugs from him in the past. That was their connection."

"What kind of drugs?"

"Weed, coke, pills. He said Max provided one-stop shopping."

"So, this mystery man is a drug dealer," Iorio said. "Any other clues about his identity?"

Desmond shook his head. He could feel suspicion slithering beneath her words. She didn't believe a mystery man existed.

"How did Klepper meet this dealer?" Reich asked.

"No idea."

"So we've still got nothing," Reich said.

Desmond could picture Klepper's puffy, almost boneless, hands reaching for donut after donut. "He told me he had a girlfriend."

"What's her name?"

"I don't know."

"So, Thomas Klepper had a mysterious girlfriend as well as a connection to mysterious Max," Iorio said. "That's a lot of mysterious, nonexistent people around him."

Even though they hadn't said the words outright, he knew they were accusing him, disputing his version of events, challenging his integrity. He rose to his feet.

"Where do you think you're going?" Reich asked. It wasn't a friendly question.

"Back to my hotel. You know where to find me. Oh, and if you want to check my alibi, find a woman who owns a chocolate lab that answers to the name of Hershey. I saw her at Lighthouse Park last night, and I know she saw me."

He walked out of the room, half-expecting them to try restraining him. He didn't look back. He could feel their eyes boring into the back of his skull.

37

His hands were still shaking with rage when he walked into the Starbucks at the corner of Twenty-third and Third. That scene at the precinct had been what his friends in the Army would call a Charlie Foxtrot. He missed the creative swearing in the service. Civilian life had never been a good fit for him.

The coffee shop was miniscule compared to the ones he knew in Illinois and Indiana. He looked around, wondering if he could sit down for a bit. What he wanted was a stiff drink, but he knew himself well enough to admit that would only lead to trouble. Instead, he'd opt for the safety of strong caffeine and faint jazz.

His best intentions didn't last long. When he sat down on a barstool in front of the window, he noticed the young woman next to him had her laptop open to a news story. BIZARRE LOVE TRIANGLE shouted the headline. Desmond tilted his head closer. Yes, that was indeed a story about his sister and Gary.

The woman noticed him hovering over her shoulder and half-turned in his direction.

"Sorry, I was just reading your screen," Desmond said.

"Oh, sure." Her voice was nonchalant. "It's a really creepy one."

Desmond tried to read it, but his brain balked at the task. Without another word, he headed outside. The wind was blowing hard, and he managed to walk two blocks north before pulling out his phone and typing his sister's name in a search engine. *Bizarre Love Triangle* was the least offensive story he found. PLAYBOY AND MIStress in death pact screamed another tabloid. There was some speculation about whether Dominique and Gary's deaths were truly accidental, or whether they had actually committed suicide together. There were anonymous sources making insane claims; one particular rumor—that the couple's naked bodies had been found entwined in a bed strewn with rose petals—had really gained traction. The reader comments were what finally forced Desmond to shut the screen down. "They deserved to die for committing adultery. That is a sin they will go to hell for," read the first comment on the *Bizarre Love Triangle* story. If Desmond could have reached through his phone and throttled the person, he would have. Marcus Aurelius had plenty of advice about keeping calm, but that wouldn't have stopped him. He tried to think of something comforting the philosopher had to say while he stood on the street, wiping tears from his eyes and trying to pretend it was from the wind. There was nothing.

Finally, he wandered back to Dominique's apartment building but, at the last minute, he changed his mind about going inside. He wasn't sure what stopped him, except that his emotions were overpowering him. They were coming on with the velocity and force of a tornado. The one swirling to the top was regret. He owed Dominique so much. It had been his responsibility to take care of his baby sister, and he'd failed miserably. There was a den in his house with a wall filled with the awards he'd earned in the service for bravery and honor. The truth was, they didn't mean much; they were props he used to convince himself he'd done right in his life. But Dominique's sad death showed him the truth: he'd always let his sister down, even if she didn't know it. He'd let his whole family down.

He walked west across Twenty-ninth Street, vaguely remembering a church Dominique had taken him to once. His sister never fit in with the modeling scene in New York. She didn't smoke or do drugs, and her occasional indulgence in champagne was about as wild as she got. She'd had a lot of boyfriends, but he didn't think she'd gotten serious with many of them; at least, that was what he was determined to think, and nothing was going to change his mind. She liked fine clothes, and her hobby was hunting for interesting churches.

Desmond was less comfortable inside houses of worship. *Whenever I walk into a church, I feel like our grandmother is watching me*, he'd admitted to his sister.

I always feel like Nana is watching me, she'd told him.

But the concept of having their grandmother's eyes on them had a very different meaning for the two of them, Desmond knew. Nana doted on Dominique. His sister was only four when their mother had gone to prison. Only four when her father had died, Desmond reminded himself. What had been a tremendous blessing for him had been a curse for her. As much as Desmond hated his stepfather, he had to admit that the man had been a perfectly good father to Dominique. He'd adored the girl, and Desmond couldn't remember the man ever shouting at her, let alone punishing her when she was naughty, which was often. He was only monstrous as a stepfather, making Desmond call him "Mr. Monaghan" and trying to distance him from the rest of the family, beating him for infractions big and small, real and imaginary. For a long time, Desmond hid the abuse from his mother, because he knew how deeply the truth would hurt her. His heart broke thinking just how badly it had devastated her when she'd found out.

The church was closed for the night when he arrived. He stood next to its low, decorative iron gate, pretending to admire the offbeat neo-Gothic façade, but his mind was trapped between past and present. He'd tried to broach the subject of *Mr. Monaghan* with Dominique once or twice, but his approach had been tentative; he'd eased off, relieved, when she didn't seem responsive, promising himself he'd revisit the subject when she was ready. He knew their grandmother had told Dominique that her father's death was an accident, and he felt an obligation to set the record straight. It hadn't been an accident at all, and he was the only person living who knew that. But deep down, he was terrified if he told her what had happened, she would cut him out of her life forever. Now that she was gone, his sadness and shame were unrelenting, because he could never set things right.

His troubled thoughts were leading him in painful directions. That was why he needed to run around New York like a maniac, he realized. As long as he was moving, he didn't have to think about all he'd lost. He stepped away from the church and walked to Madison Avenue, turning north. He thought about what to do next, and he was grateful for the distraction when he got a text. Better yet, it was from Westergren. *Got a test result. Want to talk?*

Desmond called him back immediately. Westergren was the only cop in the world he wanted to talk to. "Hey. I got your message. What's this test?"

"I wasn't sure if I should bother you about it," Westergren said. "It's probably not a big deal. But they checked the blood on the shirt they found in the sink, and it's Gary Cowan's."

"That's not a surprise, is it?"

"No, but here's where it gets weird." Westergren's voice was almost giddy. This was his first serious investigation, and he was enjoying it to the hilt. "There was blood on that nail you found. It doesn't match what's on the shirt. It's definitely not Gary's."

Desmond's breath caught, making his chest feel tight. "Could it be my sister's?"

"Nope. They tested it, and it isn't hers."

"That leaves one possibility," Desmond said. "It belongs to Max."

38

On Tuesday morning, after an endless, sleepless night, Desmond took the subway uptown. Gary Cowan's wife lived in a fancy building on Fifth Avenue, one that overlooked Central Park. The doorman had a neatly combed black mustache and a substantial unibrow, marking his face with two parallel lines, as if somebody had driven over it and left skid marks. The man was haughty as only a man with gold braid on his uniform could be. Still, his mustache quivered when Desmond mentioned Gary's name.

"Poor Mr. Cowan. We're all very sad about what happened." He looked Desmond up and down. "You're here for . . . ?"

"I'm here to see Trinity Lytton-Jones."

Desmond gave his name and the doorman called upstairs. When the man hung up the phone, he pointed toward an elevator to the far right side of the lobby. "Take that one up."

"To which floor?"

"That particular elevator only goes to one floor. The Penthouse. There's only one apartment up there. Don't worry, you'll see."

Desmond had expected luxury overkill, but even without setting foot in the apartment, he was vaguely disgusted. The men and women he'd served with in Iraq and Afghanistan had given their all for their country, and most of them had made enormous sacrifices, but there was no material reward waiting for them. There was nothing but more hardship and struggle.

When the elevator doors opened, he stepped into a broad foyer with elaborately carved double doors. The floor was tiled with a mosaic of a gold lion with one paw raised. Before he could study it, the doors swung back. A tall, slender young man with mocha skin and Caucasian features stood in front of Desmond. He was wearing some sort of archaic uniform with rows of brass buttons running up and down the front. "You must be Desmond."

"I am. You're Costa?"

"Yes. It's an honor to meet you." He came forward, extending his hand. When Desmond took it, Costa pulled him into a bear hug. "Your sister saved our lives. If it weren't for her, we'd be dead."

Desmond pulled back. He'd spoken to Costa on the phone before coming over, and he knew the man was effusive. But outpourings of emotion made Desmond wary, and this was a character who worked for Gary Cowan's widow. He didn't trust him.

"I'm so very sorry about your sister," Costa added. "What happened to her breaks my heart."

"Thank you."

"Please come in. I'll get Trin. Uh, Miss Lytton-Jones, I mean. This way, please."

Costa led him through the doors and along a broad hallway. Every inch of the walls was covered in framed photographs. Some were glossy shots, others clippings torn from a magazine or newspaper. All of them featured the same doll-like woman. Close-ups of her face and images of her body covered the walls on either side of him. As Desmond passed them, he noted a strange progression: the subject became progressively thinner and more haggard as the years went by. Her eyes sank into her skull, even as her clothing became more grand and outrageous. In the later shots, her makeup was a ghoulish mask. No matter the wealth she enjoyed, Trinity Lytton-Jones looked as if she'd lived a very hard life.

Costa led him into a living room so crammed with furniture

and decoration it could've been a showroom for antiques. More was, apparently, more. Trinity's wan face stared out of photographs in gilded frames. There was also an Andy Warhol–style portrait of her above the marble fireplace.

"Please have a seat. Would you like something to drink?"

"I'm fine, thanks."

Costa gave him a sweet smile. "Miss Lytton-Jones will be with you soon."

The man left the room quietly. Desmond looked around. There were images of Miss Lytton-Jones as far as his eye could see. The only other prominent decoration was a stuffed Jack Russell terrier on a brass base. Desmond loved dogs, but the thought of preserving an animal that way left him cold. He avoided it, instead circling over to the fireplace to study a photo. In it, Trinity was wearing a dress with a train of peacock feathers. It caught his eye because Dominique had worn exactly the same dress in a fashion show way back when. She'd sent him a photograph of it, with a note that read *Fine feathers make fine birds!*

He caught the scent of burning tobacco and he turned. The woman from the photographs had materialized in the doorway. She posed like a mannequin, with one arm raised above her head, hand resting against the wall. Her head was turned at an angle, but she was watching him out of the corners of her eyes. She wore some kind of dress that brought to mind long strips of black bandages coiled around her. It looked like it was intended to hug curves, but there weren't any to caress and so it sagged. There was a diamond-encrusted bangle on one knobby wrist and more diamonds in her ears.

"Trinity? I'm Desmond Edgars. Thanks for seeing me."

"I didn't want to see you," she answered coolly. "That was my houseboy's idea." She dragged on her cigarette and released plumes of smoke.

Her words left him off balance. It was unnerving, having those baleful, sunken eyes on him. "He seems grateful for what my sister did for you."

"I know." She sounded bored. "It's all he talks about. I wish I'd sent him on to the country house without me. It would have been interesting to see how that turned out."

That was why the woman was so lifeless: there was ice water in her veins instead of blood. "I guess you're not the sentimental type," Desmond said. "Where are the photos of your dearly departed husband? I don't see one."

"There is one in the Schiaparelli Room," Trin answered. "I'm wearing a dress by Alexander McQueen. Gary is on his knees, holding out one of my shoes, as if he were the Prince and I were Cinderella." She blew out smoke dismissively. "I only got married to wear that dress, you know. You'd think you could wear a beautiful white dress with a fifty-foot train if you felt like it, but you just can't. You have to get married."

"You got married to wear a dress?"

"Well, yes. And no. I had to have a wedding to wear the dress. Occasions are important, you know. Only, I would have married the Chrysler Building if I had the choice. It's the most beautiful skyscraper in the world. Art Deco perfection."

"I don't think you can marry a building."

"You *are* bourgeois. What about Erika LaBrie? If she can marry the Eiffel Tower, I can marry the Chrysler Building. No?" She raised her thin, penciled-in brows and cocked her head. "My father didn't like the idea, either. He said he would cut me off without a dime if I went ahead with it. Instead, he found a man for me to marry." She sighed, investing the gesture with great drama, and gave a little cough. "It was quite the disaster."

Desmond had heard so many justifications from Dominique about dating Gary. *He's not really married,* his sister would say.

He'd always written that off as schoolgirl longing on her part. Now, he wondered if she'd been right, in a way.

"You didn't want to be married to Gary, I take it?"

"Of course not. Everything about him was so common. His name. His sport. If he had been an equestrian, I could have respected that. Even an archer might have been interesting. But boxing?" She simulated a shudder. "I was ashamed of him. He didn't belong in my world at all."

Desmond was stunned into silence. Trin stepped into the room to tap the ash from her cigarette into a silver tray. "You're very easy to shock," she smirked. "Didn't my houseboy offer you anything to drink?"

"Your houseboy?"

"Costa!" she shouted, instantly losing that air of mystique she'd tried to craft with her grand entrance.

"Yes, Miss Lytton-Jones?"

"I didn't want a drink, thanks," Desmond said.

"Of course you do. Champagne, with two flutes," she ordered.

Desmond glanced at his watch. It wasn't even noon.

"Don't tell me you're a Puritan," she said. "That would make you so dull." She came closer. He wasn't entirely sure her head was on the right body. The face was heavily made up, with thick black kohl around her eyes that made her look like one of Cleopatra's handmaidens. Under the paint, her skin was puffy. Her body, by contrast, was just skin clinging to the skeleton underneath. He'd seen photographs of concentration camp survivors being liberated after the Second World War, and Trin was emaciated enough to be mistaken for one.

"Are you gay?" she asked.

"Excuse me?"

"Oh, don't be embarrassed about it. I'm not judging you. I think everyone should be free to follow their desires."

"I didn't think I was stylish enough for anyone to make that mistake."

"You don't have to be all defensive about it. I don't like straight men. I don't think they can ever be trusted."

She moved a little closer and he noticed her eyes. The irises weren't human; they were lavender, but the pupil wasn't a circle but a long, narrow slit like a cat's. She was wearing some custom-designed contact lenses to get that effect. Nothing about her was natural.

"So, why did you want to meet me?" she asked.

"I wanted to talk about Gary and my sister."

"Ah, yes, the thoroughbred." Trin nodded. "She was a very fine mannequin. Not the most graceful presence I've seen on the runway, to be honest, but she was statuesque. Queenly, almost. She wore clothes beautifully. I remember seeing her once in this Lacroix gown that was absolute perfection. I had to have it, but it never fit me the way it did her. I was so envious."

Her admission caught Desmond by surprise. "You admit you were jealous of Dominique?"

"Yes. Much to my regret, and in spite of my best efforts, I have never been able to wear clothes the way she did." She inhaled deeply on her cigarette. "Mr. Edgars, I am the bluntest person you will ever meet. I've spent my life surrounded by courtiers who would say anything to curry favor with my family. Brutal honesty is the one true luxury wealth has given me. If you want to be truly outrageous and shock people, always be honest."

"Were you jealous of Dominique's relationship with Gary?"

"Why on earth would I be?" Trin's eyebrows shot to the cavernous ceiling. "*I* certainly didn't want that big lump. I detested everything about him. He was just so . . . low and contemptible. I know this will shock you, with your dull little bourgeois ideas, but I couldn't be happier that he's dead."

39

They were interrupted by the arrival of the houseboy. "Champagne, Miss Lytton-Jones?"

"Finally," she said. She took mincing steps toward a burgundy sofa, lowering herself and arranging her legs. Trinity was maybe five foot four without those stagger-inducing high heels. He could imagine her tumbling on that polished marble floor and cracking a birdlike limb.

"Please sit down," she added. Desmond lowered himself onto the sofa opposite her, feeling himself sink deep into the velvet. It wasn't a pleasant sensation. It felt as if he were being swallowed up in a very soft, delicate trap.

While Costa opened the bottle and poured the champagne, Trin ground out one cigarette and fished a fresh one out of a decorative box on the table next to her. The houseboy lit her cigarette, made a gracious bow, and left.

"So, what are you going to do with Dominique now?" Trin asked, picking up her glass.

"With her?" Desmond was thrown off by the way she'd phrased the question. "There's going to be an autopsy. I don't know how long that will take. I'm organizing a funeral service, but I won't know the date until her body is released."

"A funeral. How traditional." Trin nodded. "Since I heard about Gary, I've been thinking of his funeral. Or, more specifically, about what to wear."

Desmond's expression gave away his opinion, and she smiled in response.

"Like I said, occasions are important," she went on. "And I should say, Gary's will be a memorial service, not a funeral. His body won't be there. Do you know what I'm going to do with it?"

Taxidermy, Desmond suspected. Like that stuffed pup on the table. "What?"

"I'm going to turn Gary into a diamond."

"You're going to . . . what?"

She nodded, suddenly animated. "I have to cremate Gary first, of course. But then I'm sending the ashes to a lab that filters out the carbon until you're just left with graphite. They heat that up in some kind of volcano pressure cooker, and voilà! A diamond."

"You've got to be kidding."

"Well, it's a *synthetic* diamond, of course. But I think it will be rather striking in the right setting." She held out her right hand and wriggled her index finger. "That's my father."

Desmond stared at the square-cut diamond in disbelief. He was speechless.

"It's rather a lovely princess cut, isn't it?" Trin said.

"You turned . . . your own father . . . into a diamond?"

"Don't look so horrified. It's not as if I *killed* him. When he was alive, my father took great pleasure in controlling my life." She pulled her hand back and stared at the ring. "Now, I control his remains. Oh, he had a long list of requirements about his funeral and burial. I had to follow those to the letter. But after that was done . . ." She held the diamond up to the light, wriggling her fingers. "Voilà!"

Desmond stared at her, realizing he was in the presence of madness. There were people on the streets, shoeless in winter, sporting tinfoil hats and screaming at invisible adversaries who were less demented than this expensively groomed heiress.

"You're so resolutely parochial, aren't you?" Trin observed. "You're not much fun." She dragged on her cigarette. "Costa!" she called.

He appeared in moments, panting slightly, as if he'd run at the sound of her voice.

"Fetch the file on my dressing table."

Costa frowned, but rushed back down the hallway.

Trin rubbed her nose. "Where were we?"

"Did you have your brothers turned into diamonds, too?" Desmond asked.

Trin narrowed her feline eyes. "No, I didn't. That hadn't occurred to me then. When Byron died, I was still at finishing school. It was . . ." Her voice trailed off. She seemed almost lost for a moment. "He's buried in London, in the family crypt at Highgate. What my father envisioned as the family crypt, I mean. It hasn't been in the family for long. And it's in East Highgate, not West Highgate." Her eyes met Desmond's. "I can see that distinction means nothing to you. Let's just say that it wasn't precisely the real estate my father wanted, but sometimes there are limits on what money can buy." She stubbed out her cigarette. "Poor Byron is all alone there."

"What about your other brothers?"

"I couldn't care less about those two." Her face was hard again, but it softened slightly. "I suppose it wasn't terribly nice of me to remove their remains, or father's, but I knew Byron wouldn't want to spend eternity with that lot any more than I'd want to."

Costa returned with a leather folder dyed the bright blue of a robin's egg, and handed it to Trin. "Computers are so inelegant," she said, grasping it and flipping through pages. "I much prefer paper stock."

Desmond watched her, vaguely fascinated. "What are you looking for?"

"Aha. Found it." She scanned a couple of pages. "Just refreshing my memory." The tip of her tongue flicked out like a lizard's. "You were divorced almost two years ago, just after you retired from the Army. Interesting timing. Easy split, no children. I suppose your wife wasn't keen to have you at home."

"How—"

"*This* is why you're so parochial. Joining the military, becoming a helicopter pilot, flying combat and reconnaissance missions." She shook her head, as if saddened by the waste of a life. "Even when you became a civilian again, you kept up all those rescue missions, flying sick children and orphaned puppies around. It's as if you're waiting for someone to pin a medal on you. Or maybe you're fueled by guilt."

"You don't know what you're talking about."

"Really? Your family history's a bit of a sob story, isn't it? Your mother murdering Dominique's father, then dying in jail. Awful stuff. Maybe that's where your rescue complex comes from." She lit a fresh cigarette.

"Why the hell would you have a file on me?"

"My father's policy was that we should always be prepared. When Gary started sleeping with your sister, we had your whole family checked out." She blew a long plume of smoke at him. "It was a very short list, which made it easy."

She wasn't just crazy, Desmond realized. There was a wide sadistic streak in her.

"When my houseboy said you were coming over this morning, I decided to dust it off," she added.

He leaned forward. "Funny you talk about family. Your father was married, what, four times? When he divorced a woman, he paid her off so he could keep the kids. Must've really screwed up your head when it came to men."

"It was an excellent cautionary tale, actually." Her eyes were hard as diamonds. "It kept me from developing any stupid fantasies about human motivation. Everyone is completely selfish and only looks out for themselves."

"And yet you married Gary."

"That was my father's decision." She stubbed out her cigarette so hard the end table trembled.

"Your father forced you to get married? You were no child bride. You obviously went along with it."

"It was that or be disinherited." She reached for another cigarette. "Which wasn't exactly a choice, you know."

"I guess after thirty years of playing with daddy's money, the prospect of getting a job must've terrified you."

"The only thing that frightens me is the idea that I might show up at a party and find another woman wearing the same dress. That's going to happen one day with that witch Daphne Guinness, I just know it."

"So you married Gary to keep up your fashion budget? That's the stupidest thing I've ever heard."

She sniffed and rubbed her nose. "It wasn't only about money. I was the only heir left. My father said it was up to me to carry on the family line." She closed her eyes and shuddered. "He didn't understand that I never wanted to marry anyone. Not ever. I might have been able to carry it off if he'd let me marry a gay man. But he had to go and select a blockheaded athlete. He told me that would breed some height and strength into the line."

In spite of her viciousness, Desmond felt pity for Trin. He didn't have much use for the poor-little-rich-girl attitude, but she was a strange, damaged creature, at once hard and harsh and yet vulnerable enough to share her most awful thoughts with a stranger. He'd been abused by his stepfather, a man who beat him mercilessly and forbade him to cry out. Trin's abuse hadn't been physical, but the scars her own father had marked her with were evident.

"That's a terrible thing for a man to do to his daughter." Desmond's voice was quiet.

She studied the diamond on her index finger again. "My father loved horses, you know. He didn't like people at all, but he treated them like horses, in a way. "

"What about you?"

She frowned. "I don't know what you mean."

"Do you treat humans like horses? Do you have someone put down after he's served his purpose?"

"You think I had Gary murdered?" For the first time in their meeting, Desmond had managed to surprise her.

"I'm wondering if you hired a man named Max to do it."

She shook her head emphatically. "No. I was going to get rid of Gary, that's true, but I was going to make sure he had nothing left first. I wanted him to suffer."

"You were going to divorce him? Wouldn't you have to pay him a lot of money to do that?"

"Oh, no, not at all. Zachary—my father's lawyer—drew up the perfect prenuptial agreement. Gary would be left with nothing. The only downside was that I was going to have to get married again."

"Trinity!"

Both Desmond and Trin turned their heads. Costa was standing in the doorway, but he hadn't spoken. Just behind him was a tall, lean man in a dark gray pinstripe suit. His skin was lightly tanned, as if he'd recently sat on a beach in St. Tropez. He was in his late fifties or early sixties, with graying hair cut close to his skull. What Desmond noticed most were his eyes. They were a magnetic blue, steady and sharp. They were the eyes of a man who didn't miss a trick.

"Hello, Zachary," Trin said. "What do you want?"

"I was concerned about you, after that scare you had on the

weekend. Why didn't you call me, or at least tell me what hotel you holed up at?"

"I didn't need anything from you," Trin said. "It's not as if I enjoy having you around."

"Dear Trinity, you are always so amusing." Those calculating blue eyes took in Desmond's face. "I believe my timing is impeccable. My name is Zachary Amberson. I'm counsel to the Lytton-Jones family."

"Desmond Edgars." He got to his feet and extended his hand.

Amberson came forward and shook it. His grasp was cold but firm. "In the future, if you have any desire to contact Miss Lytton-Jones, you may do so through me."

"He wasn't bothering me, Zachary," Trin said. "We were having a most entertaining chat."

"Actually, I've been hoping to talk to you," Desmond said. "I went to your office yesterday, but your secretary wouldn't let me upstairs. I wanted to find out what you were working on with my sister, Dominique Monaghan, and why she went to meet you at your office a couple of times."

"Your sister?" Amberson's mouth had a slight twist to it, as if sweetness had just turned sour.

"You were in touch with that woman? You were talking to her behind my back?" Trinity's fury exploded, as if it were too great to house in her tiny frame.

Amberson didn't lose his calm, assured manner. "I didn't get in touch with her, Trinity."

Trin pointed her cigarette at Desmond. "Are you saying *he's* lying?"

Amberson sighed. "She got in touch with me."

"Why didn't you tell me?" Trinity screeched, her voice losing all pretense of refinement.

"It hardly seemed important."

"You work for *me*. You report to *me*. You don't get to decide what's important and what isn't. You're fired, Zachary!"

Amberson's mouth pulled back slightly in wry amusement. "Trinity, dear, please be reasonable. You know you can't fire me."

"Get out, traitor!"

"You know your father left things in my hands, because he knew you didn't want the responsibility of running a company."

"My father left things in your hands because he was a sexist, chauvinist pig!" Trinity threw a ceramic box at him, but her pitch went wide and it hit the floor and shattered. "Get out!"

"You won't throw so many pieces of bric-a-brac at me if I stop giving you the money to replace them." Zachary's unflappability was remarkable. He sounded like a parent lecturing a naughty child.

"I hate you! Leave me alone!" Trin rushed out of the room. From down the hallway, there was the sound of a door slamming.

"Please go after her. Make sure she doesn't hurt herself," Amberson said to Costa. In a motion so slick Desmond almost missed it, Amberson's hand went from his pocket to Costa's palm.

"Thank you, sir, but I—" Costa was distinctly uncomfortable.

"Talk her down," Amberson said. "Otherwise, she might fling herself out a window."

"Yes, sir." Costa looked over at Desmond. "Will you be okay letting yourself out?"

"No problem."

"Thank you again. For everything," he said to Desmond before vanishing down the hall, following in Trin's shaky footsteps.

Amberson turned to Desmond. The expression on his face could have turned water to ice in a heartbeat. "I'd be more than pleased to speak with you at my office. In fact, I think we should make an appointment to talk. But if you turn up here again, the police will arrest you for trespassing."

"I just heard her fire you. You're not exactly in a position to make threats."

"Trinity has always been a dramatic child." Amberson's tone was carelessly dismissive. "Of course, your sister was like that, too."

"My sister was nothing like that woman."

"Trinity is an original," Amberson allowed. "I don't mean to suggest Dominique was so over the top. But they're both spoiled women, used to getting their own way. I know Trinity has quite the appetite for revenge, and I can tell you your sister did, too."

"What's that supposed to mean?"

"We'll speak later." Amberson gave him a confident smile. "We have a lot to talk about."

40

Desmond took the 6 train back to Forty-second Street, feeling a low-grade rage burning in his chest. It had started bubbling over when Trin had brought up his family. In his mind, his mother was a hero. No one could hold a candle to her, and her selfless devotion to her family made him proud. But he realized that the rest of the world didn't hold her in any kind of esteem. They looked at her as a murderer. That was a burden Dominique had had to carry through her life. Desmond, at least, got to visit their mother in prison. But their grandmother wouldn't allow that for Dominique—she always maintained it would harm the girl, seeing her mother *in such a state,* as she put it—so the last time Dominique saw her mother was when she was four. His sister had been robbed of her childhood, while their mother was robbed of her freedom.

Desmond had always assumed that, one day, he would talk to Dominique about it. He owed her the truth, even though revealing it would break the promise he'd made to their mother. *Swear to me, swear before God, that you will never tell anyone what happened here tonight.* When he closed his eyes, he could hear his mother's voice demanding that vow from him. More than anything in his life, he regretted making it. There had been blood on his mother's hands when she'd said it, blood from the oozing wound in her husband's head. She was kneeling beside the corpse, and her voice cracked, even though her eyes were dry.

Coward, he chided himself. *You are nothing but a coward, hiding behind a promise. You should've died, not Dominique.* He couldn't shake the uneasiness. He could never set things right, and he was starting to see he'd have to live with that sickening realization every day for the rest of his life.

He picked up a sandwich inside Grand Central's subterranean food court and went up to his room at the Hyatt. The maid had been in, so the bed was made and he had fresh towels. There was no view from his little cell, since it looked into an airshaft. He ate his lunch standing up, staring out the window anyway.

His greatest fear, at that moment, was that Westergren would be slapped down by his superiors and the Pennsylvania cops would sign off on Dominique's and Gary's deaths as accidental. It wouldn't surprise him if the police wanted to back off the case. Cops didn't like having an unsolved murder on the books. Accidental death made everybody happy. Everybody except the families of the victims, who saw justice moving out of their grasp like a balloon carried off by the wind.

He left a message for Westergren. Right before he hung up, he added, "Please don't give up on this." He needed to be in motion, and the thought of waiting pained him. The longer things stalled, the greater a chance Max had to get away scot-free. The trail was getting colder by the hour. He'd been assuming that Trinity would be behind the plot, but now he wasn't so sure. The man who murdered Dominique was out there, nameless, faceless, and completely free.

The phone on the desk rang, and Desmond picked it up. "Mr. Edgars? There are a couple of people here to see you. A Detective Iorio and a Detective Reich."

Hairs stood up on the back of Desmond's neck. The cops just showing up at his hotel? That set off alarm bells. Well, if they wanted to arrest him, this was as good a time as any, he figured.

"I'll be right down," he said.

When the elevator doors opened, Iorio and Reich were loitering in the lobby. "Desmond," Iorio said, and she smiled, as if it were entirely normal for them to stop by his hotel. Reich's expression made it clear they weren't there for afternoon tea, in case Desmond hadn't figured that out already.

"It's your lucky day," Reich said.

"How's that?"

"We made a few calls, and we actually found a lady on Roosevelt Island with a chocolate Labrador retriever named Hershey," Iorio said.

"Even better, she remembers you," Reich added.

"The quote from Ms. Forbus is actually pretty funny," Iorio chimed in again. "She said, 'Yeah, I noticed that guy. I figured he was either a creep who was going to kidnap a child, or else he got stood up for a date.'"

Desmond stared at them. He knew he should be grateful anyone remembered him from his fruitless trip to Lighthouse Park. But he wondered how these cops could suddenly be so lighthearted. He didn't trust a word out of their mouths. Before he could say anything to change their minds and get himself arrested after all, his phone rang. It was Westergren. "I need to take this call," he said. "Excuse me."

He walked toward the waterfall in the lobby, glad to put some distance between himself and the cops. He could feel the detectives' eyes on him, just as he had the night before. Nothing had changed, in spite of Iorio's smiling face. They were still looking at him as Tom Klepper's killer.

"You aren't going to believe what I found!" Westergren's voice was hot with excitement.

"Please let this be good news." Desmond glanced at the detectives.

"It is. I found Max."

That hit Desmond like a thunderbolt. "Talk to me. Where?"

"We got a DNA hit from a database," Westergren said. "It's a definite match for a Max Brantov from Long Island. Only . . . here's where it gets bizarre."

"He's already got a criminal record?"

"No, I mean, it's bizarre that we found him in this database."

"What database?"

"The National Center for Missing and Exploited Children," Westergren said.

"He . . . he kidnapped a child?"

"No. Max Brantov *is* a missing child."

41

I'm trying to wrap my mind around this," Desmond said. "Could you repeat that? Because it sounds like you're saying the man who killed my sister and Gary Cowan is an abducted child."

"That's about the size of it," Westergren said. "Max Brantov went missing when he was seventeen. That was seven years ago. He hasn't been found."

Desmond's mouth was dry. "What happened to him?"

"At first, his family thought he was a runaway. The brother said he'd been upset since his parents' divorce. He thought Max had run off to be with his dad. The family lived on Long Island, and the dad had moved to Arizona. But he never showed up at his dad's house, at least not according to the dad. Then the mother found Max's favorite T-shirt in his laundry hamper, and it had blood on it. That was how his DNA got into the system."

"I don't believe this." Desmond's mind was reeling. Out of the corner of his eye he saw a white glimmer, like someone moving, but when he turned his head, no one was there. "What can you tell me about the family?"

"I'm looking into them now." Westergren lowered his voice. "My partner isn't happy. He thought everything was tied up, but now we've got this and he's pissed off."

"I'm with a couple of NYPD detectives right now. Could I hand you over to one of them so you can explain this?" Desmond walked back to the cops. He handed his phone to Iorio. "Pennsylvania trooper. You really need to hear what he has to say."

She took the phone from him and talked to Westergren. From the shell-shocked expression that crept into her face, he knew she was as stunned by the news as he was.

"This is unbelievable," she breathed, her eyes darting to her partner and then to Desmond. He watched her dash off frenzied lines in the notepad she carried with her.

"So, you've got some interesting history," Reich said to Desmond. His voice was casual, almost conversational. Iorio looked up, frowning, and gave a slight shake of her head, as if warning him off, before going back to scribbling notes.

Desmond didn't respond to Reich. Cops hated that. They thought they were the only ones who could stretch silence out like a rubber band. They didn't like it when it snapped back at them.

"You got quite the rap sheet," Reich added. "Robbery, burglary, vagrancy."

"You left out loitering."

Reich's face tightened like a screw. "You think this is a big joke, huh?"

Desmond was suddenly light-headed, and something swam at the edge of his vision. He remembered Dr. Torres's warnings and swallowed hard. "What can I say, detective? I made a lot of mistakes when I was a kid. But I turned my life around after that."

"You've managed not to get arrested for anything since you were fourteen," Reich said slowly. "That's not the same as turning your life around. I've gotta say, your background made for some interesting reading. I know you told us about your mother being a killer, but you left out the really shocking parts."

The urge to punch the officer in the gut was so overwhelming that Desmond had to take his eyes off the man and cast them across the lobby. His own pulse beat inside his ears like a drum. The only thing that kept him calm was his mother's voice echoing from far away. *Let go.* When he turned his eyes back to Reich, he was composed.

"My sister is dead," Desmond said. "Her boyfriend is dead. Tom Klepper is dead. And you're standing here in front of me, proud of yourself for looking up my rap sheet? I'm forty years old. You want to talk about what went down twenty-six years ago?"

"You should've come clean with us at the station."

"You should stop playing the fool and start looking at the man who's connected to all three of these deaths."

"That's what I'm doing," Reich said.

Don't hit him, Desmond warned himself. He didn't care that he might get hauled into jail, but he didn't want to give the police a pretext to drop their investigation. "You're wasting my time and your own."

"That's enough, both of you," Iorio commanded, before returning to her phone call and politely modulating her voice. "Thank you. I can't begin to tell you how helpful this is. I'll touch base with you later today when I'm back at the squad." She handed the phone back to Desmond. Westergren had already hung up.

"You won't believe this, but Mystery Max exists," Iorio said to her partner. "His real name is Maxim Brantov. The family lives on Long Island. Maybe we should have the local PD talk to them this afternoon, see whether Max has been in touch lately."

"So, there really *is* a Max. Amazing." Reich didn't even try to hide his astonishment. He stared at Desmond. "I guess this really is your lucky day."

42

A cloud of dread followed Desmond as he drove out to Long Island that afternoon, even with Edmond Dédé keeping him company. "Mon Pauvre Coeur" couldn't soothe him now. He didn't give a damn that the police wouldn't like him talking to the Brantov family. What troubled him was Marcus Aurelius, and the fact that the words he'd been living by since he was fifteen years old weren't resonating inside him anymore. *If you are pained by any external thing, it is not this thing that disturbs you, but your own judgment about it. And it is in your power to wipe out this judgment now.* The words sounded wise, but it wasn't in Desmond's power to follow them. The more he thought about Max Brantov, the harder it was to breathe. Max Brantov was a runaway who'd turned to a life of crime. He could no more change his judgment about the man than he could bring Dominique back to life again.

He didn't know which way to turn, except to follow the only real lead he had. So he picked up his car at Newark Airport and headed east to a town called Huntington. It wasn't hard to get the address; *Brantov* was an uncommon name. Desmond breathed a little easier as he got away from Manhattan, but the pastoral expanse of land he was hoping for didn't materialize. From the Long Island Expressway, Queens was an assemblage of shopping malls and buildings and houses. If he caught sight of a patch of green, it was undoubtedly a cemetery. He'd never liked cities. Even though he claimed to live in Chicagoland, his small house in Hammond was in a quiet part of town that was a world away from where he'd grown up. He found it difficult and draining, being around people too much. Flying released him from the burden, but only while he was in the air. He was still smarting from what Trinity Lytton-Jones had said about his wife. *You were divorced almost two years ago, just after you retired from the Army. Interesting timing. Easy split, no children. I suppose your wife wasn't keen to have you at home.* He'd gotten married while he was serving in Iraq, to a tawny-eyed nurse with a Georgia accent. Everything had been fine between them when he was on foreign soil and only coming home for short stretches of leave time. That had satisfied him, but he hadn't understood how much more his wife had wanted.

It's like I'm married to a stranger, she told him a month after he retired from the service. *You have your life, and I'm just on the edge of it. You don't talk to me about anything.*

He'd tried to joke. *We're talking now, aren't we?*

No, we're not. I'm trying to talk to you, but you're running around every day finding ways to fill up your time. It's like you don't want to be with me, except in bed. I hoped everything would be different when you came home for good. I prayed it would be different. But you won't let me in. I don't know if it's me, or if you won't let anyone in. All I know is, I can't stand it.

A month later, she'd filed for divorce.

When Desmond arrived in Huntington, he found the Brantov house quickly; it was the only house on Greenlawn Road with a rusted-out mailbox with no number on it. It also had a police car parked in the driveway. He drove by and into the town of Huntington, parking his car on the street and himself in a bookstore called Book Revue. It had a little café near the front and books as far as the eye could see. Normally, that would've been heaven to him, but he was impatient and looking for a way to painlessly kill time.

He gave the cops half an hour. By the time he drove past the residence again, the police car was gone. He pulled into the long, curving gravel drive, noticing for the first time a six-foot-tall metal fence that looked like it covered three sides of the property. Unlike the mailbox, it wasn't rusted out.

Getting out of the car, Desmond stared at the wildly overgrown front yard, choked with weeds even in November, and at the house behind it. It was set far back from the road, at least forty feet. The house was a two-story box, very plain in design. Its straight lines and sharp angles were dissolving through obvious neglect. A lintel rested on two posts, one on either side of the front door, but its left side sloped down; under the dark eyes of the second-story windows, it made the front of the house resemble a skull with a crooked smile. The wooden paneling was sorely weathered, with grayish white paint clinging for dear life in small clumps. The last time the house was cleaned up, the roof probably still had all its tiles.

That was what grief did, Desmond thought. It drained you until you sank in on yourself, collapsing under an invisible weight. He felt as if he suddenly understood the Brantovs. On the train out to pick up his car, he'd read up on the family, and the articles made it sound like the father and mother had split just months before Maxim vanished. The boy had been bound for his father's and he never made it. The family would have waited for him to return, and the vigil was probably still going on somewhere inside that sad excuse for a house. Hoping against hope took up so much energy, there was nothing left over to spare for anything else.

He stood there for a while, thinking he might catch sight of someone passing by a window. Finally, he approached the house and rang the bell. He heard it echo, and then, much to his surprise, the door swung open.

"Yes?" Standing in front of him was a white-haired woman wearing a furry green robe. She was five foot eight, even with her slumped shoulders. The harsh frown lines in her ivory skin were as deeply etched as cut crystal, but if this was the missing boy's mother, Desmond knew from what he'd read that she was only in her midfifties. There was a cloud of alcohol fumes around her, almost like a vapor of fine perfume.

"I'm sorry to bother you, ma'am. Are you Galina Brantov?"

She nodded.

"I'm here because of your son Max."

The woman breathed in sharply. "You have found Maxim?" She had a Slavic accent, and she spoke with the painstaking dignity of a person who is drunk, yet aware of just how intoxicated she is.

"Not exactly. There's DNA evidence that Max was at a house in Pennsylvania this weekend."

"That is what the police said. They were just here. They said they had evidence, this DNA. They said they would come back when they found him." She swayed slightly and her head drooped lower. "You haven't found him?"

"No, not yet. Would you mind if I came in?"

"No more visitors." Her voice was stern. Then, almost as an afterthought, she added, "Are you police?"

"No, but I'm working with the police."

"The police are no good. They do nothing." Her chin wobbled. "I am so tired of questions, and then nothing. Always nothing."

"Could I come in?" he asked again.

"The police were *just here*." She said it as if he were slow on the uptake.

Desmond cleared his throat. "When did you last hear from Max?"

Galina Brantov stared down at the tangled yard, as if the truth were buried under the weeds. "He never forgets my birthday." Her voice was tender, almost shy. "He is a good boy."

"He comes over on your birthday?" Desmond asked.

She shook her head.

"Does he call you?"

She played with a gold bracelet around her wrist.

"Did Max buy you that bracelet?" Desmond asked.

She looked at him, eyes wide in wonder, as if he were brilliant for figuring that out. "Yes," she answered. A moment later, there was the sound of glass breaking inside. Mrs. Brantov turned. "You clumsy girl! What did you do now?"

There was no answer.

"I must go," Galina Brantov said. "Come back when you have found my Maxim. Tell him I love him, no matter what. It doesn't matter what he's done." Her voice choked on the last word, but she'd already closed the door in Desmond's face.

He stood there for a moment, listening. There were voices, both female, but he couldn't make out their words. Ashamed to be eavesdropping on the stoop, he backed away. When he got to his car, he noticed a curtain move. Someone was watching him from inside the house. He scanned the other windows but saw no movement. Was it possible that Max was in his mother's house? *Tell him I love him, no matter what. It doesn't matter what he's done,* his mother had said. If Max was a murderer, she'd still stand by him.

He backed out of the driveway, but parked his car in the gravel next to the street in front of the evergreens. He wasn't done yet. He walked to the neighboring house, where no one was home. Then he tried the house on the other side of the Brantovs'. A red-haired woman in her late sixties answered the door. She was wearing a woolly cardigan and fleecy track pants.

"I'm sorry to bother you," Desmond said. "My name is Desmond Edgars. I was wondering if you know the Brantov family."

"Yes, of course. We've lived here for thirty-two years. Are you a detective?"

"No, ma'am. I'm here because . . . well, it's a long story. The heart of it is that my sister, Dominique Monaghan, was murdered last weekend."

"The model?" The woman's eyes opened wide. "I heard about that. At a house in the Poconos."

"What you haven't seen in the news yet is that they found Max Brantov's blood at that same house," Desmond said. "They matched it up with DNA they had in a database of missing children."

The woman put her hand to her mouth. "They found poor Max!"

"No, ma'am. Not a body, just some blood, but it showed he'd been there."

"Poor Max." The woman shook her head. "Please come in. Harold! Turn the TV off. You have to hear this."

A man padded out of the front room. He was bald and wore furry slippers with monster toes.

"Harold, this is, ah . . ."

"Desmond Edgars." He reached out his hand to shake. The man's hand was papery yet firm.

"He's Dominique Monaghan's brother."

"Who?"

"The model they found on the weekend." The woman was exasperated. "You never know anything that's going on. All you do is watch stupid movies. You should be watching the news." She looked at Desmond. "I watch the news all the time. I like to keep my brain sharp."

Desmond smiled at her, then turned to her husband. "I was telling your wife that they found DNA evidence that Max Brantov was in that same house in the Poconos. I drove here to talk to the family, to figure out if there's some connection between Max's disappearance and what happened to Dominique, but Mrs. Brantov had been drinking."

"Galina is always drinking. She's a kindhearted woman, but she's been a wreck since Max disappeared."

"Does she live alone?"

"No, her daughter lives with her. Polina, that's the girl's name. She's very sweet, but so shy she can barely string three words together. She walks around like she's in a trance. Poor thing." She lowered her voice. "Sometimes I think she might be on drugs."

"After Max vanished, the family got really paranoid," her husband added. "I can't really blame them, I guess. They put that big fence up around their property. As if that were going to change anything. It's like closing the door of the barn after the horses escape."

Desmond frowned. "Just the girl and her mother live here?"

"The older boy, Valery, is there sometimes, but you never know when you'll see him."

The woman gave a little cough. "He's a bit of a character, that one. Even when Valery was a boy, he was very aloof. He never speaks to anyone. They're an antisocial bunch."

"I used to wonder why they came to America, since they didn't want to socialize with anyone," Harold piped up.

"Except Max. He was always such a nice boy."

"Yeah, Max was a great kid," Harold said. "Our son was a year behind Max in school, but they used to play together all the time."

His wife nodded at the decrepit yard and dilapidated house. "You wouldn't know it now, but the house and the yard used to be beautiful. Now it's just an ugly, overgrown mess. Not that we can see much, with that ugly fence they put up."

"When Max disappeared, did you have any idea what happened? The police report said he ran away."

She shook her head firmly. "Max would never have run away. He was a good kid, always thoughtful. But there was trouble in the house, no doubt about that. The family had a lot of problems. The parents drank and fought. I never understood what they were screaming at each other, but they threw things. Pots, pans, phones, you name it.

Valery, the older brother, got kicked out of high school. Everyone says he was dealing drugs. It was not a happy home. But Max was different. He was always such a sunny, upbeat kid. He did well in school, he had tons of friends, he was a great athlete. You could tell he was going to be handsome when he grew up, but he also had so much charisma."

"He was super-smart, too," Harold said. "He was going to an Ivy League school in the fall. There's no way that kid ran away."

"Then what do you think happened?"

"Foul play." Harold's voice was firm. "It had to be."

"You haven't seen Max since he disappeared?"

They both shook their heads.

"His mother said Max never forgets her birthday," Desmond said.

"Poor Galina. I don't think she can tell what's real and what isn't anymore." The woman shook her head. "She's so certain Max will come back one day. I think that's all that keeps her alive."

43

After Desmond drove back into the city, he parked his car in Hyatt's outrageously-priced-for-anywhere-but-Manhattan lot. *What a rip-off,* he thought, wondering for the umpteenth time how his sister had come to love such a ridiculous place. He had dinner alone at Michael Jordan's The Steak House, which was also tucked inside Grand Central. He'd been subsisting on bagels and sandwiches for days, so having a boneless rib eye was a luxury. Afterward, he walked down Park Avenue to Dominique's apartment. On the way down, his cell phone rang.

"Is this Desmond? Zachary Amberson. We met this morning."

"Yes, I remember." Desmond's tone was noncommittal, but he was curious. He'd been expecting this call.

"I'd like to apologize for that scene earlier today," Zachary said. "I know it was unpleasant."

"Not for me."

There was an uncomfortable silence on the other end. Then: "I'm glad you see it that way."

"Is Trinity still upset about you working with Dominique against Gary?" Desmond asked.

"She's a very high-strung girl. The least little thing sends her flying off the handle." Amberson's voice was conspiratorial. "Typical female. Overly emotional about absolutely everything."

Desmond wondered what angle the lawyer was playing, and it dawned on him that whatever dossier Trinity Lytton-Jones had on him, her lawyer knew about it as well. The smarmy creep was aware of Desmond's divorce and figured him for bitter.

"You can say that again. It was funny, her running to her room and slamming the door as if she were a little girl." Desmond's thoughts didn't match his words. He'd wondered how Amberson had convinced Dominique to help him against Gary. According to Sabrina, his sister never would have agreed to it but for those photos—sent by an anonymous tipster—of Gary and his cheerleader girlfriend. What if those illicit shots had come from Amberson himself? He had motive, after all.

Amberson chuckled, as if they understood each other. "I think it would be an excellent idea for us to discuss matters in person."

"Matters?" Desmond played innocent.

Amberson didn't take the bait. "Would you mind coming to my office? I believe you said you know the address. I'm very much looking forward to speaking in person, man to man."

There he goes again with his line of sexist crap, Desmond thought. Did Amberson assume every divorced man who'd served in the military ate that up? But he pretended to, and they made an appointment for the next day.

He was in a bad mood when he hung up, and he looked behind him, feeling eyes on him again. It was the same sensation he'd had around the cops, and it left him wondering if they'd put a tail on him. How could he tell? There were too many people on the street. But the untrustworthy cops were only part of what fueled his anger. It wrenched his guts around to accept that Dominique had effectively been plotting with Trinity Lytton-Jones and her lawyer. How much had his sister hated Gary to plan what she did? His imagination didn't stretch far enough to picture her drugging her ex with a muscle relaxant. Still, she'd plotted with Sabrina to do exactly that. If he pushed himself, he had to admit that his sister's temper could fire up like a solar flare. It wasn't impossible to see how, hating Gary for how he'd mistreated her, she'd cooked up something bad. But working for Trinity, even through the proxy of her seedy lawyer? He started to wonder how well he knew Dominique at all.

Desmond was well aware that, in the aftermath of a crime, relatives always said they never saw it coming. He and Dominique hadn't been in touch as much as they should have been. She never wanted to come back to Chicago and he had no fondness for New York, so they only saw each other a couple of times a year. They talked on the phone every week or two, and they sent email every few days. Surely, that was enough contact for him to figure out something had changed his baby sister. But he hadn't had a clue about the drama that was actually unfolding.

That brought to mind Max Brantov, missing boy turned kidnapper and killer. Thinking of the boy's mother made his heart hurt. To Desmond, there was nothing more awful than losing a child. That idea pinged around his brain, connecting the dots back to his mother. When she'd gone to jail, she effectively lost her daughter. All she saw of Desmond was his weekly visits. When he thought of how his mother must have suffered, even before the ovarian cancer grew inside her, it broke his heart. His mother had sacrificed her life to protect his, and there was no way he could ever repay that.

At Dominique's apartment, he felt like a trespasser. He went into her bedroom, straightening things up. Had the cops who'd come over dusted for prints or anything else? It didn't look like it. He opened her closet. When Dominique had been modeling, she'd loved those Italian designers whose names sounded like money when they came out of your mouth. Gucci and Pucci and Prada, hanging together like spoiled little princesses. Her shoes stood like little soldiers at the bottom of the closet.

All of this will need to be bagged up for charity at some point, he thought. That realization gutted him. He reeled against the wall, gasping for air, before dropping onto the bed with his head in his hands. He choked on the scent of roses lingering in the air.

When he got to his feet, his eyes landed on a photograph of the two of them, and he picked it up. It was taken the summer after Dominique graduated from high school, maybe two weeks after Desmond had brought her to New York. There was no stopping that girl when her mind was set on something. They both looked happy, Desmond's expression tentatively so and Dominique grinning like she had a big secret she wasn't telling. He'd taken a leave of absence when their grandmother had died, since Dominique wouldn't turn eighteen until October, and he was the only family she had. In the photo, he was wearing his dress uniform, and he could still remember his baby sister demanding that he put it on. *You look so handsome dressed like that,* she told him. *Daddy would be so proud to see you.*

No, he wouldn't, Desmond had told her, trying to keep his voice steady. *I couldn't do anything right in Mr. Monaghan's eyes.*

Daddy was a Vietnam vet, she pointed out. *He'd have been thrilled you followed in his footsteps.*

Desmond had been about to say something—something he'd thought he would regret—when Dominique put her hand over her mouth.

Oh, Des, I'm so sorry. I forgot your daddy was in the Army, too. He'd be so proud of you. He is so proud of you.

There was a little white blip at the corner of his vision, and he set the picture down. *You need sleep,* he told himself. *You're no good to anybody if you're dragging yourself around half-dead.* He checked his watch and realized it was after one in the morning. He turned off the lights in the apartment and locked the door behind him.

When he got down to Twenty-ninth Street, he turned right to head to Park Avenue South. He was so worn out he was ready to get into a taxi. It was a cold night with a harsh wind blowing. He noticed a white woman with long blond hair walking toward him, with her long black coat flapping open, in spite of the chill. Her phone was in hand, as if she were texting. He stepped to one side to let her pass but she bumped into him anyway.

"Oh, I'm sorry," she said, smiling at him.

"No problem," he answered, smiling back.

A split second later, a cord looped around Desmond's neck from behind. It was pulled tight so suddenly that nothing but a wet gurgle came out of his mouth. There was blood beating in his ears. His whole body was on fire. There was no way he could last. Desmond used every bit of strength he had to throw himself backward, knocking his attacker off balance. Desmond dropped to the ground like a dead weight. The attacker stumbled back, and the cord around Desmond's neck went slack. He hit the ground, and saw the man looming over him. He was six three and broad-shouldered, Desmond's size, dressed in black from the balaclava on his head to the boots on his feet.

The man came forward, cord stretched between his fists, when a chorus of women started screaming. The man turned and ran toward Lexington, disappearing around the corner.

44

He didn't have to wait long for the cops. It didn't even take five minutes for uniforms to get on the scene and start taking reports. The group of miniskirted, stiletto-heeled ladies who'd scared off Desmond's attacker were still riled up.

"We's just walking by and we see this freak, and he's strangling a guy," said a redhead with a particularly loud voice and strong Queens accent.

"He wasn't just mugging the guy. It was like he wanted to kill him," said another.

"It was sick. This is the kind of shit my mom worries about," added a third.

Desmond sat on the sidewalk, taking it all in and trying to catch his breath. A young Asian cop sat with him. He'd tried asking questions, but Desmond couldn't speak. When an ambulance pulled up, he patted Desmond on the back.

"Here's your ride," he said.

Desmond shook his head.

The cop seemed amused. "We can take your statement later, when you can speak, that's no problem," he said. "But somebody strangled you, and we've got to check you out."

Since Desmond couldn't really argue—at least not aloud—he gave in. At least he managed to get up and walk to the ambulance on his own. He gave the scantily clad ladies a grateful wave, since he couldn't get "thank you" out of his mouth, not audibly, anyway.

"Take care!" one of the ladies called back.

"Feel better!"

"Hope they catch that bastard!"

One of the women was a blonde in a black coat, but she didn't look like the one who'd bumped into him on the street. This woman was much curvier, and her hair was obviously dyed. What had happened to that slender blonde? he wondered. Did she run off out of fear, or was she supposed to be a distraction so he wouldn't notice the thug creeping up behind me with the rope?

The hospital was only a couple of minutes' drive away, a massive complex at First Avenue. A doctor and a couple of interns poked and prodded him before running a batch of tests. "No laryngeal fracture or upper airway edema," the doctor pronounced. "But I'm concerned about vocal cord immobility."

"I'm okay," Desmond tried to say. It was like a hiss of air escaping a tire.

"You're not very convincing," the doctor informed him. "I'm keeping you in for overnight observation."

As much as Desmond hated the idea, the combination of pain and exhaustion wrestled the last ounce of resistance from him. He gave the doctor an elaborate shrug.

"So eloquent," the doctor said.

They set him up in a room for the night, taking his blood pressure yet again before turning off the lights. He lay in the dark, praying for rest and not finding it. Instead, he remembered the last time he'd been strangled into voicelessness. His attacker that time had been Mr. Monaghan, experimenting with new and awful ways to use his leather belt.

You no-good, lowlife, piece of shit. You are not part of this family, his stepfather ranted. *You want to run with a gang? They can be your family. Get out.*

They were in the basement. Desmond's mom was upstairs, putting Dominique to bed. She was an unruly child, and that was a long process.

Mr. Monaghan threw a punch at his face, and Desmond hit the floor hard. At fourteen, he'd been small for his age. His stepfather had seemed as big as an ancient tree in the forest.

You have yourself a choice, Mr. Monaghan said. *You can get out while you can, or I'll kill you. My right hand to God, I will do it. You will not bring shame on this family.*

Desmond started to get up, but his stepfather kicked him in the stomach and he went flat on the concrete floor again. There was bile in his throat, and he choked it back. He'd thrown up before when his stepfather beat him, and that only enraged the man further.

Now you stay down. I'm gonna learn you something you'll never forget.

Desmond heard Mr. Monaghan's belt slithering off. He pulled himself into a tight little ball, bracing for the blows to rain down, but they didn't.

Stand up like a man, Mr. Monaghan ordered.

There was something under his words that scared Desmond, but he couldn't refuse. While he was getting to his feet, his stepfather looped the belt around his neck and pulled tight.

I don't know why trash like you is walking around, but I won't have it in my house. You get out tonight or you'll be dead by morning.

Please, Desmond begged with his last audible breath.

Don't you worry about your mama. I'll explain it all to her. Mr. Monaghan pulled tighter. *I already figured out how I'll kill you, and how to make it look like your gangbanger homies did it. Or maybe I'll just finish you here and now. What d'you think? Rid the world once and for all of a filthy piece of shit who never should've been born.*

He jerked the belt up, and Desmond thought he was going to

die. He couldn't see anything but fuzzy white dots in front of his eyes. His heart was pounding out of his chest, trying to break from the rest of his expiring body.

Then his stepfather flung him on the ground. The belt slithered off his neck.

Get upstairs and pack up, Mr. Monaghan said. *I won't warn you twice.*

He kicked Desmond again in the kidney with his steel-toed shoe. Desmond didn't look up, but he knew his stepfather was feeding the belt through its loops again. Then the man went upstairs and turned out the light, leaving Desmond crying silently in the dark.

By the time Desmond was able to get up, he knew what he had to do. It took some time to crawl on all fours up the stairs. He heard his mother's voice in the living room, and he was grateful she couldn't see the basement door from there. He pulled himself upstairs, one foot stumbling after the other. There was no doubt in his mind that Mr. Monaghan meant what he said. He was going to kill him.

Desmond moved down the hallway past his own room, then past Dominique's, before getting to the larger bedroom his mom shared with Mr. Monaghan. He went into the night table that sat next to the pillow where his stepfather rested his head every night, and he retrieved the pistol from the drawer. Still moving slowly, he made his way to the living room.

It's for the best, Mr. Monaghan was saying. *We'll all be better off.*

Have you lost your mind, Eli? He's still just a baby. This is his home, he's not going anywhere. His mother's voice turned plaintive. *Why do you hate him so much? He's just a boy.*

That boy just told me he was going to kill me in my sleep. I will not have him in my house a day longer.

I want you to be honest with me: did you beat him? Because I see marks on him, and he won't tell me how they got there.

He runs with a gang, Mr. Monaghan said. *He's always in trouble. Somebody must've beat him up. And you know what? I bet he deserved it.*

You didn't answer my question, Eli. Did you hit him?

I never laid a hand on him.

Then Desmond got to the doorway. Mr. Monaghan saw him first, and his face narrowed in fury. *You're a liar,* Desmond wanted to say. *You've beaten me since we moved into your house five years ago. You're the devil.* But he couldn't get a coherent word out. There was a burbling sound when he tried to speak.

You want to tell me how innocent your little boy is now, Ruth? Look at him now.

His mother turned. *Desmond, what are you doing? Put that down. Now.*

He blinked back more tears and lowered his arm.

What happened to your face? his mother asked.

Desmond shook his head.

We finished supper an hour ago, his mother said. *Someone hit you in the face since then.*

Desmond gave his head another stubborn shake.

I'm not blind, Des. I can see what's going on. I only wish I'd believed my eyes before. She turned to face her husband. Desmond couldn't see her expression, but her voice was stony. *You've been beating on my son.*

All I've ever done is give him the discipline he so sorely needs.

Don't you dare. His mother raised her hand, as if she were going to slap her husband, but Mr. Monaghan grabbed her wrist and shoved her back.

You should be thanking me, you ungrateful bitch. You should be—

Desmond stepped forward, lifted the gun, and fired right into his stepfather's face. Mr. Monaghan didn't even have time to scream. He dropped to the floor with an almighty thud.

There was a horrible stillness in the room after that. Desmond couldn't move. His mind was still trying to process what he'd done. He watched his mother go to Mr. Monaghan and touch his face.

Give that to me, his mother said, taking the gun from his hand.

I'm sorry. I'm so sorry, he tried to say, but his words were garbled. His mother understood them anyway.

No, baby, I'm the one who's sorry. I didn't want to believe he'd be capable of . . . of . . . what he did. I didn't want to believe my own senses. I failed you. There were tears standing in her eyes. *But I will not fail you now.*

Desmond could barely see her face through his tears.

I want you to get out of here. I don't want you in the house when the police come. You've been in too much trouble. They'll lock you up and they'll try you like an adult.

No, he cried.

Listen to me. She touched his face. *A black boy barely gets a start in this world. One false move and your life is over. People like us don't get a second chance.*

He wanted to ask her what she was going to do, but he could only half-wheeze words at her.

Swear to me, swear before God, that you will never tell anyone what happened here tonight, his mother said.

I swear, he whispered.

I love you. She kissed his forehead. *Now get going,* she ordered. *Not a word to anyone, ever. This is your only chance.*

Those were the last words she said to him as a free woman. The next time he saw her, she was already in a prison jumpsuit.

It was a nightmare Desmond could never wake up from. He had murdered his stepfather, and his mother had taken the blame for it. Sometimes he had dreams about that night, and he would wake up screaming. His ex-wife had mistaken it for post-traumatic stress disorder. She couldn't have imagined that it wasn't what he'd seen on the battlefield that haunted him. He'd never been able to speak about it to anyone; whenever he felt as if he were getting too close to another person, he pulled away, certain he'd betray himself sooner or later if he didn't. Deep inside, he wanted to confess. He longed to say, *I shot a man dead,* and take the punishment he knew he deserved. But that would render his mother's sacrifice a waste, and he could never let her down. The only way he could keep his secret safe was to be completely, utterly alone.

45

orio and Reich weren't impressed with him when they saw him in the hospital early Wednesday morning. "Can't stay out of trouble, can you, man?" Reich asked when he came in. The big cop was a little friendlier now than he'd been a couple of days ago, when Desmond first encountered him. Or maybe he was just amused by the idea of someone strangling Desmond on the street.

"It wasn't a random mugging." Desmond heard a whispery, scratchy quality in his own voice. It was as if his body remembered what it felt like to be strangled, and the fear he'd felt had curled up into a ball and lodged itself firmly in his throat. Still, he was grateful to have his vocal cords cooperating at all.

"You sure are a magnet for trouble," Reich said.

Reich's words echoed something Desmond's mother used to say to him. *You catch trouble like a magnet. Trouble's just attracted to you for whatever reason. You're going to have to work twice as hard as anyone ever should just to keep it at bay.*

At least Iorio had the decency to look sympathetic. "How are you feeling?"

"Peachy."

"What can you tell us about the guy who attacked you?"

"He was a solid six three and built. Other than that, I didn't get much of a look. He attacked me from behind." He took a sip of water through a straw. It felt as if it were going the wrong way down his throat. "There was a woman there, too. About five ten and very slim, blonde, and heavily made up. She was like a decoy. She bumped into me before he attacked." He looked from one to the other. "I think the guy was Max."

"Why would Max want to attack you?" Iorio asked. "It doesn't track."

"I'm the only reason you know about Max. If Dominique hadn't told me about him . . ." His throat clogged up, and he took a couple of deep breaths. "Her death, and Gary's, would've been written off as an accident."

"But you've been talking about Max since we met you," Iorio pointed out. "Before that, you were telling the police in Pennsylvania about him. So, why would Max want to get rid of you now? You've already done the damage of letting the police know about him."

"That cat's out of the bag," Reich added. "Attacking you now would only draw attention to him."

"I've been trying to figure that out." Desmond didn't want to share what was really going through his head. Was the attack retribution for showing up at Max's family home on Long Island? He had the sense Max hadn't taken that visit kindly. He knew about it, and he wanted to make sure Desmond couldn't stir up more trouble for him and his family.

"Anyway, how would Max know to find you at your sister's apartment building?"

"I had the feeling someone was following me last night, when I walked down Park from my hotel." Desmond knew he'd been stirring up hornets' nests, running around New York and asking questions no one wanted to answer. Trinity Lytton-Jones was a psycho. Maybe *she* sent the thug over.

"But why attack you?"

"Maybe Max figured Tom Klepper told me something that could be used against him."

"Not impossible," Iorio said. "But if this Max has any brains—and we think he does, because setting up a couple of people to die and then erasing your own involvement takes some smarts—he'd get out of town while no one knows who or where he is. Hanging around to take you out only puts him at risk. What if he'd been caught? That's a giant risk to take."

"Here's what's been bothering me," Reich added. "Someone strangled Tom Klepper. That's thug territory, right? But if—and I mean *if*—your sister and her boyfriend were killed on purpose, it was a kind of scarily smart plan. Not thuglike, I mean. Do you know how many people are harmed by accidental carbon monoxide poisoning in this country every year? Last year it was over twenty thousand. More than five hundred of them died. So picking it as a way of getting rid of people is kind of diabolically genius. It makes it seem like we've got two different perps here."

"I get what you're saying," Desmond said. "But whoever planned the deaths in Pennsylvania had the luxury of time to plan. I'm a new problem they didn't expect to deal with. That might have something to do with their methods." He looked from one to the other. "What about the Brantov family? You go to see them yesterday?" He feigned ignorance.

"The local PD did. They said it was a depressing scene," Iorio answered. "They talked to Max's mother and sister. The house is like a shrine to Max. They have framed photos of him everywhere."

"Plus every trophy and medal he ever won, plus his acceptance letter to Harvard," Reich said. "That's framed and up on the wall next to a Russian icon."

"They said his mother, Galina, smelled like vodka," Iorio said. "I told them vodka isn't supposed to have a scent, but apparently if you're pickled in it, you can't hide it. Galina sang Max's praises, how he was always such a good boy."

"Which is rich when you look at his record and see he was picked up at sixteen for drug possession," Reich said.

"Drug possession?" Desmond hadn't expected that. The neighbors had spoken highly of Max; it was interesting that the boy had been arrested.

"Yeah, nice family," Iorio said. "They said the sister seems to worship Max."

"How old is the sister?" Desmond asked.

"Seventeen. Her name's Polina. She was ten when Max went missing."

"Any other relatives?"

"There's a brother, Valery. He's two years older than Max. Still lives at home, but he was at work when they stopped by."

"It would be interesting to get his take," Desmond said. "The older brother would probably know what Max was really into."

A look passed between Iorio and her partner, and Desmond could feel them communicating silently, disdaining his thoughts.

"You're obsessed with this Max character," Iorio said. "The thing is, the nail they found in that house could've been there for ages. We get that it's creepy as hell, having a missing child involved in this mess. But you're getting obsessed about a kid who might've died several years ago."

"Dominique told me about Max. She met him. She talked to him. He's not some figment of my imagination." Desmond looked from one to the other, realizing it was hopeless.

"We're canvassing your sister's neighborhood to see if we can find this guy who attacked you," Reich said. "We'll be in touch if we find something."

"*When* we find something," Iorio corrected her partner.

Desmond wasn't fooled for a second. Reich had been speaking the truth. It was definitely *if.*

46

It took some convincing of the doctors, but Desmond got out of the hospital after choking down a particularly bland grilled cheese sandwich and a rice pudding. It hadn't been easy, but it was the only way they'd let him go. When he got to Zachary Amberson's office building, the guard he'd met on Monday gave him an encouraging nod of acknowledgment. "Hey, the Iron Eagle's back! You got an appointment today?"

"Believe it or not, I do."

"No way, man." The guard called upstairs. "Uh-huh. Sure. I'll send him up." He smiled at Desmond. "Your lucky day, I guess."

The elevator opened to a wood-paneled atrium. An attractive Asian woman in a winter-white suit greeted him. "Mr. Edgars? Please come this way."

She opened a heavy wooden door and led him through a long, broad corridor. There were oil paintings on the walls, and fine Chinese porcelain on spindle-legged antique tables. Finally she stopped, knocked at a door, and opened it for him.

"Excuse me, Marina. Mr. Edgars is here to see Mr. Amberson," she said, speaking to a woman in her early sixties. Her skin was white as porcelain, and her hair was dyed a dark auburn. She was wearing a black suit with a gold pin on the lapel and a double row of pearls. The look she threw at Desmond made it clear she expected him to make a grab for her necklace.

"We'll see," she said. With her accent, it sounded like *Veel see*.

She got up from her desk and walked to another wooden door, this one with a gilt nameplate that read ZACHARY K. AMBERSON.

"Yes, Marina? Ah, Mr. Edgars is here? Excellent. Please bring him in."

Amberson was standing behind his desk when Marina led Desmond in. The room was expensively decked out, but what caught Desmond's eye were the framed degrees. B.A. Princeton, J.D. Harvard, MBA Harvard. Interesting little triad. "Thank you for taking the time to meet with me," the lawyer said, proffering his hand. "Would you like something to drink?"

"No, thanks."

Marina muttered something and shut the door.

"Please, sit down," Amberson said. "First, I owe you an apology for the other day. I was aware that Gary was dead, but I didn't know about your sister. My deepest condolences to your family." His blue eyes were working hard to look earnest. Desmond didn't believe him for a minute.

"Thank you."

"I suppose this is quite a shock for everyone." Amberson steepled his fingers. "Yesterday, I made a foolish assumption. I thought you were at Miss Lytton-Jones's apartment on behalf of your sister. I suspected that, with Gary Cowan's death, your sister was looking for some sort of financial settlement. . . ."

"If you're wondering if I know about your arrangement with my sister," Desmond said, "that would be a yes."

Amberson's eyebrows went up. "I see. I see. Well, that's not really a surprise. I'm glad you know. It means I can be completely frank with you. Did she tell you how much I was going to pay her?"

Desmond found it interesting that Amberson was so eager to talk about his arrangement with Dominique. That felt all wrong. This lawyer didn't do upfront and honest; if he was revealing something significant, it had to be because he had other dirt to hide. "Why don't you tell me about Tom Klepper?"

Amberson's tongue flicked at the corner of his mouth. "Gary's lawyer? What can I tell you about him?"

"For starters, how come you took him to lunch so often at the Harvard Club?"

Amberson leaned back. If Desmond didn't know better, he'd guess the man was nonplussed. His guess had hit its mark. "Tom always wished he'd graduated from Harvard. He was in the law school for two and a half years. It's a terrible thing to be kicked out on the cusp of graduation."

"What happened?"

"Tom has always been a little too clever for his own good. I don't know that he ever cheated on an exam, but he helped other people cheat, and that was the end of his Harvard career. I don't think he ever got over that. So near and yet so far."

"I heard somewhere he had Gary Cowan throw a fight."

"You only heard about one? You're not as well-informed as you think."

"Seems funny, you and Tom Klepper being such pals. I mean, Gary and Trin hated each other. Kind of strange to think of their lawyers being all cozy."

Amberson made an elegant shrug. "It's a professional relationship. There's no room for hatred. Just because we have crazy clients, that hardly means we have to behave as badly as they do." The lawyer leaned forward again. "Which brings me back to my original point. I feel that I should honor the obligation I have to your sister. The reason Dominique was away with Gary Cowan in the first place was to get that recording she and I discussed. There is a part of me that feels—" Here, Amberson's mouth turned down in a reasonable facsimile of a sorrowful frown. He was a good actor; Desmond gave him that. "—somewhat *responsible* for what happened to her. I believe I owe *you* the money I was going to pay your sister."

"You don't owe me anything. I don't want your money." Something prickled at the back of his neck. Was Amberson trying to bribe him?

"It's not *my* money, of course. It belongs to the Lytton-Jones family, if that makes you feel any better."

Desmond resisted the urge to laugh. "Did Trinity tell you to buy me off?"

"Trinity is a child. A thirty-five-year-old willful child who refuses to grow up." Amberson sighed. "She's always been horribly spoiled by her father. He'd think nothing of buying her dresses that cost fifty thousand or sixty thousand dollars apiece. She doesn't live in the same world as anyone else. She truly believes she should be able to say 'Off with their heads' and heads will roll."

Even though the lawyer's tone was light, his words pummeled Desmond like fists. Trinity had been so upfront about wanting Gary dead, and he'd died. The widow claimed she wasn't jealous of Dominique—except for how well she wore clothes—but then she'd become hysterical when she'd found out her lawyer was dealing with Dominique. It seemed like whoever Trin disliked died. "You're basically telling me she'd kill people, given half a chance."

Amberson chuckled gently, as if Desmond were simply too amusing to be believed. "No, no, of course not. It's one thing to *say* it, quite another to do it. She is spoiled, there's no doubt about that, but to suggest she would ever harm anyone . . . well, that's absurd."

"What about Byron, Shelley, and Keats? I don't mean the poets. I'm talking about her brothers."

There was an odd light behind Amberson's eyes now. He stared at Desmond without blinking. "Their deaths were tragedies. Certainly, you're not suggesting that Trinity had anything to do with them."

"That's exactly what I think."

"Tread lightly, Mr. Edgars." Amberson leaned forward. "It would be terribly unfortunate if your understandable remorse over your sister's death were to cause you to make irrational claims against Miss Lytton-Jones. It's been my job, for more than thirty years, to protect the family. I take that responsibility with the utmost seriousness."

"You think you can cover up murder?" Desmond leaned forward to meet his gaze. "The rich can buy justice, any fool knows that, but there's only so far money will reach. Trinity's got blood on her hands. Her three brothers, her husband, my sister. That's five bodies she has to answer for."

Amberson's pale eyes pierced into him. There was no nervous tension in the lawyer, just smug condescension emanating from him, like a poisonous vapor. "Mr. Edgars, I will give you double what I was going to pay your sister to go back to your home in Hammond and forget we ever had this conversation. Two million. In your hand. Right now."

"I just told you, I don't want your money."

The lawyer smiled. "Are you a betting man, Mr. Edgars? Your odds of getting a couple million dollars forked over to you for doing nothing at all are slim. I advise you to take it."

"Since Trinity fired your ass, you want to become my lawyer?"

Amberson's lizard gaze held steady. He wasn't upset at all. "I hope you're not under the illusion that you can put together some kind of case against Trinity. For the record, her brothers' deaths were all ruled accident or misadventure. Byron was a notorious cokehead. He's the person who introduced Trinity to drugs, you know. Shelley was a maniac behind the wheel of a car. And Keats, well he—" Amberson stopped speaking suddenly. His eyes were cast downward and Desmond found it impossible to read his expression.

"What happened to Keats?"

"Please let this drop, Mr. Edgars. Trinity is a mess. You must realize that." His voice was pleading, but his eyes were hard. "I promised her father I'd take care of her."

"She's your problem, Mr. Amberson. Not mine." Desmond went to the door. "You're going to want to find her a good defense attorney."

47

He took a taxi uptown, and it moved as if on wings. Seven minutes after he left Amberson's place, he was in front of Trinity's. The doorman was the same one who'd been there Tuesday morning. "Edgars, right? To see Miss Lytton-Jones."

"That's right." Desmond was impressed with the man's recall. He waited while the man called upstairs.

"Costa says you can go on up."

Desmond took the private elevator to the top floor. The houseboy was waiting for him.

"You came back!" he said, excited. "After the other day . . . well, let's just say I'm glad you're here. Trin—um, Miss Lytton-Jones owes you an apology."

Desmond had been planning to crash inside and accost Trinity, but seeing Costa gave him another idea. "I don't care about her saying sorry. But I was wondering what happened on Friday. You said Dominique saved both your lives. What happened?"

"Miss Lytton-Jones got a call around seven-thirty. It was a police officer—at least, that's what he claimed to be. Detective Lee, that was his name. He told her Gary had been in a horrible accident. He'd driven his car into a tree up by the Hudson Valley house, and he died."

"How did Trinity react to the news?"

"She was psyched. She said it was the best thing that ever happened to her." Costa looked guilty. "I feel bad saying this, but she had me open a magnum of Krug Brut 1988."

"That's champagne?" Desmond asked. Costa nodded. "I get the feeling she's always drinking champagne."

"But I drank some with her," Costa said. "I still feel guilty about it. But she was so overjoyed."

"What happened after that?"

"It took her awhile to pack. The detective—or whoever it was who called—said she had to identify the body. We were just starting to drive up when your sister called." Costa swallowed hard. "That changed everything. It wasn't just what your sister said. Miss Lytton-Jones suddenly realized how strange it was that Detective Lee had called her on her cell phone. Hardly anybody has the number. Wait, that's not true. Plenty of fashion people like Anna Wintour and André Leon Talley have it, but they never call her. Her personal shoppers have it, Mr. Amberson and I have it, Gary had it . . . I don't know who else. But her phone doesn't ring very often."

"So, you never spoke to Detective Lee?"

"No. Trinity had me turn the car around, and we drove to the Plaza Athénée. She got us a suite, and then she had me call the police and hospitals in the Hudson Valley. I couldn't find anything about Gary. The number Detective Lee had called from just rang and rang." Costa closed his eyes, as if his life were flashing in front of them. "It was some kind of trap. I believe that with all my heart. Someone wanted to kill her."

"Do you have any idea who?"

Costa shrugged. "If you asked me that a week ago, I would have said Gary. Those two hated each other. But otherwise . . . I don't know. She doesn't have any friends."

"What about a boyfriend?"

Costa looked incredulous. "Never."

"Okay, a girlfriend, then?"

"No. You don't get it. She doesn't have relationships with people, just things."

There was a sound of clattering heels coming down the hallway. "Is that my delivery?" Trinity called out.

"No, Miss Lytton-Jones. Mr. Edgars is here."

Trin's pinched, angry face suddenly peered out the door. "Get him out of here. I am not speaking with him again."

Before Desmond could say a word, Costa was answering her. "You don't get to do that. His sister saved our lives. You should be grateful."

Trin's hollow eyes shriveled to the size of raisins. A muscle next to her eye twitched and she bit her lip. Then she threw her lit cigarette at Desmond.

It didn't burn him, but it scorched a little patch on his white dress shirt, not far below his throat. "What are you, three years old?" he asked.

"Get out!" she shrieked at him. "Out, out, out!"

"I can't believe you did that," Costa breathed.

"Take him downstairs before I ship you back to Argentina," Trin seethed.

"That's your big threat, *cara rota*? I might have to go back to Buenos Aires?" Costa flung his hands up. "I quit!"

"You can't do that, you stupid nothing."

"Yes, I can!" Costa said. "You know what's funny? You're the stupid nothing. You can't do a thing for yourself. You're as helpless as a baby." He turned to Desmond, throwing his arms around him in a hug. "I apologize for all of this rudeness." He brushed by Trinity and she pulled back, as if he carried contagion. "I am packing my things now."

Trinity stared after him as if she'd been struck. "You can't do that!" she screamed.

"Looks like it's hard to find good help these days," Desmond said. "I wonder if Max will turn on you as quickly as your houseboy."

"Get out!"

"Happy to go. But you'll be answering to the cops before the night is through."

He pressed the elevator button and the doors opened. The advantage to having a private one was that it was there whenever you wanted it, he guessed. But, like every other advantage Trinity Lytton-Jones had, it was wasted.

He went down to the street, calling Detective Iorio as soon as he left the building. "Trinity Lytton-Jones just assaulted me, and I want to press charges. Her lawyer tried to buy me off for two million dollars. I'm in front of her building right now. I have the feeling this bird is trying to fly the coop." He left the address and hung up. He had no intention of budging until the cops arrived.

He might not be able to hunt down Max, but he could hand the police Ms. Lytton-Jones. Sure, it seemed lame to press charges for her tossing a lit cigarette at him, but he was positive she'd crack under pressure as soon as she was hauled to the police station. She was ultimately responsible for Dominique's death, even if Max had been the one to do her dirty work. When Desmond thought of his sister's life, and everything that had happened in the aftermath of her death, he envisioned it as a spiral, twisting wildly and growing bigger and taller, until it consumed everything. Trinity was finally going to be swallowed up by it, too.

What if you're wrong? asked a voice in the back of his mind. *Everything we hear is an opinion, not a fact. Everything we see is a perspective, not the truth.* He shook it off. There were facts in this case that couldn't be ignored. Trinity was the person who benefitted from the deaths. Well, from Gary's death. Obviously, she got some sick satisfaction from Dominique's. Klepper's . . . who knew. The woman was twisted.

He crossed the street, keeping an eye on the entrance to the building and fending off creeping doubts. One thing that had never made sense to him was why Trinity would want to kill Gary at the very time Dominique was gathering evidence against the man. Clearly, Amberson hadn't told his client what he was doing, but wouldn't she have some clue things were moving on the screw-Gary front? And Costa's story about Detective Lee bothered him. It suggested that Trin was actually being set up. Now, obviously Gary wanted her dead, because he would be free—and rich. But how big a coincidence was it that Trin and Gary had conspired to kill each other on the same weekend?

Just as that thought went through his mind, he noticed a beautiful blonde walk by. There was something familiar about her. She was tall and model-slender. Her long blond hair bounced over her shoulders like she was in a shampoo commercial. She spoke to the doorman, and he nodded. Desmond crossed the street again to get a better look at her. He watched the blonde get into the elevator, the private one that led to Trinity's apartment.

There had only been one apartment on that floor.

He realized exactly where he'd seen her before. That woman looked an awful lot like the one who'd bumped into him in front of Dominique's building just before he was attacked. Was that just another coincidence?

Desmond's hands clenched into fists. It was time to finally get some answers.

Part Three

POLLY

48

When Polly went upstairs, Costa met her at the door. "I'm so glad you're here! You look gorgeous," he said, kissing her on both cheeks.

"Why aren't you wearing your uniform?" Polly asked. "I thought she threw fits if she sees you in normal clothes."

"She does, but I just quit. No more monkey suit."

"But doesn't that mean you have to go back to South America?"

"No." Costa looked almost giddy. "My boyfriend and I have been talking about getting married."

"That's wonderful!" Polly exclaimed. In the background, she heard the woman screeching, "Costa! Come here!"

"Ugh. She doesn't believe I've quit. She thinks I should be waiting on her hand and foot. She's a horrible person." He reached to the side. Polly hadn't noticed his packed suitcase. "Good luck. Don't worry about locking the door when you leave. It's her own fault if someone breaks in and robs her."

Polly hugged Costa, then watched him get into the elevator. He gave her a sweet, childish wave before the doors slid shut. Polly turned around.

"Costa!" The Unsmiling Tsarevna was coming along the hall-way. That was how Polly thought of Trinity Lytton-Jones. Of course, in the Russian fairy tale, the Unsmiling Tsarevna one day met a man who made her laugh. Polly didn't think that was ever going to happen to Trinity.

"I haven't seen you in months, and now you're late," she ranted, a cigarette burning at the corner of her mouth. "How dare you keep me waiting!"

"If it's a problem, I can leave," Polly suggested. "Just like Costa did."

Trinity grabbed her wrist and yanked her forward. For such an emaciated wreck of a woman, she still carried some strength in her. "Don't you dare." On second thought, that was just the power of her addiction.

"Our courier was running late," Polly said, walking into the grand apartment. "It couldn't be helped."

"Where's my package?"

Polly gave her a lingering glare and strolled deeper into the apartment. The Unsmiling Tsarevna was always so nasty. Polly had been making semiregular deliveries to this apartment for four years, and in all that time, Trinity had yet to say thank you. She just grabbed for what she wanted with those bejeweled knobby-twig fingers of hers. Let her twist. Let her wait.

"It's already paid for, isn't it?" Trinity whined, smoke pouring from her mouth and nose.

"Is it? Perhaps I should check while you wait."

"It's always paid for in advance! You know that."

The Unsmiling Tsarevna never touched money, of course. A princess never had to do that, Polly surmised. That was the job of a handmaiden like herself, a woman who was born to work.

In the living room, Polly saw that Trinity had already laid out her silver tray and the other accoutrements of her addiction.

"I don't even have a pill left," Trinity whined. "Your employer stinted me last time."

"He wouldn't do any such thing. He is very careful." Polly eyed her. "But if you're unsatisfied with the service, perhaps you should find another supplier." Polly would never get away with talking back to her brother. Sniping at this horrible woman, and a few of her brother's other customers, was one of her rare freedoms.

"Just give me the package." There was heat in the Unsmiling Tsarevna's voice, desperation winding through it, taut as a violin string.

"All right." Polly pulled the package out of the inside of her jacket. There were a dozen tiny white pills, plus a gram of white powder.

Trinity's eyes went round as she took it. "What's this?"

"Your order."

"But . . . there's only a gram here." She was panicking, even though she was getting down on her knees in front of the coffee table to prepare her fix.

Polly's instructions from her brother had been more complicated than usual. Her normal job was only to drop off packages for Trinity. Tonight, she was supposed to ignite the woman's perpetual panic and fan the flames of her fear. Her brother hadn't explained why. All he'd said was to make sure Trinity snorted the powder quickly.

"I told you, our courier had an issue. We've got more product coming in, probably tonight. I'll be over again later if at all possible. We just didn't want to keep you waiting any longer."

Trinity was busy inhaling the cocaine through a silver tube, first one long line into one nostril and then switching sides.

"Okay, I get it," she said, cutting two more lines and inhaling them. She pressed one hand to her chest. "You can go."

"Sure," Polly said. "See you later."

She walked down the long corridor, thinking how hideous the apartment was. What woman puts up photographs of herself everywhere? The Unsmiling Tsarevna probably deserved pity, but Polly couldn't find any in her heart for her. What an easy life that spoiled woman had. When had she ever had to exert herself? Polly had been working her whole life, it seemed, and she didn't imagine that would ever change.

She took the elevator downstairs and said goodnight to the doorman. He smiled and gave her that little half-wave he always did. She walked out the front door, zipping the front of her coat. She almost walked into the tall man standing like a wall in front of her. He was big and black as the night. His teeth shone white when he smiled.

"Good evening." His voice was surprisingly soft, barely above a whisper. "Don't I know you?"

"No, I don't think so. Excuse me."

He blocked her way. "Even if you don't know me, I know you."

"You're mistaken."

His dark eyes gleamed. "Now that I see you up close, I know I've seen you more than once before. You're Tom Klepper's girlfriend."

At the sound of Tom's name, she froze. "Who-who?" she asked, sounding like a defective owl.

"I bet you didn't know Tom kept photographs of you," the man said.

"I don't know what you're talking about."

"So, why were you visiting Trinity Lytton-Jones?" the man asked.

"Who?"

"Come on. You're not even trying."

"I don't know her."

"Then who were you visiting? That elevator only goes to her apartment, you know."

Polly just stared at him.

"Let's go talk to Trinity, see what she has to say." The man put his hand on her back, propelling her into the building.

"You back already? I guess you forgot something upstairs?" the doorman asked them. He was an idiot, that one. He wouldn't even try to stop them.

The man pushed the elevator button and it opened immediately. He nudged her inside.

"Please." She was almost whimpering. "Let me go. You'll get me in trouble."

"With who?"

She couldn't tell him that. The cardinal rule, should she ever be so stupid as to get caught, was to never say a word. She'd always been careful, and the combination of her youth and her beauty let her fly under the radar of suspicion.

At the top, the elevator doors opened to an empty foyer.

"Why don't you ring the bell?" he suggested.

She did. They waited. There was no sound from inside the apartment.

The man touched the knob and pushed the door open. "Didn't even have to bump the lock on that one," he murmured.

There was no sound inside the apartment.

"Trinity?" he called out. "It's Desmond. Where are you?"

No answer.

He walked along the corridor holding Polly's arm.

Trinity was in the living room, sprawled on the rug. The man rushed over to her, touching the Unsmiling Tsarevna's neck. "What the hell did you do to her?"

49

The man got to his feet and Polly froze. He came close to her, grabbing her shoulders and shaking her. She could feel her brain rattling in her skull. "Tell me what you did!"

"I didn't do anything!" Her voice was a whisper, but there was urgency in it. "Please let go of me."

The whites of his eyes were stark against his skin. The more they showed, the more frightened she was. She'd seen that look in her brother's face, and it always terrified her. It meant there was going to be a fight. It meant there would be blood.

"You're going to tell me who you are and what you were doing here. How did you kill her?"

"I don't know what you're talking about."

"Stop playing games with me!" The man's harsh voice crashed through her head. She hated noise, and shouting made her want to curl up in a fetal position.

"I'm not!" She tried to stay calm. Her brother didn't like it when she cried. He'd punished her for weeping enough times that her eyes stayed dry now, no matter what happened.

"Why did you try to kill me last night?"

"I didn't do anything."

"You distracted me so your brother Max could strangle me."

"No!"

"I hate to tell you this, Polly, but Costa already blew your cover. I talked to him when he came downstairs. He didn't know your real last name, but I do." He stared at her, as if figuring out a riddle. "You're Polina Brantov."

She tried not to react.

"What do you know. Polly Brantov." The man's voice was soft, but she wasn't going to let it fool her. He was capable of violence. "You have two brothers. Their names are Max and Valery."

She inhaled sharply, feeling suddenly as if she were drowning.

"It's okay," the man said. "You don't have to answer. I know about you, and I know about your family. My sister knew your brother Max. Or Maxim. What does he prefer to be called?"

"Only our parents call him Maxim," she answered. "No one else does."

"Did Max tell you anything about my sister? Her name was Dominique Monaghan."

"Dominique?" The name was familiar, like a fragment of a nightmare she'd forgotten. She tried to remember where she'd heard that name. When she did, a shiver ran down her spine, as if someone stepped on her grave.

The man took her reaction for bafflement. "What about my name. Desmond Edgars?"

She shook her head.

"What did you do to Trinity?"

"Nothing!"

"She's dead, Polly. You were just up here. Seems like quite the coincidence. And I don't believe in coincidences."

"I don't know what happened. She was sitting there, snorting up cocaine when I left. She told me to leave. That was all that happened."

"That's strange. You deliver drugs to Trinity and she dies. Just the other day your boyfriend got himself killed."

"My boyfriend?"

The man stared at her hard. "Tom Klepper. You know he's dead, right?"

His voice washed over her like a tidal wave. She didn't consider Tom her boyfriend. She only spent time with him because her brother said she had to. But, even so, she had a tender spot for Tom. He was kind, but also so silly, so hapless. She thought of him as a *domovoi*, a house spirit covered all over in hair. That wasn't an unfair description of Tom. Naked, he was grotesque.

"But . . . how did he die?"

"He was strangled."

"I don't believe you!"

"Google it if you don't believe me. The police are investigating it. They're searching for his killer."

Her head swam. For a minute, she thought she might faint, and she put her hand up to her temple. She stared around the room and noticed that the Unsmiling Tsarevna's foot was twitching like a fish flopping about in a boat.

"What's that?"

He turned his head to look. "What the hell? Is she alive?" He went to Trinity's side, kneeling and pulling out his phone. When he spoke into it, he gave the police their location. He wasn't watching her. She crept down the hallway, then broke into a run, tearing out of the apartment and into the elevator. Just before the doors shut, she saw him, enraged as a bull, rushing at her. She heard him crash against the doors, but by then she was headed down, down, down.

50

She rushed out of the building, ignoring the startled door-man and his reflexive half-wave. Fear had burrowed into her chest back in the apartment, but her brain was surging on adrenaline now.

Get out of the building, she ordered herself. She had a head start. The elevator went directly from the lobby to the penthouse. The man was going to have to run down eighteen flights of stairs.

Head across Fifth Avenue, directly into Central Park. It would be a lot harder to identify a person jogging in the park than a woman running along a well-lit street.

Somehow get back to my brother. She didn't want to, but she had no choice in the matter.

She ran across Fifth Avenue, even though she didn't have the light and there were cars and a city bus racing toward her. But she made it to the other side and scrambled down the block. She looked around as she went in, catching sight of the man, diagonally across the avenue and one block up. He was fast, she had to grant him that.

She ran into the park, emptying the pockets of her coat, pulling out her phone and her hat, and tossing the coat on a bench. Within a minute there'd be some homeless person claiming it.

She ran off the path, pulling her hat on and tucking her hair inside. She heard running footsteps behind her. A man was yelling. She went deeper into the darkness. Her mother had, early on, instilled a fear of parks at night into her, but she'd shed that fear along with her coat. It was cold, but her head was clear.

A man grabbed her arm.

"Where you going in such a hurry?" he hissed. There was alcohol on his breath and a strange, sweetish smell coming off him. This was why her mother was afraid of parks at night. Polly had no time and no patience. She didn't care if the man only wanted to shake her down for money. How could she tell? She swung her elbow around and hit him in the throat, just like her brother had taught her. The man went down, making a pathetic, wet gurgle.

She kept running.

Finally, she exited the park on the west side, just as an empty cab rolled by.

"Kind of a cold night not to have a coat," the driver commented.

"Seventh Avenue and Forty-second Street, please," she told him. She couldn't go straight to the hotel, because she didn't want the driver to remember the odd girl with no coat.

"Seriously, you're going to catch a chill without a coat."

Inwardly she groaned. Most of the time, New York taxi drivers didn't speak to their clients. Many of them barely spoke English. But occasionally, you would get a chatty old-school type.

"Sorry. No English." She stretched it out to *Eeeeengleesh*. She'd grown up with Russian tales and worries embedded in her soul, but she knew almost nothing of the language. Her parents had never tried to teach her. That was their private vocabulary for fighting.

"Oh." The cabbie sounded disappointed. "Where you from?"

She opened her eyes wide, as if working to understand him. "Seventh Avenue and Forty-second Street, please?" she repeated.

The cabbie muttered something and turned up the radio. Polly sank back in her seat, relieved.

At Forty-second Street, she handed some bills to the driver and got out. She headed back up Seventh Avenue, because the cab driver couldn't follow her in that direction. If that seemed paranoid, fine.

You never knew what detail people would remember. She turned west at Forty-third Street and rushed to the hotel, which was really at Eighth Avenue. When she got to the Westin, she went in and kept her head down. She took the elevator up to the room. She rapped on the door before using her key. *Always knock first,* her brother told her, countless times. When she went into the room, she found him, sitting by the window, his computer propped in his lap.

"How did it go?" he asked, not even looking up.

"It was awful."

That got his attention. He lifted his eyes. "What happened?"

"I think she died, Val."

He gave her a small smile. "Silly Polly. She could be dead, or she might be in a coma. Don't worry about it. If she ever wakes up, she'll be brain damaged."

"You . . . you did this on purpose?"

Val observed her dispassionately. "That was the whole point, Polly."

51

Y ou sent me over to *poison* her?" Polly's voice had a catch
in it. Her brother had trained her to be his accomplice in
many things. He'd taught her to fight in the most brutal
way; she could bring down an opponent with a single,
swift strike to an eye or throat. He'd used her as a carrier pigeon,
delivering messages and packages. He'd used her as a spy. He'd
used her as a . . . she didn't want to say call girl, but that was surely
Val's idea, holding her out as a soft, warm lure when he needed to
catch something slippery. But this was different. "You made me a
murderer."

"You aren't, Polly. You delivered a package, that's all. You're as
responsible for what's inside as a helper monkey would be."

"You tainted the drugs. She sniffed up the cocaine right away.
You mixed something in that?"

Val nodded. "I didn't have a choice. We had to do it for Max."

"I don't believe for one second Max wants to kill anyone."

Val looked pensive, as if he were weighing the truth against a lie
in his head. With the scar on his face, he always appeared severe.
"Of course Max didn't want that. But Max is mixed up with some
terrible people, and if we don't do what they say, they'll hurt him.
They could even kill him, Polly. I don't want to risk that and I
know you don't, either."

Polly stepped forward and threw herself on one of the double
beds. "Why did they want to get rid of her?"

"I don't know all of it," Val said. "Except that she's the heir to a huge fortune."

"This was about money?"

Val went back to his computer, suddenly bored. "It's always about money, isn't it, Pretty Polly?"

"Won't the police be suspicious when someone else inherits all this money?"

Val shrugged. "It doesn't matter to us. We just do what we're told."

"There's more I have to tell you," Polly said. "There was a man at the apartment."

"The houseboy?"

"No, it was the black man . . . the one who you attacked last night."

That caught Val's attention. "No. He couldn't be there."

"Do you really think I'd make this up?" Polly asked. "Desmond Edgars was at the apartment."

"Then you should have turned around and left!" Val leapt up, ready to strike her.

"He wasn't there when I went in! Trinity answered the door and dragged me inside. She was desperate to get high, and I gave her the drugs. She laid out lines in front of me and started snorting it up. She told me to leave, so I did." She took a deep breath. This was the part that involved some fancy footwork. If Val knew she'd made it down to the first floor before she was accosted, he'd beat the living daylights out of her for being so stupid. Why hadn't she run away? She'd been frozen. Transfixed, even. "The man came out of the elevator when I was coming out of the apartment. He recognized me immediately. He said he knew me, that I was Tom Klepper's girlfriend."

"How could he possibly know that?"

"I have no idea!"

"Hmm." Val would be coming back to this subject later, no doubt about that. He was like an eel in the water, subtle and invisible until he was ready to strike. "What happened then?"

"He said his sister knows Max."

"And you believed him?"

"Why not?" She suddenly felt desperate. "It *could* be true."

"It's pathetic, how gullible you are, Polly. All someone has to do is tell you they know Max and you're all over them."

"No, I'm not." She turned it over in her mind. Well, maybe it was a little bit true. "I miss him. I don't understand why he can't see me. . . ."

"Max is trying to protect you, Polly. He can't come home. You know that, and I know that. Mama won't accept it, but we can't do anything about that."

She wanted to curl up in a ball and cry. "The man, Desmond, told me Tom Klepper is dead. He said Tom was strangled. Is that true?"

Val held her eyes. "Yes."

"Did you kill him?"

"Yes." His voice was colder this time.

"How could you?"

"I was under orders, Polly." He sat next to her on the bed. "I thought you didn't like Tom? You said he was disgusting."

She wiped her nose. "He was a big, stupid lump with twelve hands. But that doesn't mean I wanted him dead."

"Well, Pretty Polly, you don't get to choose. Okay, back to that rich bitch Trinity. What happened next?"

"I talked to that man for a little while. I tried to leave, but he blocked my way. Then he dragged me back inside the apartment. He wanted to talk to Trinity about me. He wanted to know why I was there. When we went in . . . she was on the floor. We thought she was dead, but then her foot started moving. He called 911, and I ran. I got downstairs and went into the park. I had to throw away my coat because it would make it easier for him to recognize me. Another man tried to grab me, but I hit him in the throat like you taught me and kept running."

If she'd been expecting a pat on the head for her quick thinking, she was sadly mistaken. Val's eyes were intense as a cobra's, only colder.

"That mad animal came to our house. Somehow, he got on Max's trail, and now he's on ours, too. He's stalking us, Polly. We need to get rid of him."

"How?"

"Don't worry, I have a plan." Val smiled at her, but there was no warmth in it. "Don't I always take care of you, little sister?"

"What are you going to do?"

"The less you know, the better." The was Val's standard line. "I'm going to make a couple of calls. Then I'm going to talk to Max. You're going to wait here. Don't go anywhere." He pulled on his black leather jacket and started out the door before stopping suddenly and swiveling around. "Here. Take one of these."

He watched her put the pill into her mouth. She swallowed it without water, and for a blissful time, she was floating in a warm, tender sea without a care in the world.

52

Polly knew she was being followed on Thursday morning. She pretended not to see the tall, black man across Forty-second Street as she talked on her phone. She was wearing a quilted black coat Val had bought for her and her black cap, but her blond hair fanned around her face, and the man recognized her from the night before. He did a double take and stopped in his tracks. She watched him in the glass, and when she was sure she'd been spotted, she turned down Park Avenue, looking as agitated and frantic as she could.

Since she was ten years old, her family had impressed upon her what a dangerous place the world was. Nowhere was safe, and there was no one you could trust, not outside of your family. The traditional Russian folk stories about Koschei the Deathless, who abducted many a good girl from her home, became cautionary tales. When she came into Manhattan, with its noise and sirens and catcalling men, she was always on edge. Her way of dealing with it was to will herself invisible; sometimes, she even believed it worked. Keep your eyes down, and your hair in front of your face, and people didn't quite see you. They were so wrapped up in their own lives that unless you immediately caught their eye or got in their way, you were only so much background scenery to them.

But she wasn't invisible to this man. She knew she was in his sights, and it was only a matter of time until he caught up with her.

She watched his reflection in shop windows, and she sped up her pace. She walked south, turning east on Thirty-seventh Street.

The man was just behind her, not even trying to hide the fact he was following. By that point, he had to know where she was going.

How bad was he? She'd asked Val this last night, when he came back to the room and told her what she had to do. *He's an evil man, and if he gets the chance, he'll murder Max,* Val had said.

She would do anything for Max.

Polly got to Tom Klepper's brownstone apartment, fumbling for her key in front of the door. There were bits and pieces of yellow police tape loitering around the doorframe. Val must have run out of time to remove it.

"Polly."

She turned at the sound of Desmond Edgars's voice, and she cringed against the door as she pretended to suddenly recognize him. "You."

"What are you doing at Tom Klepper's house?"

"I . . . I . . ." She tried to remember her words. Val had gone over them with her last night, and again that morning, but her mind was suddenly a blank.

"What the hell happened to you?" He seemed stunned. Polly had almost forgotten her black eye. Val had given it to her when he'd come in late at night.

We need to make sure he's off guard, Val had said.

Okay, she'd answered.

He's the kind of man that will respond to a damsel in distress.

Okay.

So, when he sees you've been brutalized, he'll be sympathetic.

O—

Val had punched her in the face before she'd gotten the second syllable out.

"Nothing," Polly stammered.

"Somebody punched you in the face?" His raspy voice rose, as if he really were concerned.

"I'm fine." She tried to put her key in the door, but she dropped it on the ground and had to stoop to pick it up.

"No, you're not." The man was right behind her, his hand on her arm. He wasn't pulling at her, as he had the night before. He was trying to gently coax her.

"Look, I need to go inside. Please go. Just forget you ever saw me."

"I can't do that, Polly."

She started to turn the key. "Well, then—"

"What are you people doing!" shouted a man with a heavy accent. It wasn't a question so much as a shrill accusation. Polly looked up and saw a furious man glaring down at them. She recognized him as Tom's superintendent.

"I call police NOW," he yelled. "You get away from that door."

"But I—," Polly started to say. She looked around, now genuinely frantic. It was her job to get Desmond Edgars inside Tom Klepper's apartment. If she failed, Val really would want to kill her. The next time he hit her, it wouldn't just be for effect.

"We're going," the man said. "Come on, Polly." He tugged her arm.

"But I have to—"

"Police!" yelled the angry little man.

"This way. Come on." The man dragged her back toward Park Avenue. Polly looked back at Tom's apartment, wondering if Val had heard the commotion. He was waiting inside, and she knew exactly how furious he'd be when he realized she'd screwed up yet again.

53

W e need to talk," the man said. "Look, there's a Starbucks across Park. Come on."

Polly didn't try to resist as they crossed Park Avenue. What could she do, anyway?

"You'd better not run off again, before you hear what I have to say," the man warned her. "If you do, I'll come after you and I won't stop until you've heard me out."

"I won't run." She was resigned. Maybe after they talked, she could get him to come back with her to Tom Klepper's apartment. Then Val could deal with him. If she couldn't manage that, she might as well throw herself into the East River, before Val could do it.

"Have you had breakfast?" he asked, once they were inside.

"No." That was the truth.

"Okay, let's get something to eat."

When she thought about it, she was actually starving. She grabbed a sandwich and a fruit salad and a cookie and a bag of salted nuts, and she ordered a hot chocolate. When they sat down, the man said, "I told you who I am last night, but it's not like we've been properly introduced. My name's Desmond Edgars." He waited for her to speak. She didn't. "And you're Polina Brantov."

"No one calls me Polina except my mother. It's Polly." She glanced around the café. "Everyone is staring at us."

"They're staring at your shiner. It's pretty bad. They're also wondering what I'm doing, having breakfast with a high school student. You're seventeen, right?"

She nodded.

"Why aren't you in school, by the way?"

She didn't want to explain anything to him. "I stopped going."

"Your mother's okay with that? My mother would never, in a million years, have let me quit school. Though when I was thirteen, fourteen years old, I wanted to." He gave her a smile, but it looked sad to her, like something that had broken long ago. "My mother was afraid I was throwing my life away and she . . . she stopped that from happening." His shoulders hunched slightly and he shook his head.

"Your mother's dead?"

"Yeah. She died a long time ago. Right after I went into the Army." He gave her that same fractured smile. "Sorry. I get emotional when I talk about her. My mother sacrificed so much for me."

"My mother doesn't care what I do. I don't think she even realizes I stopped going to school."

"What about Max? Does he care?"

She eyed him warily. "He won't like it, when he hears about it. School's a big deal to him."

"Right. Somebody told me he got accepted to Harvard. That's really something."

She nodded, warming to the subject. "Max is brilliant. Going to Harvard was always his dream."

"But he didn't end up going, did he?"

"No. He . . . he got into some trouble and . . . he couldn't."

"What kind of trouble?"

Polly wrapped her arms around herself. "I can't talk about it."

"Okay. Let me tell you about my sister instead. Her name was Dominique Monaghan. You ever meet her?"

"No, but I think—" She tried to stay cool, as if she didn't really care. "I think I might have heard the name Dominique. But I'm not sure."

"You'd remember if you met her. She was such a sweetheart. She was ten years younger than me, so I thought she was a pain in the neck when we were kids. But later . . . I loved having a baby sister to take care of. It was a bit like having my own kid." Desmond looked down, but Polly could see enough of his face that she caught the tug-of-war between sadness and sweetness.

"You're talking about her in the past tense," Polly said.

"She's dead. I'm still trying to get used to that idea, but she is." His eyes weighed heavily on her conscience.

"Dominique is dead?" She couldn't hide her shock. "How did she die?"

"She was in a house in the Poconos. You know where that is? Upstate Pennsylvania. Pretty area. Anyway, she was there with her boyfriend, Gary. Max was at the house, too. Dominique and Gary died of carbon monoxide poisoning. Somebody set up a problem in the furnace, and he sealed all the windows, so no air could get in."

"But she . . ." Polly's voice trailed off. She remembered standing inside that pretty country house in the Hudson Valley. Val never let her go away anywhere, so she'd been thrilled about the trip. He'd described his little project like a game. *All you have to do is stand there with a gun, Polly. . . .*

A gun? That part had frightened her.

It won't be loaded. Don't worry, you'll be fine. You'll be completely covered up. No one will know it's you. Just don't say a word. This is kind of a delicate job, so I don't want to use one of my freelancers. I want you to be the one in the room with me.

At that house in the Hudson Valley, all she'd had to do was stand silently and point an unloaded gun. After Val put the man and the woman in the van, he gave Polly the keys to a shiny green car and told her to follow him on the highway. They drove for two and a half hours before Val signaled her to stop at a campsite. She sat there, waiting in the car for hours and freezing. When Val came back with the van, he'd wiped the car down for prints, even though she'd done what he said and wore gloves the whole time.

Where's the couple? Polly asked.

They're settling in for a romantic weekend right about now.

That hadn't made any sense to Polly. All this, for a romantic weekend?

That's how it's going to look, Val told her. *Don't worry about it. I'm driving you home now. Tomorrow I'll come back and deal with the loose ends.*

What happened to your neck? she'd asked him. *That looks like blood.*

Val had put his hand to it, and he'd cursed long and loud. He never told her what cut him.

"You said . . . Max was in the house, too?" Polly asked Desmond.

Desmond nodded. "Definitely. Max's blood was found there. He might have fallen and hurt himself. The police don't really know. Dominique told me about Max on the phone. That's the only reason I knew he was there."

Max was there? Polly squeezed her eyes shut. Why hadn't Val let her go with him to the house? Sometimes she hated her brother with such a passion. Val was forever going on about how they had to do something to help Max, when the only person being helped was Val himself. Polly felt sorrow for Desmond's sister and the man who died, but she was grateful Max hadn't been harmed.

"I'm very sorry," she said. "About your sister."

"What I wonder is how Dominique came to die, and if Max knew that was going to happen."

"If Max knew, he would have tried to save her." There was a vehemence in her voice that made the man widen his eyes.

"Did your brother give you that black eye, Polly?"

"Yes," she whispered. "But it was my brother Val, not Max. Max wouldn't hurt anyone."

"Was it Val who set you up to run into me today?"

She looked up, realizing she'd given away far too much. Every word out of her mouth was a nail in her coffin. When Val found out—and with Val, it was always a question of when, not if—he would do terrible things her. If she were lucky, he'd snap her neck and be done with it quickly. The other possibilities were too awful to face.

"Please let me go," she begged. "I can't stay here. He'll know, and he'll be angry with me."

"I'll deal with Val," Desmond answered.

She could feel her soul curl up in misery inside.

"What did he want?"

She glanced at him, trying to measure his motives. She tried to remember the last time she'd had a conversation with anyone outside of her family. Her mother had made her afraid of everyone since Max had gone. Yet, strangers were never the ones who'd hurt Polly; the pain she knew was inflicted by her brother and, to a lesser degree, by her mother. "Are you telling me the truth about your sister? Is she really dead?"

Now it was his turn to nod. His face was fierce like a stone angel's. "I still can't believe it. She's the only family I had. Now that she's gone, all I care about is getting justice for her. I don't know what else to do. Nothing else matters to me."

She understood him so well. Max was the only real family she had, and he was all she cared about. Her parents had always been blind to whatever happened to her. Val was a monster. She wasn't family to him, but a tool for him to use, a body to send on errands. It didn't matter to him that she was his sister. He'd shown her that enough times. But Max . . . he was different. She remembered how he used to pick her up from school every day and walk her home, even though he was in high school. Boys that age didn't like to walk hand-in-hand with their baby sister. Of course, that had all stopped long ago, but thinking of Max always made her heart warm up. Most of the time, she felt like it was encased in ice.

"I want to find Max, more than anything in this world." She gazed at Desmond. "If I help you get justice for your sister, will you help me find Max?"

"I will. I promise." He took a deep breath. "You're going to have to tell me the truth about a lot of things. Will you do that?"

"Yes."

"Let's start with Val's plan. What does he hope to get?"

"I don't know what Val wants," Polly admitted. "He tells me nothing unless he absolutely needs to, or else if he feels like bragging. He says it's my job to do what he tells me."

"When's the last time you talked to Max?"

"Not in a very long time," Polly whispered. "He sends me notes and cards sometimes, but he won't come to the house."

"Is Max afraid of Val?"

"Everyone is afraid of Val."

"Was it Val who poisoned Trinity Lytton-Jones last night? Did he put something in the drugs you delivered to her?"

"Yes. I asked him and he admitted it."

"She was a regular customer of his?"

Polly nodded. "For years. She was a terrible addict. Tons of pills, mountains of cocaine."

"How did she come to be Val's customer?"

"I don't know. The arrangement goes back a long time."

Desmond's eyes narrowed to slits, and he was silent for a moment. "What I don't get is this: Val deals drugs, and Trinity is a really great customer. I mean, she probably spent a lot every week, right?"

"Yes. I don't know exactly how much. I didn't collect the money."

"You didn't get paid by Trinity?" His black eyes were shiny with curiosity.

"Never. Everything was paid for before I made a delivery."

"Who paid?"

"I don't know. The money goes straight to Val. I don't know how he gets it."

Desmond looked pensive. "That's interesting. But my point was this: why kill the Golden Goose? He just lost what had to be one of his best customers."

"He said . . ." Her voice quavered. She shouldn't be telling him anything, but she liked him, especially because she believed he loved his sister. He was like Max in her mind—a good man. She felt pity for him, too. "He said it was because of her family fortune."

Desmond sat stock-still, his gaze sliding away from her face into some far-off place where Polly couldn't follow him. "Does Max deal drugs, too?"

"No. He wouldn't."

The expression on his face told her he didn't quite believe her. He didn't understand that Max and Val were like day and night. Max was kind and gentle, while Val . . . she didn't like to think about what Val was. There were Russian fairy tales about a creature called Tugarin Zmeyevich, which was cruelty personified. Sometimes it looked like a knight, or a dragon, but it was always an incarnation of evil. That was Val.

"I'm pretty sure the police told me Max was arrested for drug possession when he was sixteen or seventeen," Desmond said.

"That was Val's fault!" Polly's reply came out of her mouth like a bursting dam. "Max doesn't use drugs or sell drugs. Val does, and he got caught once. He claimed the drugs in his car were also Max's. That was why Max was charged." She stared at the table. "Max didn't want Val to get in more trouble than he was already in, so he went along with it. It was a lesser charge for Val since the quantity was split between them."

"What exactly does Max do?" Desmond asked.

"I don't know."

"You don't know, or you don't want to know?"

She closed her eyes. Thinking of Max was sweet, yet painful. "Both."

"But, basically, he works with Val."

"I . . . I don't know. Val likes to pretend he's just following orders, but I think he gives the orders. He tells me I have to do what he says, or Max will get hurt." She lowered her eyes. "What I think sometimes is that Val tells Max to do what he demands, or else Val will hurt me."

They sat quietly for a while, and then Polly's phone rang, breaking the silence between them. She pulled it out of her jacket. "It's Val."

"Answer it. Let's hear what he has to say."

"Hello?" Polly said.

"Are you still with him?" Val asked.

"Yes."

"Do you think he trusts you?"

"Yes."

"Good. What you need to do now, Pretty Polly, is to lure him back to Mama's house. Tell him all the evidence he's looking for is out on Long Island, and you'll show it to him."

"I . . . I don't know if I can."

"Don't be a dummy. Just get him out here."

"But what if . . ." *What if he sees it's a trap?* Polly wanted to ask.

"Don't worry. He won't figure it out. He's too desperate to think straight." Val's voice was cold. "You'd better not ruin everything this time, Polly. This is all on you. You make one false move, and no one will ever think you're pretty ever again."

54

So, what did Val have to say?" Desmond asked after she hung up.

Polly shrank back in her seat. She was terrified of Val, but she couldn't let that keep her from finding Max. "He wants me to get you out to our house." Her voice was almost inaudible, even to her own ears.

"You mean, he wants to get me out to Long Island to finish me off?" Desmond didn't sound worried.

"He didn't say it exactly, but . . . yes."

Desmond pulled his own phone out of his coat. "Here's the part where I call the police."

Polly leapt out of her seat, as if she'd been scalded. Desmond stood and put a reassuring hand on her arm.

"I can't talk to the police!"

"No one's going to make you do that," Desmond said. "I told you, *I'm* going to talk to the police. You can decide what you want to do."

She nodded, slowly lowering herself into her chair again.

"I take it he hasn't been home since last night?" Desmond asked.

"No. Why?"

"Because the NYPD knows you were at Trinity's apartment last night. I'm pretty sure they've got the cops on Long Island watching your house."

"Did she die?" Polly asked suddenly.

"Last I heard, Trinity was in the hospital. I don't think she's woken up." He hit a couple of buttons on his phone. "Never thought I'd have cops on speed-dial," he murmured. "Detective Iorio, this is Desmond. Give me a call as soon as you can. We've got more to talk about."

"What are you going to do?" Polly asked.

"First, I'm going to talk to the cops. Then, if they think it's a good idea, I'll go out to Long Island with you."

"But Val—"

"Val is planning bad things for me. I know." Desmond sighed. "That's why I'm talking to the cops first." His phone rang while he was speaking. "Oh, now that's interesting," he said, just before he answered it. "Edgars." He listened for a bit. "We had a long talk last night. Oh, they are? I know they certainly wanted to talk to you." Another long pause. "Sure, that's fine." He glanced at his watch. "Give me ten minutes." He hung up without a goodbye.

"I'm going to meet up with the cops," Desmond said. "I'd like it if you came with me."

Polly shook her head. "I can't."

"Polly, what happened last night wasn't your fault. You made a delivery. An illegal delivery, but I'm pretty sure no one is even going to think about locking you up, not with what you've been up against."

"You mean, they'll want to lock my brothers up. They'll want me to testify against them." Her voice was bitter. She wiped her eyes. "What about coming to my house? Val . . . he won't be happy if you don't."

"I know. I head out with you immediately afterward. You come uptown with me, and you can sit at a bookstore or something and wait for me, okay? Then we'll go out to Long Island."

Outside, they crossed Park to get a cab heading north. Desmond held the door for her to get in, then gave the driver an address on Park Avenue.

"What will the police do to Max if they arrest him?" she asked Desmond.

"It depends on how involved he is. My sense, from what you've told me, is that Val is the ringleader. If Max has been involved in bad things because he's protecting you, that changes things a lot." Desmond gave her a searching look. "I can't help notice you're not so worried about what would happen to Val."

She cast her eyes down. Val. Whenever there was suffering and misery, there was Val. She'd known it, even as a young child. She'd heard her parents arguing about him. Her father saw Val for what he was, but her mother never had. Of course, her mother's gaze was directed toward a bottle of vodka most of the time. Then her father had left the family, and Max had been the only one willing to challenge Val's domination. Then even Max had left, and there was no one to protect her from Val's attentions.

"You don't have to say anything, Polly. Every time you mention Val's name, I can tell how you feel. He sounds like my stepfather."

"I thought you said you didn't have any family."

"I don't. My stepfather died when I was fourteen. And he was *never* my family."

They were silent after that, hurtling up the broad boulevard.

"I've got to do this," Desmond said when the cab stopped at Fifty-fourth Street. "Will you promise to wait for me?"

"Yes."

"I don't know how long I'll be."

"It's okay. I'll watch for you."

"What'll you say to Val if he calls you again?"

That stopped her short. "I don't know."

"Maybe you should think on that a bit." He looked thoughtful. "I don't want to get preachy, Polly, but you know I'm an older brother, so it comes naturally to me. Here's the thing. Most people go through life without making decisions. They wonder why things happen to them, why they've got no power to change. The thing is, they do have the power, they just don't choose to use it."

"You're telling me to stand up to Val?"

"Not exactly. This might not be the best day for that change to happen. But you need to root yourself somehow. You can't let yourself go through life letting people hit you. Do you know who Marcus Aurelius was? He had this saying—okay, he had a lot of aphorisms, but this one's the best. 'Do every act of your life as if it were your last.'"

"Were you bossy like this with your sister?"

That made him smile, and he actually looked happy for a moment. "I tried. Dominique didn't put up with much, though." He touched her arm. "Be careful, Polly."

She watched him cross to the west side of Park Avenue and enter a building, head up and shoulders squared. Silly as it seemed, he reminded her, just a little, of Max. Almost as an afterthought, she realized she knew the building. She didn't remember what it was called, but she'd been there before. She stood on the block, staring at it, trying to remember why it was familiar. On the next green light, she crossed the street, hoping to see a name that would jog her memory.

Instead, she saw a woman with dyed red hair, dressed all in black, hurrying out of the building. It hit her suddenly, like an avalanche, what Desmond had just walked into.

55

Aunt Marina!" Polly called.

The woman stopped and squinted. Her coat was plain black wool, her stockings were opaque black rayon, and her shoes were black leather with just the tiniest lift of a heel. Underneath was undoubtedly a black dress or suit. Marina always thought dressing in black made her a stylish New Yorker. "Polina? What are you doing here? Does your mother know?"

"Val sent for me."

"He did?" Marina's face scrunched in confusion. "Mr. Amberson made me clear out the office, but he wanted me to stay. Then Valery insisted I go. I don't think Valery wants anyone else there."

"Knowing Val, he doesn't want an audience. All I know is, he wants *me* there, and I don't want to make him angry," Polly said.

"No, of course not." Just like everyone in the family, Marina was afraid of antagonizing Val. "Come with me."

Marina took Polly's arm and returned to the building. "This is my niece," she told the security guard, sweeping Polly past the desk, and firmly ignoring the guard when he tried to say they should still sign in. "As if I need a security photo of my own niece." Marina's voice was laced with contempt.

"I haven't been here in years," Polly said. "It still looks like a movie set to me."

"It's only impressive when you don't know what goes on behind the scenes." Marina thrust an electronic key card at her. "This will get you in upstairs. Everything is locked down, so you'll have to use this card to open every door."

"Thank you." They kissed and Marina went out again. Polly got into the elevator.

As usual, Val was one step ahead of everyone else. How clever of him to call her and tell her to bring Desmond Edgars to Long Island, when in reality, Val had laid a trap in Manhattan.

She unlocked the outer door and found herself in an antechamber. Through another door, the lobby expanded into something grand, with a waterfall trickling down the wall. Over its peaceful gurgle, she heard voices, and she followed them down the hall. She used the key card to get into the suite where her aunt worked. The next door lay open. The first sound she heard was Desmond's voice.

"You've gone a few steps past plausible deniability. Even if I hadn't called the police just before I came over here, it would be all over for you," he said.

"Really, Mr. Edgars?" That voice wasn't entirely unfamiliar to Polly, but she couldn't quite place it. She'd heard that cool tone and icy diction before. "I fear you've put too much faith in the police. No one will search further than your body, you see. You tie together all the threads quite well, even for a conspiracy theorist."

"Really? How's that work, exactly?"

Polly moved closer. She could see an older man speaking. He was thin, with a high forehead and gray hair. His black suit was perfectly tailored. Amberson, that was his name. He'd been Aunt Marina's employer for close to thirty years. He had been very good to her aunt, Polly knew. Marina was always bragging about how he'd done something or other that was extraordinary for her. Because of Marina, Max had been allowed to work for a couple of summers in Amberson's office, and the great man himself had written a recommendation for Max to get into Harvard. *Max owes Mr. Amberson so much,* her aunt would say. *We all do.*

"Allow me to explain. I've put a fair amount of work into this narrative, so I may as well lay it out for you. You'll point out the flaws," Amberson said. "Here goes: you came to New York, distraught over the untimely yet entirely accidental death of your sister. Anyone could understand that sentiment, and your subsequent madness."

"My madness?"

"Oh, yes, Mr. Edgars. You see, you blamed Tom Klepper for your sister's death, and so you killed him."

"There's a few witnesses who saw me visit him at his office in the Empire State Building," Desmond said. "They saw us leaving together, and then part ways. There's a witness who saw me on Roosevelt Island."

"Excellent points, Mr. Edgars, but easily answered. You did go to Lighthouse Park, but you stopped at Tom Klepper's apartment afterward, because you knew he'd set you up. That repulsive toad tried to deceive you, and you were smart enough to realize it. So you went to his apartment in the dead of night and strangled him."

"I went to his place the next day," Desmond said. "What are the odds I'd do that if I'd killed him?"

"Pretty good, actually," Amberson said. "In this day and age, we're inundated with information about crime. Everyone knows that killers often like to go back to the scene of the crime. They like to *help* with police investigations, too, you know."

"The cops won't buy it."

"I think they will, especially because of what you did next."

"I can hardly wait to hear this," Desmond said.

"Obviously you murdered Trinity Lytton-Jones."

"Now you sound like a nutcase."

"No, Mr. Edgars, you're the obsessive stalker who was certain poor Trinity was involved as well. No one would have trouble believing that. Some people may even sympathize with your antipathy toward Miss Lytton-Jones, given her vile statements about your sister. This is, after all, a woman who made corpses into diamonds. If you knew what I've had to deal with over the years with that vile little creature, I think you'd actually feel pity for me."

"I already feel sorry for you, but that's because the story you're spinning is pathetic. Your henchman with the gun over here, he's the one who killed her. No one is going to have any trouble figuring that out, least of all the police."

"On the contrary, the police are going to have a very different picture of you when they examine your hotel room later on," Amberson said. "That's when they'll find your stash of cocaine."

"What are you talking about?"

"My henchman, as you called him, will plant several samples, both pure and tainted. Don't worry, Val won't leave any prints. He's very careful that way, albeit clumsy in others. We'll make it clear that you were involved in Trinity's death. I believe in thoroughness."

"Everyone who knows me knows I don't do drugs."

"But you have that record trailing after you, from your wild, errant youth." Amberson's voice had a lulling quality to it, as if he were relating a fairy tale. "Once you earn the notice of the police that way, there's always a cloud of suspicion over you. Look at poor Val here. When he was young, he couldn't keep out of trouble."

"It wasn't my fault," Val said. That was the first time Polly heard her brother speak up in this entire exchange.

"Come on, Val," Amberson said. "When I let you work here for a summer, you stole from me."

"You shouldn't have left bundles of cash around." Val's voice was low.

"Blaming the victim," Amberson said, with a dramatic sigh. "But I realized, troubled though he was, this boy had certain intriguing talents, and I could make use of them. Of course, there was rather a lot of training involved."

"Let me guess." That was Desmond's voice again. "You trained him to kill for you."

Amberson chuckled. "Val was already a killer. I had nothing to do with that."

"When I turn up with bullet holes in me, the cops are going to smell a rat. And you're the biggest rodent in this story, Amberson."

"We won't shoot you unless we have to, Mr. Edgars. There are other ways for you to die. I'd hate to have to clean blood out of that rug you're standing on. It's a Persian antique and it cost me a hundred thousand dollars."

"I had a feeling about that," Desmond said.

"About what?"

"You and your expensive tastes. You've had a series of showgirl wives. That must've cost you a bundle."

Amberson cleared his throat. "Aside from my wives, I like to be subtle, you understand. I don't approve of showy deaths that scream 'murder.' I refuse to use guns for that reason. They're the fail-safe if nothing else works. You see, I like quiet, accidental deaths. Misfortunes. Misadventures. Like the carbon monoxide poisoning I arranged for your sister and Gary. For the record, I had nothing to do with Tom Klepper's death or with the attack on you in the street. That was all Val's initiative, which was why the execution was so clumsy and ham-fisted."

"Thanks for confirming my theory," Desmond said.

"Oh? What's that?"

"Max is dead. There's somebody who wants his mother and his sister to believe he's alive, which is why they get cards and presents in the mail, but Max has been dead for some time. You and Val planted evidence in the house to confuse the investigation."

"Ah, Mr. Edgars. You're not as clever as you thought," Amberson said.

"I know Max Brantov isn't just an alias Val made up. And I'm certain he's dead."

"Oh, no, you misunderstand me," Amberson answered. "I meant that no one planted evidence about Max in the house. That was a terrible mistake on Val's part. You see, Max Brantov was a very intelligent young man with a promising future. Of course, he's been dead for several years. But Val could tell you far more about that than I could. Val's the one who murdered him."

56

P olly didn't realize it, but a scream escaped from her throat. Amberson came to the doorway, staring at her. His eyes were bright blue, and they regarded her curiously. "Excuse me, my dear, but what are you doing here?" He turned his face to one side. "I believe your little sister has found her way into my office, Val."

"Polly?" Val came into view. "You are not supposed to be here. Get out."

"What happened to your eye, my dear?" Amberson frowned at Polly. "Did someone hit you?"

Polly ignored that. "What did you say about Max?" she wailed.

Amberson gazed at her in obvious wonder, before his eyes slithered over to meet Val's. "Your sister has no idea what happened? How on earth did you manage *that* all these years?"

"Did you ever tell the Lytton-Jones family that you lost literally a *billion* dollars of their money by being such a pathetic gambler?" Val shot back. "Or that you keep bundles of cash around for tipping strippers?" He stared at Polly. "Don't believe a word out of his mouth, Polly. He's lying because he wants to see you cry. He loves messing with people's heads."

"Actually, Val, what I love is money." Amberson gave Val a withering look. "You're the one who plays creepy mind games. When I gave you the money to hire a girlfriend for Tom Klepper, I didn't expect you to prostitute your own sister."

"I didn't—"

"Oh, please. Tom was such an easy mark. I took him out for the occasional lunch at the Harvard Club and had him eating out of the palm of my hand. It was that simple. All you had to do was find a girl for Tom, and make sure she got her picture taken cuddling up with Gary. Did you really need to pimp poor Polly for that? Being completely honest, that made me think less of you."

"Yeah, well, let's really be honest. Why don't you tell everyone why you killed off that whole rich Lytton-Jones family?"

"I didn't kill them *all*." Amberson rolled his eyes. "Byron didn't need help killing himself with drugs."

"He's been controlling their family fortune for years." Val's voice boomed. "But he's used up so much of it on his gambling addiction and on whores that there's almost nothing left! It's a house of cards. That's the real reason he had to kill Gary Cowan. It's because Gary was poking around in the family finances." Val turned and looked at Desmond. "You know what he called your sister? 'Collateral damage that would add to the ambience.' That's a quote."

"Well, Dominique *was* a win-win situation. If she'd gotten what we needed from Gary, we could have squashed him like a cockroach, without anyone dying in suspicious circumstances. But she kept stalling, and Gary came up with his masterly kidnapping plan. It was too irresistible an opportunity to pass up."

"You think you can manipulate anyone," Val said. "You're always talking about how everyone has their weakness, and all you have to do is find it. *You're* the twisted one who screws with people's heads."

Amberson kept his composure. "Really, Val? Being criticized by a man who murdered his own brother in a fit of jealousy is a bit much." He turned to Polly. "You must remember that Val was always jealous of Max. Val was always in trouble, and Max was the golden child. Straight-A student, star athlete, and actually a surprisingly sweet boy."

"Yes, I remember," Polly whispered.

"It was the acceptance to Harvard that did it, I think," Amberson said. "That pushed Val over the edge."

"You're a liar. Polly isn't stupid enough to believe you," Val seethed. "Shut up now."

"Or you'll do what?" Amberson asked. "You forget, I have all the evidence I need tucked away. If anything happens to me, your life is over. You're my helper monkey, Val. I know where Max's body is buried." He chuckled. "Imagine, murdering your brother over his admission to Harvard." He shook his head. "That's rather pathetic, don't you think?"

"That wasn't why Val did it," Polly whispered. Blood was roaring in her ears, and all of those terrible dreams she used to have came crashing in on her like a tsunami.

"No?" That got Amberson's full attention. "That's what I always thought, my dear. What happened?"

There was a panicked expression on Val's face. All those years. All those lies. Still, Polly's memory was buried underneath, like a shipwreck at the floor of the ocean. "Max came into my room when Val was . . . when he was . . ." She choked on the words she couldn't say. She locked eyes with Val and realized she had never hated anyone in the world but him. He was her torturer, her jailer, her drug dealer. But she couldn't express herself and tears started to trickle down her face.

"You poor thing," Amberson said. "Why don't you sit down, Polly?"

"This doesn't make any sense," Desmond said. "Max's DNA is in a database of missing children. You can't fake that."

"Come on, Val, why don't you explain how *your* DNA was mistaken for Max's. That's a fun story." Amberson turned to Polly. "Val was so jealous of Max, you see, that he stole a T-shirt Max got on his Harvard visit. A T-shirt! Can you imagine the pettiness?"

"Yes," Polly whispered, remembering Val coming into her room. At first, she'd thought it was Max, because he was wearing that crimson T-shirt with the big logo in the center. But it was Val, who'd snuck into her room before when he thought everyone else was sleeping. *I don't want to play,* she told him, but Val had forced her, as he always did. Then Max came in and pulled him off her, and the two had started fighting. *Let's take this outside,* Val said, and the two of them disappeared downstairs. She waited and listened, but Max never came back. Deep down, she'd believed it was her fault that he left.

"Val was stupid," Polly whispered. Val stared at her with frozen fury. "He didn't even realize his own blood was on the shirt, and he threw it in the hamper."

Out of the corner of her eye she saw Desmond throw himself toward Val, grabbing for the gun. And then the pistol went off with a boom that made her jump.

57

Everything was still for a second after the gun went off. Val and Desmond faced each other, both breathing hard. They didn't even turn to regard the attorney sliding down the doorjamb, his eyes wide and his mouth open in a small, curious O.

As Amberson hit the ground, his torso crumpled forward. Polly saw the bullet wound on the back of his head. It was just red pulp with tufts of hair sticking out now. That single bullet had sheared off a chunk of his skull.

Desmond roared as he wrestled the gun out of Val's hands. He took a step back. "Don't make a move, or you're dead. Polly? You okay?"

Polly couldn't say a word. Her breath came out in ragged gasps.

"Polly?" Desmond called. "Did you get hit?" When she didn't answer, he turned his head slightly so he could see her. "You're okay? Call the cops *now*."

There was another boom.

Desmond's mouth contorted and he shouted as he dropped to his knees. Val stood there, his face an impassive mask. He was holding another gun.

"I like to be prepared," he said. "I was never the boy scout Max was, but I understood 'be prepared' a lot better than he did."

Blood stained Desmond's shirt, and even though his trousers were black, the blood pouring out of his gut rendered them a darker shade.

"Polly?" Val called.

She couldn't find her tongue, but she moved forward with a jolt, like a sleepwalker.

"Come here, Polly."

She inched around Amberson's body in the doorway.

"Is Zachary Amberson dead, Polly?"

She nodded.

"I can't hear you."

"Yes," she whispered.

"Shit. Now I have to go through his files," Val muttered. "Polly, I want you to get the gun out of that man's hand. Don't worry, he can't hurt you. He's in too much pain from his wound. Besides, he knows I have a gun trained on him."

Desmond's hands were crossed over the side of his torso, as if he were trying to hold his guts in. Polly reached for the gun, moving as slowly as she did in her dreams, as if she were swimming in warm water. She took the gun from Desmond's hand.

"Now give it to me," Val instructed her.

She turned toward him, firing into his stomach. Val emitted a screech like a wild animal. It was something between a gasp and a scream. The shot to his abdomen doubled him over in pain.

"You murdered Max," Polly whispered. "You told me it was just a nightmare. But I remember. I didn't want to believe it. I thought I'd die if it was true. So I pretended Max was alive."

"I'm the only family you have left, Polly," Val gasped, lifting his head. "Without me, you have nothing and no one. Our mother's a drunk. The state will lock you up."

"You mailed me cards and signed them from Max. You pretended Max sent me birthday gifts. You sent cards to mother signed by Max. You made us believe he would come home one day! All this time, he was dead."

She fired again, directly into Val's head. He went down, but she kept shooting until the gun click-click-clicked. Then she stood, still aiming the weapon, waiting for Val to look up at her. It took a moment for the reality of what she'd just done to hit her.

"Polly." Desmond's voice crackled.

She let her arm drop to her side and turned to him, kneeling on the bloody carpet.

"Put my phone in my hand, okay? It's in my coat." He groaned and sank a little lower into the ground.

She retrieved it.

"Now wipe down the gun," Desmond ordered.

"What?"

"Get your prints off it. Use your scarf."

She unwrapped it from her neck and rubbed it across the gun. She touched the trigger gingerly.

"Okay, put it in my hand," Desmond said.

"Why?"

"Because we can't pretend the lawyer and your brother shot each other. The missing part of Amberson's head will give that explanation the lie. Give me the gun."

"But the police will think you shot Val."

"That's the idea. He shot me and I shot back. It's self-defense. But if we say you did it. . . ." He groaned softly. "You've suffered enough, Polly. More than anyone ever should."

She put the gun in his hand.

"Run and get help. Make sure the doors stay open behind you. Otherwise the medics can't get in." He sighed. "Get ready to tell the police about all the people your brother hurt."

"Okay." Dizzy and dazed, she got to her feet.

Desmond grasped the phone in his left hand. The other, still holding the gun, covered his abdomen. As Polly backed away, she heard a woman's voice coming from the phone. "What's the nature of your emergency?"

"I need an ambulance. I've been shot," Desmond said. "And I shot a man dead."